Invisible Threads

by

Sharon Heath

Invisible Threads

Cover photo by Ante Gudelj on Unsplash.com. https://unsplash.com/photos/red-heart-shaped-hanging-decor-P-JX1Agg0Ts. (Public Domain under the Unsplash License)

Bourne, Wm. Oland. Now I lay me down to sleep. (Public Domain)

Poe, Edgar Allan, et al. The Raven. New York: Harper & Brothers, 1884. (Public Domain)

Scriptures taken from The World English Bible. (Public Domain)

Tolstoy, Leo. Anna Karenina. Fort, Paul Leicester (1899). The New-England Primer. New York. (Public Domain)

Library of Congress Control Number: 2025938312
1. Contemporary fiction 2. Literary fiction
ISBN 10: 1-950750-58-2
ISBN-13: 978-1-950750-58-0
Thomas-Jacob Publishing, LLC, Deltona, Florida USA

In memory of my father, Charlie Karson, the first man I ever loved, who sang like an angel and who taught me to recite—with feeling—every word of "Annabel Lee."

One

THE PATIENT IN bed two stirred, making thick, molasses-mouthed sounds on her slow passage back to consciousness. Once she finally found a way to re-inhabit her mind, she cursed herself for having bothered. Really, she should have known better. Anyone who'd worked with the elderly and infirm for nearly fourteen years should have gotten the message that a hospital is hardly the place to take the measure of your life.

She'd entered Cedars-Sinai's fifth floor recovery room lost in an anesthetized limbo. The ruddy-faced surgical aide who wheeled her in had all the finesse of a trucker on speed. Without a word, he deposited his load and took off down the hall.

The gurney sat in the middle of the hectic room like an orphan at a new school, until a petite Filipina nurse abandoned her paperwork to push the incoming lumpectomy into a space against the wall between a surprisingly voluble hysterectomy and a bleary-eyed young ulcer. Welcome or not, consciousness returned to the woman in the middle, but at first only in patchy islands poking up through a fog.

"Evelyn. Evelyn Kerr?" Nurse Cory Subharto adjusted the flow of liquid into the elongated cocoon of energy beneath her, suspended between the netherworld of death and the over-loud voices and beeping monitors of the blindingly bright recovery room.

Like everyone else in post-op, Nurse Cory was chronically overworked. Attuned to the struggle of heart and lung to re-establish their familiar rhythms, she could hardly be expected to spare a thought for her patient's muddled mind, where the barest hint of something crisp and weightless nosed its way through clumps of underwater reeds.

Evvie Kerr couldn't quite grasp whether she was a woman or some weaving mound of abraded flesh. And she couldn't tell if it was better to try to fight toward the distant shore of familiarity or let herself dissolve into the powdery murk at the bottom of this sea.

Sound came at her in incomprehensible waves. "Evelyn? Can you hear me? It's all over. You did great. You're okay."

Navigating the entire evolutionary sequence in a matter of minutes, Evvie landed into full consciousness with a grunt. She was no longer a fish, but almost recognizably human, her body hostage to a cosmic flu.

Every part of her was uncomfortable. She was above ground, but she really didn't belong here anymore, especially since some lunatic was trying to convince her that everything was hunky dory, when she was clearly unfixably broken and nothing, nothing was okay.

***

Dawn brought spiky shafts of sunlight, throbbing pain, and the other three members of the Kerr tribe to Evvie's fourth floor hospital room, but if the family members seated around her narrow bed had any inkling of her radically altered state, they weren't letting on. To be fair, she didn't look sick. Despite the uncomfortable dryness of her naturally moist, coral lips and the slightly sallow tinge to her flawless olive skin, her prominent cheekbones and big, dark eyes were as arresting as ever.

"Hah!" her father Michael was saying. "He should have made it Curse instead of Kerr." While his words were harsh, his lingering glance at her sister Miriam was intimate and glowing, as if he were speaking to her alone.

Miriam wasn't paying him any attention, too busy sneaking a look toward the open doorway of the small adjoining bathroom, where her teenage son Ben was just visible trying to pop a zit in front of the mirror.

Evvie's right breast ached despite the Darvocet she'd been given half an hour ago. She wriggled under a thin cotton blanket as her fingers struggled to loosen her hospital nightgown from its binding fit.

She forced a smile of feigned interest. How many times had she been subjected to the same story over the course of her forty years?

Michael Kerr sat forward in his visitor's chair. "Picture it. Seventy-seven years ago. Nineteen-twenty-three. Eighteen miserable months, sneaking across a series of borders in the middle of the night, navigating half of Europe on foot before sailing steerage class across the Atlantic. Most of us were sick and dehydrated by the time we landed at Ellis Island. They had one lousy clerk entering the names of all of us 'tired and poor' in his big black book. Even at nine-years-old, I knew we were in trouble when I noticed his weasel-faced boss standing behind him, sneering like some Jew-killing Cossack from Kasrilivka. The sonofabitch stood there paring himself a juicy red apple, knowing we were all famished and dying of thirst." Michael leaned confidingly toward Miriam. "By the way, Dick and I used that scene in *Lamp of Liberty*. Pauline Kael said the guy playing weasel-face would have rated a nod for Best Supporting Actor if he'd had a few more scenes."

Evvie tried again to loosen her nightgown, until it occurred to her that it was the bandage that was causing her sense of constriction. Relentlessly, her father went on. "I knew it was a bad omen when the sadist sliced his thumb at the very moment the clerk was writing down our name. His blood spurted onto the page like a geyser, smearing the ink so that the letters were barely legible. Sure enough, when our papers were sent to us a few months later, we'd gone from being the Kirschons to the Kerrs, a couple of petty bureaucrats cutting us off from our roots more effectively than a shitty sea journey."

Evvie leaned her weight onto her palms and gingerly shifted her body a little to the right. God, he was an angry man. But as her father reached his finale, spitting out the familiar mantra of her childhood— "What else would you expect from the capitalist sons of bitches? You think it's much better for immigrants these days under Clinton?"—the hairs prickled up and down her arms. She put a hand to her bandaged chest.

Her eyelids grew heavy, and the contours of the hospital room began to dissolve. In her dream she'd become lilliputian, staring in no little awe at a larger-than-life version of a breast. A jagged line of red stitching stretched above its nipple like a primitive archway, out of which a small boy emerged. Three or four years old, he stood on a patch of dusty ground that was surrounded by a cluster of small buildings. The air was crisp. Smells of burning wood and horse manure stung her nostrils. Just a few feet away, a cluster of chattering peasant-skirted women was gathered around a well. One of them lowered an ancient-looking pail by a heavy rope, her hands as thick and calloused as a man's.

As if he alone were aware of Evvie's presence, the child signaled her with a nod of his curly brown head. He disappeared inside a small hut whose chimney spat coils of black smoke. She followed him, swerving around an odd jerry-rigged outdoor pantry that reeked of curing meat. She had to duck her head to clear the shallow doorway.

It was a single-roomed dwelling, with a gray cement floor and a few holes cut into the walls for windows. She guessed that the thin wooden boards leaning against the walls were used to fit into the openings and block out at least some of what must become a bitter cold at night. The atmosphere was pungently suggestive of human sweat, cooking onions, goat cheese. A pot simmered on a cast iron stove. Curled in an alcove above the stove, a ginger cat blinked lazily at her before slipping back into sleep.

The boy stood in a dim corner, stretching his hands toward a teen-aged girl whose fiery braids reached halfway down her back. She was painstakingly transferring a network of stretched red yarn from her hands to the boy's in a complex cat's cradle maneuver. She danced away from him, past a rustic worktable where a length of floral fabric spilled across an open sewing basket. Pulling the half-finished garment across her chest and making a graceful pirouette, she collapsed in a fit of giggles onto a pile of blankets that looked like it might make do for a family bed. The web still taut in his hands, the boy stumbled after her, laughing with abandon.

Evvie wanted in the worst way to join in. But now she felt like she was falling, and suddenly an irritable voice was telling someone to get off a bed. She opened her eyes and saw her sister Miriam's blue ones, glittering with anxiety, just inches from her face.

Miriam looked so pale that the dusting of freckles across her chiseled nose stood out more sharply than usual. Her long red hair fanned around her head as she darted an accusing glance at Ben, who stood beside his seated grandfather at the foot of the bed.

4

Evvie smiled uncertainly at her visitors. Her father's expression was blank, Miriam was shooting sparks out of her eyes, and Ben's young face wore a stricken banner of apology. Even though her seventeen-year-old nephew towered over his grandfather like a giant sequoia, Evvie couldn't help but feel protective of him. She fidgeted under her covers and signaled him with her eyes, willing him not to feel bad.

Ben leaned forward and patted Evvie's blanketed ankle. His expression relaxed as she murmured, "Mm, that feels good." She was well aware that the crooked grin he gave her had conquered half the female hearts at Uni High. He'd conquered hers the moment he was born.

"Sorry, Auntie. It just felt weird to leave without…some kind of contact. I didn't think that a little touch on the foot would wake you up."

His mother broke in. "Didn't think? I warned him, but he never listens to *me*." Ben inclined his head sheepishly.

Evvie's tongue felt thick as she spoke up to defend him. "S'okay. Shouldn't be sleeping through your visit, anyway."

Was that all it had been—a dream? It had seemed so real, as if she'd been transported back in time to the Ukraine of her father's childhood. Surely, that child had been him. She put a hand to her forehead and licked her anesthesia-cracked lips. Sensing movement in the room, she looked up to see her father rise stiffly from his chair. He moved purposely toward the door.

Ben had noticed how dry her mouth was. He fetched a moist washcloth from the bathroom and gently dabbed her lips. She shot him a look of gratitude, then heard her father say to no one in particular, "Evvie's as strong as a horse. She'll be back in form in no time."

Evvie struggled to sit up straighter so she could make eye contact with her father before he left, but found herself calling, "Bye, Dad," to an empty doorway.

Her cheeks burned, but a glance in her sister's direction made her laugh for the first time in days. Miriam had grabbed an empty paper cup from the bedside table. She'd clapped it onto her head and was rolling her eyes comically. "Well, I guess we're going, too, or the next story we'll have to sit through is how he had to walk all the way across

LA to get home." But for all her sarcasm, Miriam hurried to conclude their visit. She slid the phone a little closer to Evvie's bed. "Will you call me just as soon as Dr. Manning comes?" She glanced at her watch. "Jesus. Nearly noon. I love how they tell you he'll be doing his rounds before ten and only get around to mentioning he's had an emergency after you've been waiting a couple of hours."

But when her surgeon showed up, Evvie was hardly in shape to remember her sister's request. Her latest hit of Darvocet was pulsing through her bloodstream. Her eyes traveled up Dr. Manning's lab coat to meet his earnest gaze. She decided he resembled a kindly seal.

"Evelyn, I'm sorry I've made you wait. Actually, it's a bit of luck that I was delayed, since we've just received the initial lab results."

Cruising along a road of pleasantly dulled feeling, it was hard to keep track of what he was saying. The few words she managed to catch—"margins" and "nodes" and "Dr. Abrams"— bounced off her brain like snowflakes against a windshield. She tried to nod in all the right places but was mesmerized by the physical sensations of her gown being carefully lifted off her shoulder. Long, tapered fingers gently coaxed her bandages away from her breast, nearly imperceptibly tapping the skin bordering her incision. She looked down and with unwelcome clarity saw a dark red gash, land-mined with black stitches. The puckered skin alongside the incision looked swollen and weepy, but as he tenderly reattached the bandage, Dr. Manning assured her it was doing very nicely.

Shuddering, she closed her eyes. She'd rather risk another dream of her father's childhood any day over this ravaged battlefield her body had become.

Two

MIRIAM WOULD HAVE liked to sleep forever, but the number crunchers of managed care had dictated that her sister would be released from Cedars-Sinai the day after her surgery. Which was why Miriam was even awake at such an ungodly hour, bustling around Evvie's bedroom in their shared condo near the sprawling Westwood campus of the University of California, preparing for her sister's return home.

Their upscale neighborhood was typically serene, at least at this time of day, and the room was so quiet that Miriam could hear her sister's clock ticking the seconds. She glanced at Evvie's pine dresser, where an art nouveau timepiece sat amid a host of framed photos, primarily of Ben at various stages of his young life. The marble clock was one of a kind, sculpted in the form of a sinuous dancing woman with the clock face set like a jewel in her navel. It was a gift from their father's estranged second wife Moira, who was also one of a kind.

An all-too-familiar refrain oozed from the rear of the condo. Miriam stifled an impulse to yell at Ben to turn the damned Nirvana CD down, settling instead for slamming the bedroom door. The perspiration that pearled her forehead had little to do with the exertion of stuffing a down quilt into its jacquard duvet cover.

Noticing that one of the cover's buttons hung by a loose thread, Miriam hurried through the adjoining bathroom to her own bedroom and extracted her well-worn sewing kit from one of her dresser drawers.

Everyone in the family said that Miriam could never sit still. Certainly, at this moment, she was a study in nervous animation. Returning to Evvie's room with a satin pincushion and a spool of burgundy thread, she sat on the edge of the bed and tugged enough of the duvet across her lap for her needle to flash in and out of the cover's fabric.

She'd selected the elegant, floral material months ago, but thanks to the film she'd been working on at the time running way beyond schedule, she'd barely finished sewing it the night before Christmas. The hassle had been worth it. Evvie's doe eyes had radiated pleasure when she opened the oversized box on Christmas morning.

On the whole, it had been a satisfying Christmas. Even their father had been on best behavior. He'd groused about the hypocrisy of a secular Jewish family celebrating Christ's birth ever since his second wife Moira had finally put her foot down and insisted on bringing home their very first Christmas tree in the early eighties. But this year he'd actually seemed to enjoy himself. After a little coaxing he'd treated them to his soulful tenor version of "Danny Boy," wolfed down two helpings of Evvie's roast beef and Yorkshire pudding, and grinned with delight over Miriam's gift of a limited edition of Poe's poetry. He'd told her that the way she'd wrapped it in red silk fabric reminded him of a girl named Golda, who'd lived in his village "in the old days."

Miriam had her own version of "the old days," vague memories of her bedridden mother Riva. Long before she lost her mom at the age of eleven, Miriam had known something was terribly wrong. It occurred to her now that her mother's bed must have been like a prison to her, her spine entwined by metastases of the breast cancer that would claim her life just before her forty-ninth birthday. And now her older sister had gotten hit by the fucker at an even younger age.

Miriam squeezed the fabric tightly before flinging the duvet onto the bed. She marched up the hall and banged on Ben's door. "Turn that damned thing down! Do you want to go deaf?" Ben flung open the door, blasting the hallway with sound. Her face pinched with rage, Miriam shook a finger at him. "You'd never pull that kind of crap if Evvie were home."

Ben did an about-face and strode to his CD player, switching it off so forcefully that it nearly crashed to the floor. He returned to the doorway and crossed his arms. His expression was determinedly neutral, but Miriam saw that his ears were flaming red. An image came to her of steam shooting out of his ears. She struggled to keep a straight face.

"What are you laughing at?"

It took them both a moment to register that someone was ringing the doorbell.

Ben's athletic stride got him down the hallway in seconds. Miriam knew he was only too relieved to get away from her. Damn it, she'd lost it. Again. She could almost see Evvie's disappointed gaze shaming her.

A familiar voice sprang into the apartment. "Darlings! Did you miss me?"

Miriam froze, then turned to see Moira, her blue-black hair flowing over a silvery cape. Moira wrapped herself like a human octopus around a stiff-postured Ben. She peered over Ben's shoulder at Miriam, made a sad face, then held Ben at arm's length. "God, you're still growing. I can't believe it. And what a hunk!" Finally letting him out of her clutches, she gestured to a pair of Louis Vuitton suitcases at the condo's entryway. "I hope I'm not intruding," she said, as Ben bent to pick up her bags.

Miriam repressed a sigh. "Of course not. Evvie'll be glad to see you."

Moira sailed up the hall, preceded by her signature Chanel No. 5 scent. She kissed Miriam on each cheek, murmuring, "Mm, you smell delicious." Then she let her violet-lipsticked mouth sag with genuine worry, whispering in Miriam's ear, "I know it's a pain in the ass having company now, but after talking to you on the phone last night, I couldn't not come."

Miriam stood very still. She realized with a pang that Evvie being diagnosed with cancer was so big and terrible that it even upstaged Moira's penchant for putting herself first, Miriam second, and the rest of the world way behind. But where was she going to put Moira? Moira had moved up to Berkeley after divorcing their father, and usually Miriam shared her bed with Evvie when their stepmother visited. That was out of the question now. As was sharing her own bed with Moira, who'd proclaimed a couple of visits ago that, at her age, needing to pee multiple times in the night precluded sharing a bed with anyone.

Miriam reached up to pat Ben's cheek, thinking better of it when he glared at her. "Honey," she said, "those bags must be heavy as hell. Just put them down for now and we'll figure out where they need to go in a little while."

But Ben wasn't going to give her an inch. He set the bags down without a word and lumbered back to his room, securing the door with an emphatic click of the latch.

Moira arched an eyebrow.

"Never mind," Miriam sighed. She ushered Moira into the kitchen, where—until two weeks ago, when a routine mammogram had changed everything—Evvie had whipped up nourishing dishes from scratch nearly every night for Ben to deliver to Michael. Evvie had never complained, but it drove Miriam crazy that her father refused to hire daily domestic help when he could well afford it.

Miriam yanked open the Sub-Zero and pulled out a half-full bottle of the Chablis her new boyfriend had brought over a few nights ago. Her eyes narrowed. James was good-looking, and she was a sucker for his British public school wit, but he was unbelievably deficient in the empathy department. He'd selfishly assumed that she would go to bed with him, with her newly diagnosed sister sobbing in the next bedroom.

She slapped the bottle and two glasses sharply onto a floral-painted tray. "Given the circumstances, I don't think it's too early, do you?" Before Moira could respond, Miriam gestured with her head and carried the tray toward the living room, where she set it down between two oversized, slipcovered sofas holding court at the center of the room. "I have to tell you, though— this business of being responsible is the shits."

Her stepmother shot her a commiserating look before sinking down onto one of the sofas and kicking off her heels. "I know, darling. But tell me, how's Evvie? Have you talked to her today?"

"Yeah, but she still sounds pretty groggy. I finally got the call from Dr. Manning, her surgeon, a couple of hours after I talked to you. He said he was fairly confident he'd gotten wide margins around the tumor, and we already knew that the BRCA tests were negative. I tried to emphasize to Evvie what good news that was, but I know she's still on pins and needles, waiting to hear from Abrams whether it's spread to her lymph nodes and what stage and type of breast cancer she has." She played with a lock of hair, which resembled a little flame around her forefinger. "We all are. Moira, it's so unbelievable. I keep waiting to wake up from this nightmare. It feels like just yesterday we were celebrating her fortieth birthday, for Christ's sake. Everything going along just fine, and then, whammo!"

"I know, love. It's been a terrible shock." Moira reached over and patted Miriam's leg. "But Evvie's going to beat this. I just know it. It won't end up like … she just needs a little time to get her bearings. You'll see, you'll have your big sister taking charge of things again before the year's out."

Miriam eyed her dubiously. "You think? God, I hope so." She laughed nervously. "*Somebody's* got to save me from my father."

"Why? I'd think worrying about Evvie would make him a little more—"

Miriam interrupted. "Oh, Moira, you of all people should know better. Dad's predictably oblivious, still wanting his supper provided every night. With Evvie out of commission, that means that yours truly has to drop everything to get Jerry's Deli to deliver something here each afternoon, which I re-package in our casserole dishes so he thinks I cooked it myself." Registering her stepmother's look of disbelief, Miriam shrugged. "I know, I know. I'm a chicken when it's anything to do with Dad, but you know what he's like. At least I have the excuse of having been born his daughter. How in the world a woman like you could have married someone so impossible …"

Moira threw her an impatient look. "Oh, come on, Miriam. Your father's still as handsome as hell, and running off with the elder states-men of the anti-war movement was a delicious 'fuck you' to everything my family stood for. I mean, really. My aunt and uncle were giving so much money to the San Francisco Archdiocese that the Archbishop came to dinner once a week."

Miriam felt a flicker of envy. It had to be some kind of crime to have no regrets, with such absolute confidence in your own point of view. "Yeah, but look what you let yourself in for. Don't tell me Evvie and I didn't cramp your style."

"Not on your life. It's true, I wasn't exactly the earth mother type, but I fell in love with the two of you on the spot. Oh, I knew I could never replace Riva. And, well … to be honest, I *was* a little intimidated by Evvie. She was so serious and protective of you. But you, Little Miss Antsy Chatterbox. I got your number as soon as I moved my loom into the house. The way you'd stand by my bench for ages with those baby blue eyes of yours, I realized soon enough I had a budding artist on my hands."

Moira was right. Her stepmother's weaving had been better than a magic show, the rhythmic clack and whirr of the loom turning separate skeins of yarn into wall hangings and blankets and garments that could caress a woman's shoulder or provide warmth around a man's neck, bringing warring hues to new life in the blending. Miriam still recalled the first time she'd watched her stepmother adjust the tension on the warp threads, solemnly declaring, "My Irish nana liked to say, 'the tighter the weave, the stronger the cloth.'"

It was too bad that what her stepmother could accomplish with yarn she was hopeless at in her relationship with their father. That complementary pairing of opposites had broken down when Miriam was sixteen and just beginning to fantasize a creative career of her own.

"You know, I remember that. I used to pretend you were my fairy godmother. Which you literally became when you defied Dad to pay for me to go to the Fashion Institute." Her eyes grew moist.

"No, no, we'll have none of that," Moira said, but Miriam could tell she felt gratified. "Listen, what's up with Ben?"

Miriam's voice took on an edge. "Oh, you know Ben. What do you expect? He's seventeen." She began pouring Moira a second glass of wine, then paused to look helplessly into her sympathetic black eyes. "Life sure doesn't get any easier."

Moira took her by surprise by breaking into laughter and pointing at her hand. Miriam looked down and saw that she was spilling Chablis all over the tray.

"Oops." Her laughter loosened her face from its spell of tension. "I don't know about you," she said, clicking glasses with Moira, "but I'd give anything to be Ben's age again, without a worry in the world."

Three

THE SOUND OF the women's laughter from the other room grated out of all proportion as Ben sat at the edge of his unmade bed, his head buried in his hands. He couldn't believe Moira was here, taking all the attention away from Aunt Evvie.

He made a bitter face. Maybe he should be grateful. At least his mom would have somebody's shoulder to cry on, rather than leaning all over him. He knew what she was up to. Feel shitty? No worries—she could always perk herself up by ragging on her only son.

He fell back, cushioning his head with his hands and stretching out his blue-jeaned legs so that they nearly overshot the foot of the bed. He stared at the ceiling, longing for some music, but reluctant to get into it again with his mom. Maybe Fiona Apple? His mom's latest boy-toy liked her stuff, so she could hardly object to *her*.

But really, it wasn't like Nirvana was heavy metal or hardcore rap. It wasn't the music, but Kurt's addiction and suicide that his mom was uptight about. That and his abandonment of his daughter Francis Bean. It wasn't as though Ben saw Kurt as some kind of role model. Couldn't she get that he just liked his music?

At that moment, it came back to Ben that his first exposure to Nirvana had been when Evvie had taken him to Amoeba Music for his fourteenth birthday. They'd had *All Apologies* playing good and loud on their sound system. Evvie hadn't been thrilled by the music, but she'd bought him the CD anyway.

Ben chewed an already-shredded thumbnail. Maybe it was because he was an only child, but it was hard to imagine how someone as nice as Evvie could be related to his mom. They certainly didn't look like sisters. You'd never mistake Evvie for a Christian, certainly not once she started talking, her hands gesturing like crazy, her strong nose wrinkling for emphasis, her dark eyes reaching right inside you to make a connection. His mom was another story. People were often surprised to find out she was Jewish, and he always thought it said something about her that she liked to brag about it.

By all rights, Evvie should have been the one to have a kid, rather than the other way around. It had been damned lucky for him that his aunt had been there to pick up the pieces after his mom got knocked up by Simon Warwick. It was just like his mom to bitch about Simon bailing the moment he learned she was pregnant, when she herself took off for the Fashion Institute as soon as she popped out her only son. Sometimes Ben thought everything would've been a lot easier if his mom had never returned from New York. His life sure as shit would've been a lot less complicated.

The phone rang, and Ben dove to pick it up, cursing his mother for taking away his cell phone as punishment when she found out he'd been cutting class with Tony. At least he and Tony had managed to keep their mothers in the dark that they'd been forging their names on absence slips to hang out with Opal and Natasha.

It was Tash on the phone now, and he nearly died when she said, "Ben, I want to see you, baby. Wanna meet me at Opal's? Her parents are at work." She paused for a heart-stopping beat and laughed teasingly. "I can hardly wait to fuck your brains out."

His hand went involuntarily for his crotch. "Jesus," he whispered, "you can't say that." He glanced anxiously at his bedroom door. "My mom could pick up the phone any second."

He didn't dare tell his mom about Tash. She'd want to meet her, but even though his new girlfriend had a mother who'd once run for office on the Peace and Freedom Party ticket (and would be considered, at least by his grandfather, one of the tribe because of it), his mom would shit a brick if she set eyes on Tash. Tash was like a walking advertisement for unsafe sex. Her sultry features and the way she carried her unbelievable body screamed that she was up for almost anything. His mom would kill him if she suspected the kinds of chances he was taking with his new girlfriend.

Ben shuddered as he remembered the contempt with which Tash had greeted his offer to put on a rubber when their first heavy make out session looked to be leading where he desperately wanted it to go. She'd said in that snaky voice of hers, her eyelids heavily shading her dark eyes, "Don't you want to feel me, baby? I know I want to feel you." He'd flung the embarrassing condom onto the floor, worrying how much of a pussy she thought he was. For a minute, anyway. Once they got going, she'd made him feel like a total stud.

Hanging up the phone, he darted into his small bathroom, relieving his straining dick of at least some of its load by urinating. He ran a hasty comb through his shiny chestnut hair, checked out the status of the solitary zit on his chin, then walked briskly down the hall, stooping to poke his head through the arched doorway to the living room. "Back soon."

His mom was already on her feet and right behind him by the time he put his hand on the doorknob. His stomach lurched. He had to get over to Opal's house soon or Tash would get royally pissed off.

"What about your aunt?" his mom demanded, her hands on her hips and her eyes flashing.

Oh God. Evvie. "When are you bringing her home?"

"Three o'clock. They said we could get her any time after three. Beady said she was going to try and come, but she wasn't sure she could get away from work on time. Don't you think I could use a little help getting her in and out of the car?" With a furtive glance toward the living room, she hissed, "I hardly think Evvie would want Moira along on her ride home."

He snuck a look at his watch. He could just make it. He touched his mother's arm and, as she shot him a startled look at the rare physical contact, he promised her, "I'll be back in an hour, I swear," before rushing out the door.

Four

PREPARING FOR HER discharge was taking every ounce of Evvie's patience. She knew the nurse was trying to be helpful, but having a stranger dress her like she was a child—efficiently tugging her blouse over her head and then skidding it over her tender, bandaged chest—was just about the limit. And trying to make it easy for the nurse by holding her hands more or less straight up in the air, with her armpit tight and sore from its separate incision for the lymph node sampling, was simply a joke. Her recalcitrant right arm reminded her of the time a bougainvillea branch had snagged her car antenna as she'd backed out of the driveway, bending it permanently at a ridiculously skewed angle.

God oh God oh God. Her whole right side hurt, she felt drugged and dizzy, and she had nothing to look forward to but finding out from her oncologist whether the malignancy had spread to her lymph nodes and how lethal and advanced her cancer was.

My oncologist, she thought dispiritedly. She supposed that someday she'd get used to saying those words. She tried looking on the bright side. While her doctors had warned her that she could probably count on a couple of months of daily radiation, they were hoping she might be spared the constant nausea and hair loss of chemo. Everyone kept pointing out how great it was that she didn't need a total mastectomy. Only radiation. *Hoop de doo*.

With some difficulty, she swallowed. Her mouth was dry as dust from the anesthesia and pain pills. Not to mention unrelenting anxiety.

She didn't dare tell anyone how bad she felt, how end of the line, or they'd stick her on suicide watch for sure. As if sensing the turn of her thoughts, the nurse shot her a quick look. Betrayed by her welling eyes, Evvie turned away in shame. The nurse put a hand on her shoulder, but Evvie shrugged away from the stranger's touch.

A light tapping on the hospital room door broke into the silent adagio between the two women. "Knock, knock." The door swung open a crack, and a *cafe-au-lait* complexioned face crowned with a wild array of corn silk frizz peered through. "Are you decent?" Beady's green eyes crinkled slyly. "'Cuz I've got Tony with me and he's getting too old to be looking at your white ass."

Evvie burst into laughter. She couldn't think of anyone she'd rather see right this minute than her oldest friend. With Beady around, you never had to pretend. Couldn't, really, because the woman was guaranteed to see through bullshit like it was Saran Wrap.

Evvie eyed her friend admiringly. Even dressed simply, as she was today, in jeans and a faded blue t-shirt, Beady was a visual feast. With a high rounded forehead, dimpled cheeks, and a luxurious mop of nearly platinum hair a striking surprise against her chocolate skin, she was one of those mixed-race stunners who transcend the best of Black or white.

It wasn't her looks, though, that had propelled her to the top of her field. Though lacking in anything vaguely resembling maternal solicitude, Soleil Blanchette had bequeathed a hell of a genetic legacy to her only child, though Beady had frustrated her mother's pretensions to grandeur early on by refusing to answer to her given name, Belle D'Antoinette, retaining only its barest of bones in her chosen sobriquet, "B.D."

As for Beady's gene pool advantage, the story went that, during Soleil's reign as a Mardi gras beauty queen, she had hooked up with a young poet from Paris who'd traveled across the ocean to see the festivities firsthand. The fact that the Frenchman with the gorgeous green eyes had mentioned he was a distant relative of Albert Camus certainly hadn't lessened his luck with the snooty Soleil, nor had it hurt the IQ of the child she bore nine months after Antoine Compain had returned to the Sorbonne.

Her hands settling gently onto Evvie's shoulders, Beady peered so intently into her face that Evvie felt she was looking right into her soul.

"Girl, I thought you'd look like shit, but you only look like crap." She flipped the bird at the ceiling. "If there was ever proof that God was an unfair, sadistic son of a bitch, it's this. No, really. How you doin', baby?" Evvie merely shook her head. Beady grumbled hoarsely, "*Tsk, tsk, tsk.* Ain't this a bitch?"

The nurse, as if distressed more by Beady's language than the recent assault on Evvie's existence, excused herself with tight lips and sidled out of the room.

Beady gave a cynical laugh. "Remind you of anybody we know?" Her curious eyes traveled the contours of the room. Evvie's bed covers were bunched like a camel's hump at the foot of the narrow hospital bed. An assemblage of wet washcloths, used tissues, and plastic cups with orange-pulp-slimed straws sticking out of them littered the rolling side table. A robe with suspicious pinkish stains on it was flung over a beige Naugahyde chair. The window dared them to try to look out at a heavily trafficked Third Street through its blinding glare.

"Nice place." Beady walked around the bed and began stuffing Evvie's possessions into the plastic bag the nurse had left on top of a juice-and-spittle-stained pillow.

As Evvie opened her mouth to object, several more people entered the room, and it seemed suddenly oppressively crowded and noisy.

"Let me do that," Miriam was saying as she reached for the plastic bag.

Out of the corner of her eye, Evvie saw Ben and Tony grin at each other. The two boys looked as comfortable together as she felt with Tony's mother. They tapped knuckles and she heard Ben say, "S'up, bro?" and Tony simultaneously utter, "Hey, dude." It struck her how readily kids bypassed the culture's racial divides by adopting shared idioms.

Had it been like that in the seventies, when she and Miriam had competed for best friend status with their next-door neighbor, who was always inventing some new game or crazy project that would capture their imaginations for weeks at a time? She couldn't remember even being aware that Beady and her family were Black, not until

Beady's *oncle* Jean-Jacques came to visit Soleil a few months following his conversion to the Nation of Islam. After just a few hours' exposure to his angry shtick, Beady had bolted to Evvie and Miriam's house and tearfully announced that Jean-Jacques objected to her playing with *ofays*.

That was one of the few times that Evvie's father had come through for her. Heartsick, she'd been unable to fall asleep that night and had crept into her parents' bedroom, full of questions about why Beady's uncle would think of her and Miriam as foes. She knew her pig Latin just fine, but the weird politics of her family had ill-prepared her for the even weirder prejudices of the wider world. Michael taken her into the living room to avoid waking his already sick wife, and he'd gently explained to her about the roots of Black rage in centuries of slavery and oppression, telling her that her own mother had marched with Martin Luther King, Jr. for justice before Evvie was even born. And—as if rewarding her for needing the kind of lesson he just loved to dole out—he'd planted a kiss on top of her head before tucking her back into her own bed. That was one of the rare bonuses of having an ex-communist for a father. He was on the caring side of a whole host of social issues, though he'd been as wrong as could be in thinking of Mother Russia as some kind of promised land.

Evvie looked up, startled, as Beady waved a hand in front of her face.

"Earth to Evvie. Come on, girlfriend. We're springing you from this joint, and by the looks of it, not a moment too soon."

Five

WHILE EVVIE SUFFERED the indignities of being ferried to the parking garage in the obligatory departing patient's wheelchair, across town her father Michael sat buried in a worn leather armchair in the living room of his two-story Hollywood Hills home. He barely noticed the raucous pair of crows in the sycamore tree outside his front window. He was equally oblivious to the glass of Russian tea and the plate of apricot *hamantaschen* on the claw-footed mahogany table at his elbow, as well as the rousing tones of the Red Army Chorus that filled his living room. His favorite book, read and re-read more times than he could count, lay open on his lap.

It was Tolstoy's opening lines that had gotten to him. With a sick feeling, he read them again. "Every happy family is alike. Every unhappy family is unhappy in its own way."

He'd pulled *Anna Karenina* off the floor-to-ceiling bookshelves for much the same reason that he'd put the Red Army recording in the tape player. Nostalgia was one of the prerogatives and pleasures of the very old. And with acid reflux giving him the business, his bowels mulishly unbudgeable, and his right leg cramping like a son of a bitch ever since his early morning walk, his advanced years were more than a little on his mind. He'd caressed the book's worn green cover, seeking refuge in Anna's story much as Count Vronsky had in her passionate embrace. But instead, he'd been halted at the tale's frontier.

It was one family member in particular who was troubling him.

Michael's eyes strayed to a large photograph in an antique burnished frame that hung on the opposite wall. His first wife had been captured throwing back her head in laughter, so close to the delivery of their first child that her fingertips barely met as she clasped her bulging belly.

Michael felt blindly for one of the pastries, its two corners folded like a little blanket over the fruit filling, and popped it into his mouth, barely registering the familiar tangy-sweet taste.

Riva's round face beckoned him, but he turned away. Hers were lying eyes. Eyes that implied she'd be with him forever.

He could never forgive her for dying on him. Oh, he was ashamed of those feelings. They weren't rational. But he couldn't help it. After making it through his early twenties without even contemplating marriage to any of the Young Communist League girls who'd unashamedly thrown themselves at him under the banner of Free Love, Riva Sikorsky had snagged him with her generous heart, her love of literature, and an insistence that he was more than the plumber he'd set out to be. When she suggested he consider writing a book review column for the *Daily Worker,* she had no idea what she was setting in motion. It was at a Malibu Colony fundraiser for the paper that he'd met Dick Shea.

A series of clattering sounds broke into Michael's reverie. He struggled up from his chair to scowl suspiciously out the window. With a snort of laughter, he hurried to the entry hall and flung open the front door. "Well, speak of the devil. I was just thinking of you, you bastard. What're you trying to do —break my window?"

The delinquent winked, dropped the rest of his pebbles, and clapped him heartily on the back. For a brief moment Michael saw through the stooped frame, wrinkled features, and tufts of white hair to the tall and large-boned man of decades earlier, whose black button eyes, caterpillar eyebrows, and big winsome grin had made him resemble nothing less than a giant teddy bear.

"Well, you old fart, aren't you going to ask me in?"

In no time, the two of them were faced off across Michael's wooden chess table, glasses of tea perched by their elbows. They studied the board intently. Their chess games tended to take forever, even more so when they were working on a screenplay. They'd take refuge at the board whenever they hit a wall.

They both knew that, if he chose to, Michael could beat Dick in a heartbeat. Once a team publicist for Notre Dame's Fighting Irish, Dick wasn't the most incisive thinker, but he had a musical turn of phrase and an instinctive grasp of what made people tick, as long as they weren't one of the women in his life.

Dick looked up from the board. "How's she doing?"

"So far, so good. Her surgeon got wide margins, and her oncologist is betting that it's going to be easy to treat. As far as I can tell, her situation is completely different from ..." He rubbed his forehead fretfully.

"Ah, she was a helluva woman, Mike. It's a lucky thing you two were already married when I met you, or we might have ended up as competitors rather than partners."

"Now that's a horrifying thought."

Dick's eyebrows arched in feigned offense. He was used to being teased for screwing up four marriages in a row. "Pass me one of those pastries, will you?" He spat crumbs as he asked, "Does she have to have chemo?"

"We won't know for sure until Monday, but if the lab work comes back with the results they're anticipating, it'll probably be just a little radiation."

"So, how're you doing with it, sport?"

"Me? It's not my body on the rack. It's a lousy piece of luck, but she's a strong girl." He scratched his chin thoughtfully. "I just wish she had a man to take care of her."

"Maybe she doesn't want one. It's different for this generation. They're not the hopeless romantics we were. Seems like the more intelligent they are, the less inclined they are to marry. At least before their mid-thirties or forties. Which portends pretty scarily for the species, when you think of it. Turns Darwin on his ears. Survival of the dumbest."

"I know what you mean. The Catholics and Orthodox Jews are cranking them out like rabbits."

Michael saw a telltale glaze come over his friend's eyes. Dick stood abruptly and began pacing the living room. "That's it! A farce with

23

three couples. A working class Irish Catholic couple. Boston. No, Detroit. Husband works on an assembly line. No, New York. The melting pot. Husband works in construction. Wife takes in kids for day care. Couple number two—Jewish, upwardly mobile. He's in investment banking. No, stupid stereotype. He writes for the *New Yorker*. No, too intellectual. We want to get financing. He's an editor for *The Times*. She's a museum curator. Lots of ambition on both sides. They're nearly forty, but in great shape, work out five times a week. They've left it pretty late, and she's having trouble getting pregnant. The first couple are overweight, couch potato types. He smacks the kids around a little, and she wimps out on protecting them. Let's see now. Couple number three. They're just living together. Maybe African-American and Puerto Rican. They're *mensches*. She's got a couple of master's degrees but chooses to teach high school on the Lower East Side. He's a lawyer for the EPA. They're too busy and passionate with their respective callings to even think of having kids."

"Oh, come on, Dick. I'm getting too old for this. I thought we'd agreed to rest on our laurels."

"Yeah, but we can get some good licks in with this one."

Michael's expression was shrewd. "So, what's the story? How are you going to weave them together?"

"I don't know." Dick sat back down at the board. His gnarled fingers toyed tentatively with a pawn. Then he grinned. "But I think there's a statistical likelihood that *you'll* find a way."

Dick knew him better than he knew himself. By the time Michael let him out the door, the gears were already beginning to turn.

A natural pessimist, Michael had always relied on Dick's enthusiasm to rev him up. The alchemy between them worked surprisingly well. They'd written enough successful films together to enable Michael to buy this house for cash. Riva had fallen in love with it on the spot. She'd fantasized tearing down the wall between the kitchen and the family room, putting a low serving bar between them so that she could keep the girls company while she cooked. Instead, she'd gotten sick just six months after the close of escrow and had spent much of their childhood valiantly struggling to stay alive.

The room darkened, as a long gray cloud fingered past the sun. Despite the sudden gloom, Michael's palms felt sweaty. He looked down and saw his hands repetitively clenching and un-clenching of their own accord. He placed them down on either side of him and laboriously pushed himself up from his chair, groaning as his leg muscles protested.

Shuffling toward the guest bathroom, the beginnings of a thought teased at him. It was Evvie again. He clutched his belly, rock-hard with constipated cramping. Evvie was so like Riva, with her dark eyes and warm smile, how quickly she leapt from joy to challenge to an almost maternal concern. Was everything he loved cursed? Was he going to have to lose her, too?

As he passed the telephone nook in the hallway, Michael struggled with the temptation to pick up the phone. He might be able to catch Evvie before she left the hospital, but maybe it wouldn't be the wisest thing to call when he was feeling this down. The last thing his daughter needed right now was her father filling her with his own fears.

Six

IT WAS ONE of the unspoken taboos of the Kerr tribe that no one dared mention Moira's name to Michael when she came to town. The two hadn't talked since the night his teenaged daughter had blurted out that she was pregnant. Michael had been apoplectic, but it wasn't until after the girls had gone to bed that he'd accused Moira of aiding and abetting Miriam in her affair with a dissolute poet a good ten years her senior. Consumed as Michael had been with helplessness and fury, Moira's retort about the irony of his outrage over the age disparity had been lost on him. Instead, with the discipline of a man who'd weathered more disappointments than he cared to count, he refused to utter one more word to his ten-years-younger second wife until she gave up and moved back to Berkeley.

But that didn't mean she had erased him from her own mind, nor would she have dreamed of losing touch with the extended family she'd gained by marrying him.

Awaiting Evvie's return to the condo, Moira fretted over how Michael was weathering the current crisis until she realized she herself was freezing. Padding barefooted across the terra cotta tiled kitchen floor, she nudged aside a wall hanging that concealed the plastic thermostat. Miriam had unerring taste in converting what had once been a boring 1980's condo into something that would be at home on the Amalfi coast, but she kept the place as cold as a morgue.

Moira had left her Charles Jourdain pumps behind in the living room, and her silvery cape lay draped across the arm of the overstuffed sofa she supposed she'd be sleeping on that night. Heels and gauzy shawls were nothing but a hindrance when you were cooking, which was how she'd decided to atone for arriving unannounced on her step-daughters' doorstep. She was determined not to be a burden to Miriam, even more so after catching her grim expression as she hustled Ben out the door to pick up Evvie from the hospital.

Moira turned back to the cutting board, which she'd blanketed with tomatoes, Crimini mushrooms, red and yellow peppers, fresh basil, and shaved Parmesan. She paused with her dicing knife mid-air, recalling how Miriam had hesitated at the front door, surveying the hall with haunted eyes, as if she could see something, or someone, that Moira couldn't. Even after she and Ben had gone, Miriam's anxiety permeated the condo like the smell of leaking gas. And if Miriam were showing visible signs of strain, Ben had looked downright agonized. But that was to be expected. Evvie had virtually raised the boy.

It was awful to think of Evvie facing this kind of ordeal. Radiation, chemotherapy. Some of Moira's more homeopathically inclined neighbors in the Bay Area wouldn't submit to those nuclear bombs of modern medicine, claiming they poisoned your body more than they helped it. But whatever the treatment, it wouldn't last forever, and if anybody could handle it, it was Evvie.

Moira licked little clumps of tomato flesh off her perfectly painted fingernails as she stared down at the colorful array of vegetables on the cutting board. It would be awfully nice to surprise her eldest step-daughter with a beautiful throw blanket, something soft she could nestle into while she was recovering. She pictured Evvie's olive-tinged complexion, naturally coral lips, and dark hair complemented by these deep crimsons, greens, and yellows, with strands of cocoa woven in. Yes, these hues were just right. Evvie had the kind of looks that belonged to the earth. The way she moved was like a big cat, sensuously slow and lazy one moment, then rising to alertness when the occasion demanded. Unlike Miriam, who was more like a deer or a springbok, skinny and nervy and always on the verge of sprinting away at breathtaking speed.

The phone rang once, and Moira dashed for it, praying nothing had gone wrong at the hospital. "Hello?"

It was Michael, his tone impatient. "Miriam?"

"No, Michael, this is Moira. How are you?" She held her breath until he finally responded.

"Fine, fine. Is Miriam there?"

"No, she's still at the hospital. Michael, I'm so sorry about Evvie—"

"Yes, well, what about Benjamin?"

"He went with her. They should be back any time now. Listen, I'm making a light meal for everyone. Would you like to—"

"No, no. Just have them call me when they get in."

The sound of his voice gave way to the dial tone. She stared at the receiver. "I'm fine, too, Michael. Thanks for asking." Eighteen years of silence, and this was the best he could do?

The last time she'd seen Michael, he'd been beside himself over Miriam's defiant confession of her pregnancy. Moira had been stunned herself, but Michael had been correct on one count—she *had* known about Miriam's relationship with Simon. What had *not* occurred to her was that a man of twenty-six wouldn't have had the good sense to use a condom.

Moira glanced at the London Underground wall clock Miriam had purchased for a song at a Covent Garden antique shop last month on the same trip that she'd met James. At least, Moira *thought* that was his name. Ever since Simon, Miriam had led the most active sex life of anyone Moira knew. "But that's just it," she grumbled. It was the quantity of Miriam's affairs that tended to stand out, rather than the quality. James was only the latest of a long string of pretty boys who'd woven their way through Miriam's life like flashy costume jewelry. Most of them were variations on the same theme, *artistes* who could never seem to pay their dues enough to actualize their artistry. Really, she didn't know which of her stepdaughters was in worse shape in the man department—Evvie, whose love life was a desert, or Miriam, who inhabited a rain forest of unrealistic desire.

The sound of a key turning in a lock broke into Moira's awareness. She looked up sharply, then hurried toward the condo's entryway, where she nearly tripped on the Oriental hall runner before managing to right herself just as Miriam threw open the front door.

Miriam's eyes were wide and liquid, her lips chalk white. She looked less like a springbok than a nervy racehorse about to bolt from the starting line. "Jesus! I thought we'd never get her out of there."

Ben appeared next on the threshold, firmly grasping Evvie under her left arm, his tall frame bent over his aunt as if he were trying to shield her from the thunderbolts of Zeus.

But it was Evvie, shuffling through the doorway like an old woman, her face open and raw, who made Moira feel suddenly helpless. *Oh my God*, thought Moira, even as she told Evvie that she hoped a nice healthy frittata would erase the taste of hospital food from her memory. What she really meant to say was, *Can this really be happening?*

As Ben led Evvie down the hall, Moira turned to Miriam, hissing, "Jesus! Do you want me to leave?"

"No, no. But I'd better see to her. She's hardly going to want Ben to help her undress." The doorbell rang. "Shit, that's probably Beady and Tony. They followed us here from Cedars. I don't think any of us realized … Anyway, can you …?"

"Go on. I'll get it." Moira turned to the door, muttering gloomily, "Maybe they'd like some frittatas."

***

When Moira finally got the other four seated, it was as if a dark cloud hung over the dining table. Even Ben and Tony—who ended up devouring six frittatas and four glasses of milk between them—were unusually subdued.

Moira started as Miriam abruptly pushed back her chair. "I'm going to check … Maybe she's awake." Her eyes wandered over the nearly-licked-clean dishes littering the table. "And hungry."

Moira exchanged a look with Beady, who sighed. "I should've known that she wouldn't be up for a visit."

"No, no," Moira replied. "I'm sure it meant so much to her that you came."

Miriam returned and slid back into her seat. "Dead to the world. Oh, God, I didn't mean—"

"Of course, you didn't." This was awful. Moira turned to Tony, forcing her lips into a gracious smile. "Gads, it's been ages since I last saw you. I don't think your voice had even dropped. And now Miriam tells me you've got the rest of your life mapped out."

Tony's cheeks flushed. "It's still pretty preliminary."

"Where are you planning to study? You do have to go to college to—"

"Yeah, unfortunately." He flicked a guilty look at his mother. "Naw, I'm just kidding. They've got a pretty good program in land-scape design at Cal, but I might want to study abroad. The University of Manchester is one possibility. Anyway, I don't have to pin myself down for another year. Not like this dude."

Ben frowned. "Thanks for reminding me, bro."

Beady put down her cup of coffee. "Tony, leave that boy alone. Let's hope you have the same problem as Ben when the time comes. It's not everyone who does well enough to have their pick of the Ivies."

Miriam tore at her napkin. "Yes, but if he doesn't pick soon, he'll end up at Santa Monica College."

Moira sensed that Ben had just about had it. She gently admonished Miriam. "Oh, come on, love. Give him a little credit."

"I'm happy to, but if he doesn't let one of these schools know soon—"

Ben stood, his ears flaming. He avoided meeting his mother's eyes. "Now that you've dissected my life … Tony, let's go, man." Tony shot the women an apologetic glance before following Ben out of the room.

All three women flinched as they heard Ben slam his bedroom door.

Miriam was on the verge of tears. "I've done it again, haven't I?"

"Darling, I think any single mother who manages to raise a son to adulthood deserves an award."

"Please, don't even talk about awards." Miriam held up two fingers. "The buzz is that two of the people I went to school with are going to be up for Costume Design this year. Two! Do you believe it?"

Beady leaned forward, her cornsilk frizz falling across her eye. "Girlfriend, you can't let that shit get to you. You know how political those things are."

"Easy for you to say."

"But that just proves my point. No offense, but when you make a documentary about disadvantaged Black kids and there's nothing up that year about the Holocaust, you're a shoo-in for an Oscar."

They all laughed.

"Too true," said Miriam, "but when your own father has a cabinet full of trophies, you get a little hungry for one of your own. Or at least *something*. Even Moira rated an article about her upcoming show in the *LA Times*."

Beady glanced curiously at Moira. "What show is that?"

"Oh, pish. No big deal. I'll be hanging in the Worth Ryder Gallery at Cal. It was just a little blurb."

Miriam made a face. "Blurb, *shmurb*. All *I've* gotten so far is my name scrolling the screen at a zillion miles an hour while everyone's leaving the theater."

Moira was finding the conversation increasingly tiresome. "For heaven's sake, Miriam, what's with the envy? You're a creative woman, and every one of your projects has offered you a new challenge. Most people's jobs are boring beyond belief. Look at Evvie—stuck with humoring a bunch of decrepit seniors day after day. Besides, the only reason they mentioned my show is that one of the schools the proceeds will benefit is LA High."

Beady put down her coffee cup. "You used to give weaving lessons there, didn't you? Soleil had this little rap she liked to do"—she screwed her face into an imitation of her mother's sour mien—"'I don't know why they'd hire some rich white woman to teach weaving to a bunch of ignorant ghetto kids who can't even read.'"

"None of us can be held responsible for our parents. If you don't hold the O'Shaughnessys against me, I won't hold your mother against you. Besides ..." Moira's hand flew to her mouth. "Oh, for God's sake, Miriam. Your father! I forgot to tell you he called."

"Oh, great." Miriam sprang out of her seat and edged behind Moira on her way to the phone. "I'm a shitty mother, a pedestrian costume designer, my sister might die from the same disease my mother died of, and now my father's gonna kill me. Did I do something awful in some past life to deserve this?"

Moira skewed around in her chair, just in time to see Miriam nearly collide with Evvie, who was standing in the doorway, her face pillow-creased and her dark hair every which way from sleep.

"Sorry to be such a pest," Evvie mumbled to the floor, "but do you think it's too soon to take another pain pill?"

***

Evvie was out of it, but not so much that she'd missed the look exchanged by Moira and her sister when she'd announced her presence. Under better circumstances, she might have found her sister's self-involvement laughable, but at this moment it merely added to her pity party. When Miriam offered to follow her back into her bedroom to tuck her in, Evvie hastily downed her Darvocet and brushed her away. "No, I'll be fine now. Go on back and finish your meal."

Detouring into the bathroom on her way back to bed, she caught a glimpse of herself in the bathroom mirror. No reassurance there. Her high-perched breasts had once been the envy of every woman she knew. But that was "B.C." Before cancer.

Christ, if Simon Warwick could see her now. Dull hair, puffy face, major bags under her eyes. It sure as hell wasn't the face that, though not nearly as lovely as her younger sister's, he'd once said was exotic and soulful.

She lowered herself onto the toilet and lingered there with little result, cursing the Darvocet for making her bowels so recalcitrant. They said that if you altered one little thing in the past, the future would turn out entirely differently. Would she be leading some deliriously thrilling life right now if Simon hadn't come up with the idea of storing all those kilos of weed in her father's never-used garage while her dad and Moira were out of the country on a series of press junkets?

Evvie pulled up her pajamas and shuffled back into bed. She knew she should stay away from thoughts about Simon. This was hardly the time to indulge in the kind of self-punishment she'd perfected ever since he'd left. But, if anything, her weakened state seemed to leave her even more vulnerable to obsessively replaying the events of the day that she'd driven Simon to her home on Wonderland Avenue with a trunk load of marijuana in her car. He'd rewarded her with an unusually enthusiastic hug, whispering in her ear, "Baby, you're not going to regret this. This shit's going to finance our move to Berkeley. You can transfer your studies up to Cal. We'll rent ourselves a big old house, paint, write, grow our own vegetables, and make the kind of life together most people don't even dream of." She'd lapped up his praise like a helpless puppy until she caught sight of her sister strolling unhurriedly up the street, a notebook balanced fetchingly on her hip. Crimped hair swirling around her delicate face like an aureole, Miriam was like a vision from a Botticelli painting.

Simon had grumbled when Evvie pushed him away, but when he followed her gaze, his expression gave way to astonishment.

Really, who could blame him?

And who'd be twenty-two again? Anyone with half a brain would have recognized that something was up when, six months after meeting her sister, Simon had left a cryptic message on Evvie's cell phone that he was moving up north, since things had gotten "a little complicated down here." She'd continued to delude herself that he would come back to her until Miriam blurted out— during what turned out to be the last dinner of Michael and Moira's marriage—that she was pregnant.

Evvie hadn't dared to ask Miriam who the father was, and their dad hadn't seemed to care, merely pronouncing with dangerous calm, "Then you'll have to get an abortion." To which Miriam spat back that she was already four months gone. When their father stalked out of the room, Miriam had thrown herself onto Moira's shoulder, crying hysterically that she was going to be one of those pathetic teenaged mothers on Welfare.

And then, like one of Pavlov's predictable canines, Evvie had felt her mouth open of its own accord, offering to put her own plans on hold to take care of the baby. Making it sound like a mere inconvenience to delay her gerontology internship while Miriam completed her two-year course at New York's Fashion Institute.

Pretty nuts, but then again, pretty predictable. Long before they'd lost their mother, the one thing she simply could not bear was hearing her sister cry.

Evvie tried rolling onto her right side but caught herself as her bandaged breast complained. How long was it going to take for the Darvocet to kick in?

It occurred to her that she'd lived her life on a river of unquiet. Under the surface lurked a continual flow of worry and guilt and blame. At night, when the waters threatened to overrun the banks of her defenses, she kept her regrets at bay by physically shifting around in her bed like a mad kayaker. But with this mangled right side of hers making the slightest movement miserable, how was she ever going to manage to hold back the tide?

"For fuck's sake," she muttered, "let it go. Why can't you let it go?" Wasn't it bad enough getting cancer? What if she ended up dying from this shit? Did she really want to ruin her last months on the planet nursing some ancient grudge?

Seven

DARVOCET WAS A dubious savior. Evvie sluggishly registered the new day after a fitful few hours of nightmarish sleep.

Her household's familiar morning routine nudged at her senses. Coffee beans rattling in the grinder. The hum of the dishwasher. Ben's shower running. The phone rang, and she heard the quick clatter of a woman's shoes on bare wood, followed by Miriam's briskly challenging "Hello?"

Someone was wielding a toothbrush in the adjacent bathroom. Evvie realized with surprise that it must be Moira, up early for her if Ben hadn't even left for school yet. The joint was certainly jumping.

Evvie fretfully scratched at an edge of the layered bandage that covered her aching breast. She felt about as energetic as a lumpfish. *Except that I don't have a lump anymore, do I? More like a hole.* Hearing her own bitter laughter was strangely satisfying, as if there were someone in the room with her who actually got how she felt.

Ha ha. A fish with a hole. A whole fish. She hated it when a dinner companion would order a whole fish at an upscale restaurant, where most waiters seemed to feel obliged to wheel the damned thing to the table on a sizzling platter, de-boning it with extravagant finesse. While everyone else ooh-ed and ah-ed, she would feel less like an appreciative audience than a witnesses to an execution, unable to disregard the sour downturn of the creature's mouth and its round eye fixing her with a stony look of accusation.

She wished she knew whom *she* could accuse for getting her carved up like some sacrificial offering. Corporate executives using the earth as a garbage pail for toxic waste? Herself, smoking a pack a day in her twenties? Going on estrogen replacement when her periods stopped prematurely? Her mother, for passing along cancer-vulnerable genes? God? Better watch out for that one. In her current condition, she couldn't afford to alienate Him. Besides, hadn't Simon insisted that laying one's personal woes at the feet of God was hopelessly naive?

It took Evvie a while to realize there were sounds coming from just behind her bedroom door.

She heard Moira ask in a low voice, "Who was on the phone?" and Ben's response: "It was Beady, calling from the set."

"*Shh*," she could make out Miriam hissing, "I'm not sure she's awake yet."

"Then I'm cutting my morning classes," Ben replied. And then, as if his mother had flashed him one of her looks, "For Christ's sake, Mom, do you think I can listen to some stupid history teacher when I don't even know how she's doing?"

Evvie stayed curled in her bed, facing the door. She heard Moira's faint assent, then Miriam mumbling, "Of course. I don't know why I assume it's easier for you than the rest of us. I just wish to Christ we could have the test results now. It's torture to have to wait until Monday to find out what we're up against."

At this, Evvie snorted. "You've got to be joking if you think I can't hear you." She struggled into a sitting position, patting the bedcovers at her side as soon as Miriam swung open the door. "Well, come on," she laughed shakily. "I suppose you want a post-mortem."

The three of them gingerly arranged themselves around her on the bed.

She scanned their faces and nearly broke down. Moira, in particular, was looking at her with such pity that she worried that her family knew something she didn't. Her oncologist had told her it was likely, since she'd already entered an unusually early menopause, that her own cancer would turn out to be very different from the aggressive type that had claimed her mother. He'd said that, if the lab tests proved him right, she'd come out of this just fine. But what if that was all bullshit? Her mother's doctors probably said the same thing to *her* before she died. And from what she'd heard Miriam say last night, her sister was thinking along much the same lines herself.

She felt herself slipping into quicksand, but then Ben squeezed her hand. She forced a grin. "Actually, I'm feeling pretty good." The three of them stared at her disbelievingly. "That obvious? Okay, if you really want to know, it *is* aching a bit. Dad may think I'm strong as a horse, but I feel more like a tower of Jell-O." She paused. "Actually, I'm worried about him. This is too much like … well, you know. I hope you guys are keeping close tabs on him."

Miriam shot a glance at Moira. "He's fine. He already called this morning. Ben's going to bring him over here for dinner tonight."

"What?" Evvie looked over at Moira. "With you here? No offense, but—"

Ben burst in, his voice thick with emotion. "Aunt Evvie, is there anything we can do?"

Before she could respond, Moira slid off the bed and interrupted, arms akimbo. "What your aunt Evvie needs is a healthy breakfast. Fresh food to stimulate her immune system." She glided toward the door. Evvie thought that she looked like one of those gracious but slightly arty hostesses sometimes harpooned in *New Yorker* cartoons, with her well-fitting black silk toreador pants and black scarf knotted casually just-so below the scoop neck of her white cashmere top. "Don't worry, darling. You won't need to deal with some godawful reunion between your father and me. Turns out I've got to fly back this afternoon. My assistant Poppy broke her leg—skateboarding, of all things, the little idiot—and I've got to find someone else to help mount my show. But I've got a couple of hours. How about if I rustle you up a fresh fruit brekkie? Lots of vitamins and minerals and natural fiber." She winked. "Actually, we could all benefit from eating the way you should now."

Evvie nodded compliantly, more to get her out of the room than because she had any appetite. Sometimes Moira's upbeat largesse was like the sun. You didn't want to stare at it for too long or you'd go blind.

Ben shifted closer to Evvie. He whispered softly, "I love you, Auntie."

Evvie nearly lost it then. Ben had always favored his mother's family in looks, with a forehead as high as Michael's and with Miriam's mischievous grin, but once he went through puberty, his voice was a ringer for his father's. Evvie took a guilty pleasure in having a living reminder of Simon in her own home, as if she were cheating destiny in this way.

But you couldn't really cheat the Fates in the end, could you? If they wanted you to have little and you reached for more, you paid. Her mother had tried mightily to counteract that message before she died—clutching Evvie's shoulders with her emaciated claws of hands, fixing her gaunt eyes on her, saying, "Go for it, my darling, go for the gusto. I'll be watching over you, rooting for you." Evvie had been more consumed with guilt for being repelled by the strange smells emanating from her mother's broken body than listening to the words that were pouring out of her chapped lips.

"Evvie?" Miriam's intensity called her back to the present. "Where'd you go?"

Evvie bit her lip, debating whether to risk it. "Oh, I don't know … But, Miriam, do you ever miss Mom? I know she was sick much of the time when we were growing up, and you were younger, but does that stop you from missing her? I know it's weird, but this cancer crap's got me dwelling on the past. And not just about Mom." Observing her sister's blank stare, Evvie pushed away the resentment that hovered like a homeless person at the edge of her mind. "Dad, too. Do you ever wonder what he was like before, well, before he became our father?"

Her words were lost as Moira burst into the room like a firecracker, and Evvie couldn't help but notice that both Miriam and Ben looked relieved. So much for true confessions.

Moira strode proudly to Evvie's bedside, bearing Miriam's new floral tray. On it, she'd set a dish of neatly cut banana circles, topped with yogurt and a scattering of fresh raspberries. Three red roses sprung from a small vase on the tray. Several petals from one of the flowers had fallen and had assumed a decidedly fish-shaped pattern over the tray's delicate design.

Moira placed the tray across Evvie's lap. "Ta da," she sang.

As Evvie fought for breath, Moira prodded her. "Well, let's not stand on ceremony, honey pie. Eat up. Let's get you well. You know what they say. Healthy food makes a healthy body. You are what you eat. And, of course, you've got to do a lot of creative visualization." She got up and walked across the room, straightening one of the curtain panels. A shaft of sunlight bisected Evvie's face. "But you're the psychologist. I don't have to tell you how important it is to avoid negative thoughts."

Eight

IN THE SCRUBBY foothills above Burbank where dozens of classic TV Westerns had been filmed, Beady was having a hell of a time keeping her own dark thoughts corralled. "Cut!" she cried, brushing an errant strand of hair off her forehead and tucking it back inside the wild puff barely restrained by her headband. In an instant, the set broke out in small talk, actors and crew bolting for their breakfast like there was no tomorrow.

Tensely rubbing her shoulder, she picked her way through a web of cables, lights, and folding chairs. The last shot had been tricky, and they'd wasted nearly an hour because of some mechanical trouble with the camera crane, but her mind was miles away from the Ford commercial she was directing on this stretch of land just beyond the reach of LA.

Instead, she wondered if it was too soon to try Evvie again and whether her friend was feeling any better. But who was she kidding? Evvie wasn't likely to feel normal any time soon. Oh, she had grit and was no delicate flower. But the big C? That shit could kill you before you even knew what was going on.

Beady cradled her elbows with her hands, and pensively rocked back and forth between her heels and the balls of her feet. Those doctors had better do right by Evvie. Maybe she should ask her *grand-mère* to make her one of her famous *asafetiddy* bags to wear around her neck.

She approached one of several white-clothed banquet tables, where small flames flickered under huge stainless steel chafing dishes that kept mounds of creamy scrambled eggs, piles of moist sausages, and scads of streaky bacon strips hot and aromatic. There were overflowing baskets of baked goods—oversized blueberry and bran muffins, raisin-rich scones, scores of crusty baguettes and soft brioches, and a wide selection of water, egg, and onion bagels to go with the finest smoked salmon and cream cheese that Ford Motor Company could buy.

Beady found herself reflecting, not for the first time, that for all the money the major corporations lavished on their TV commercials, poverty could be vanquished, not only in the U.S., but in several Third World countries as well. But the sad truth was that, unlike the agencies and organizations whose grants sometimes underwrote her documentaries, the corporate bastards did pay handsomely. And on time. If Ford unwittingly contributed generous sums to her production of documentary films actually geared to the public good, she could handle the creative compromise she made in occasionally directing high-end commercials like this one.

A craft services staffer, wearing ten thin rings crawling up her ears like silver spider legs, held out a heavy-duty paper plate. Beady declined but forced herself to take a few steps down the line and survey what was on offer. She tore off a piece of Brioche and popped a few grapes into her mouth with such lack of enthusiasm that they might as well have been pieces of Styrofoam popcorn.

One of the sound men strode purposefully up to the table, his beer gut preceding the rest of him. Unaware of Beady's unwonted pickiness, he nudged her with his elbow. "Well, wuddayaknow? If it isn't Miss Blanchette. And here we are again, sidling up to the trough together."

Startled, Beady looked up into Kevin O'Connolly's friendly blue eyes. The slow smile that spread over her soft brown face was like the sun that was just beginning to break over the foothills. "Hey, lover." She poked Kevin's protruding belly with her last grape, then dropped it exaggeratedly onto his paper plate. "What're you gonna have? A side of beef? A couple of horses? A house?"

He took no offense. They played this game every time they worked together. He looked down at her other hand, which still held the piece of bread. "Hell, what are you this morning—Gretel about to leave a little trail in the forest so somebody can find you?"

Her eyes sparkled, and her dimples deepened beguilingly. "Only if that somebody's you."

Kevin's riposte was quick. "I wish." He was laughing, but his expression was genuinely wistful.

Their repartee was interrupted by the sound of deliberate footsteps. Beady looked up. A mahogany-skinned woman had come to a stop just behind Kevin. She wore a pair of rose-tinted sunglasses and an expensive looking black coat.

"Desiree!" Beady exclaimed. She turned to excuse herself to Kevin, but he was already walking toward another table.

Beady embraced the newcomer, whispering into her ear, "The coat's great, but girl, you'd think you were traveling to the North Pole." Looking over Desiree's shoulder, she spotted a rumpled-suited man politely hanging back a few feet. A dark shadow of stubble blanketed his otherwise attractive cleft chin and angular Semitic cheekbones, and his eyes had gray circles under them, but he scanned the bustling commercial set with lively curiosity.

Desiree pushed away from Beady and held her at arm's length, her teeth like shiny pearls against her rich dark skin. She laughed lustily. "Honey, I don't know how you expect me to get up at the crack of dawn, pick up Ezra from LAX and drive us out here to No Man's Land to fit your crazy schedule, and not run the risk of freezing to death." She put a hand on her hip, and her coat flared open to reveal one perfectly tailored charcoal wool pant leg. "Look here, I don't care if it's warming up a little now. At five-thirty my beautiful black ass nearly iced over." She motioned to the man who'd come with her to join them.

"Well, here he is," she said. "Just like I promised. Beady, this is Ezra Rosenberg, right off the plane from Chechnya. Poor baby, I didn't even give him time to shave before bringing him out here. Ezra, this is the woman you need to know. Beady Blanchette."

Beady found her hand being seized by both of Ezra's and shaken vigorously. "It's an honor," he said.

Beady immediately warmed to his raspy voice, candid brown eyes, and the genuine smile that creased his intelligent-looking, slightly olive-tinged face. "From what Desiree's told me, the honor's rightfully mine. C'mon, I've got a few more minutes before getting back to serve my slave masters at Ford. Wanna smoke?" She grabbed a canvas-backed director's chair and scraped it along the ground to set beside two folding chairs. Without ceremony, they all sat down, then scooted the chairs closer together as they realized they had to raise their voices to be heard against the sound of someone's radio.

Beady impatiently fished inside her big leather handbag, overflowing with notes for the shoot, and extracted a pack of Benson and Hedges Ultra Lights. She offered it around. Both of her visitors declined, but, as she lit up and inhaled deeply, she did notice that Ezra was unabashedly studying her. Oddly, she didn't mind. Somehow, she knew he wasn't putting the make on her. Just as surprisingly, given his attractive manner, she hadn't the least temptation to flirt with him. Was it because something told her he was already taken? She glanced at his left hand. No ring. Men didn't always wear them. But now he was leaning forward in his chair. Beady raised her eyebrows, inviting him to begin.

"Okay. I know you're right in the middle of it, so I'll try to make this brief." He frowned for a moment. "Here's the thing. I've got the footage. Chechnya, Kosovo, Rwanda, Jenin. You name it, I've been there. Most of the stuff, I've had to turn in to *my* masters at CNN." He flashed her a quick grin, then resumed talking, his voice hoarse. Beady realized that this man must be bone-weary, and she worried that he might see her as some kind of media brat, making him come all the way out here, straight from a grueling flight and Lord knew what else before that. She frowned, but he didn't seem to notice, just determinedly pursued his pitch. "But I always make sure to shoot as much as I can on my own nickel once I'm off the payroll." He glanced quickly over his shoulder. "Matter of fact, most of what I'm talking about is sitting in a bunch of boxes of Betacams in Desiree's trunk." He rubbed his chin. "Amazing, when you think about it. Evidence of the slaughter of the innocents in Desiree's shiny red BMW."

Beady blinked, surreptitiously glancing at Desiree, but Desiree just kept nodding enthusiastically, like one of those old jiggle-headed dolls that kept bobbing up and down. Well, this was certainly a first. The Desiree she knew was usually quick to take righteous offense at anybody who even hinted that a Black woman wasn't entitled to every bit of the material goodies that White America craved with every fiber of its collective appetite. And Desiree was just crazy about her "shiny red BMW."

Ezra rushed on. For one distracting second, his wide gestures called her attention to the dense black hairs on the backs of his big, capable-looking hands. "It's the youngest kids who suffer the most in these conflicts. It puts a whole new spin on what Freud claimed were the formative years. Forget about Oedipal this and child abuse that." He gave a bitter laugh. "If parents trying to kill off their neighbors doesn't end up murdering all the children, it absolutely mutilates their spirits. Turns them into permanent victims. Or worse yet, another generation of victimizers." Ezra halted, then continued more slowly, as if he'd finally recognized his own exhaustion. "I've got the footage and maybe a little bit of the overview, but not much else, certainly not the ability to cut it all together into something that says what needs to be said. That's where you come in. That is, if you want to. I've known about your work for a long time. You're pretty famous out in the field. When Desiree told me she knew you, well ..."

Beady jerked as the red-hot stub of her cigarette reached her fingers. She dropped it hastily and ground it into the dust with her sneaker. Her Assistant Director Richard Marilla, Kevin's boss Joe Newton, and Freya from Wardrobe were gathered in a small group a few feet away, shooting impatient looks in her direction. Richard pointedly tapped his wristwatch and inclined his head toward the camera.

Beady ran a hand over her glistening hair. She addressed her words to a point just slightly above Ezra's head. "Shit. Listen, there's no way I can do justice to this right this second." When Ezra opened his mouth to speak, she put up a hand. "But I'm definitely intrigued." She turned to Desiree. "When can we meet again?"

Desiree assumed the brisk tone of the cameraman's agent she was. "Baby, you know I love you, but Ezra's only got a few days in town before he's off to cover the World Trade Organization shindig in Zurich. If you can't commit to this, I've got to round up a couple of other prospects real quick."

Beady spoke hurriedly, pleadingly. "Don't do me like this, Desiree. You don't have to threaten me with the competition. I'm definitely interested, but it's impossible to even think right now. You can see how it is." The crew, its appetite for food and chatter at least momentarily satisfied, had started to buzz into frenetic activity like a hive of worker bees.

"What about getting together tonight?" Beady asked. Then, clapping a hand to her forehead, she amended hastily, "Shit, I have no idea how late we'll be shooting. Where can I reach you?" She tried to beam her genuine interest at Ezra. He was frowning, and she noticed for the first time that he had some kind of orange stain on the white shirt he wore under his wrinkled brown suit jacket. She could just see him absent-mindedly spilling orange juice all over himself on the flight over. Had his masters sprung for Business Class or left him to the claustrophobic mercies of Economy? Suddenly, she felt very close to him, almost like he was family. She grabbed his hand. "Listen, you look like you could use about a thousand winks. How's about I call you when I finish? I'll probably be so wired that I won't be able to sleep anyway, and if you get yourself some z's before then, we can really get down to it." She let go of his hand and nervously twirled a lock of hair. "What you're proposing we work on together will probably give me nightmares from now until doomsday." Her face suddenly split open in a wide grin. "Call me a masochist, but I think I'm game. I just need to take a look at your footage and see exactly what you've got. Can you get hold of a Betacam deck? I know it's short notice ..."

She saw Desiree glance questioningly at Ezra, and she herself was holding her breath. As for Ezra, he merely sat awhile, staring fixedly at some point next to his dusty brown loafer. Then he stood up, stretched his arms into the air and yawned like an unselfconscious lion. Almost as an afterthought, he said lazily, "Sounds good to me."

Desiree gave Beady a quick hug. "That's my girl. He's amazing. You won't regret it."

Beady watched the two of them walk toward Desiree's BMW. Beady had been trying to figure out what her next film project should be, dealing out her Tarot cards almost every night as her *grand-mère* had taught her, looking for some kind of sign, but she'd never imagined she'd be getting up to her eyeballs in international affairs. She was already feeling that particular lightheadedness that signaled she was onto something. Something that cried out to be done. A couple of possible titles even bubbled up. Maybe *The Spoils of War.* Or *Their Fathers' Sins.* She couldn't wait to tell Evvie. With her sympathy for the underdog, she'd undoubtedly be thrilled.

But then she flushed with shame. What in the hell was she thinking of? This was one time when Evvie needed to be thinking about nobody but herself.

"Fuck," she muttered, grabbing a notepad before coming up behind Richard, who was squinting through the lens of the camera. He shot her a paranoid look. "Sorry," she said. "Not you. I didn't mean you."

She turned her attention to the SUV they were filming, sparkling in the sun like a sacred icon. Richard stepped back to let her peer through the lens. She forced an enthusiastic smile onto her face and gave the DP a thumbs-up sign. "Looks like a million bucks," she said.

Nine

WHEN MONDAY FINALLY crawled around, Evvie had Beady's Creole upbringing to thank when she stepped into the elevator at Cedars-Sinai's outpatient wing and was instantly forced to the side by the unceremonious flight of its entire group of occupants. As the elevator car climbed to the fifth floor, she hastily untied the noxious *asafetiddy* bag from around her neck and stuffed it into her purse, issuing a silent apology to Beady's *grand-mère*.

She tried keeping a pleasant smile on her face as she signed in at the reception desk, but being perky wasn't exactly second nature when you were about to hear the final verdict on how lethal your cancer was. She sat on the only vacant chair left in Dr. Abrams' cramped waiting room, her eyes seeking commiseration with the potpourri of patients crowding the room. Most of them were considerably older than she. Five out of six of them had a similar yellow tinge to their complexions, and Evvie speculated that the ghastly glow came from chemo or crummy liver function or something equally terrifying. They looked down at their shoes as if some latent mystery resided there; they stared into space with hollow, baggy eyes; they leafed listlessly through dog-eared *Newsweek* and *Redbook* magazines. They did everything, in fact, but acknowledge that another patient, *another cancer patient*, had entered the room.

Nor was the suite's shoddy décor any comfort. When she'd gotten the disturbing results from her mammogram, she'd shopped the top oncologists at Cedars like some hard-core Macy's bargain hunter, except it wasn't money she was looking to save but the discomfort of having the wrong doctor on her case.

She'd nearly gone with Harold Rosenzweig, a charming and reputedly brilliant man whose successful practice took up nearly a whole floor, with an *Architectural Digest*-class waiting room stocked with *Vanity Fair, Daily Variety*, and *Rolling Stone*, an espresso coffee maker; heaping baskets of healthy muffins and Noah's bagels; and a giant, glass-fronted fridge filled with fresh fruit juices lining one wall. But Rosenzweig's huge chemotherapy room, with two facing rows of reclining people who might have been Barcalounger testers but for the IV lines in their arms, had given her the *heebie-jeebies*. She didn't quite fancy being some assembly line patient when it was her own fucking life on that particular line.

You certainly couldn't accuse David Abrams of running a slick operation. His waiting room was circa 1970, the chairs some kind of ersatz leather, each of them scooped by thousands of seated asses into a kind of bowl shape that made you feel like you were perched directly on your tail bone. In one corner resided a dusty fishbowl, whose two salmon-and-cream-speckled inhabitants traced an incessant infinity sign above a few sprouts of fake greenery and a couple of plastic deep-sea divers probing the bottom of the bowl.

But David Abrams was a *mensch*. She got her first clue to that one when the short, salt-and-pepper mustached man, dressed in slightly rumpled slacks and a plaid flannel shirt, opened the door to the examining area himself and called out her name. She got her second when, ushering her into his consulting room, he pulled his chair around from behind his desk to sit closely facing her, cocking his head with genuine interest as he said, "So, how are you? I would imagine you're scared shitless right now, but I want you to know that, if this does turn out to be cancer, we have a whole host of treatments available that we didn't have even five years ago. And they're good. But I'd imagine that's faint comfort to you right now."

Her third clue had come when, looking up toward the ceiling to try to coalesce some of the four million questions she wanted to ask, she saw two cheaply framed black and white photographs tilting haphazardly above his various diplomas. One was a shot of a bashfully grinning Bobby Kennedy, his sleeves rolled up to his elbows, reaching down to shake hands with migrant workers from the bed of a truck. The other showed Martin Luther King, Jr. facing the camera with such simple serenity that you just knew he'd already been to the mountaintop.

There was something about the idealism of those two, brought forward like a couple of time travelers to this brave new millennium via Dr. David Abrams's earnest spirit, that she'd wanted on her side. She'd breathed deeply, leaned forward, and began to tell her new oncologist exactly how crappy she felt.

But that was then. Now she realized that she hadn't even known the true meaning of crappy. It was one thing to suspect cancer and another to know the fucker had you by the tail. Well, anyway, tit. It was another to contemplate the possibility that the lab tests had proved all her doctors' optimistic predictions wrong.

Just her luck now, Abrams was running late. When the receptionist poked her head out the door and announced that fact to the roomful of people, Evvie had to stifle an impulse to groan aloud. The impassive reaction on the part of the others in the room didn't help. Not a visible emotional blip on any one of their faces. They just went on reading and staring. All but one old bald-headed man, who fished interminably in his pocket until Evvie wondered if he was masturbating. But then he pulled a handkerchief out of his pocket, honked into it a couple of times, then stuffed it back in and stared down at his shoe.

By the time the waiting room had cleared, and a harassed-looking Abrams called her name, Evvie figured she'd aged a decade or so. Saint that he was, Abrams started talking before they even hit the consulting room.

"You'll be pleased to know it's just as I'd thought. Clear margins, no nodes, barely one centimeter, estrogen-receptive, minimal breast cancer. I couldn't even call it a Stage One. Evvie, once you've had your radiation and we put you on Tamoxifen, this is going to be a cure." He pulled out a chair for her and sunk heavily into his own. "I'm not worried about you."

"Well, at least that's one of us." Traitorous tears were running down her cheeks.

He scooted closer to her and took her face in his hands. "It's going to take a while, but I promise you, you're going to look back on all this one day as if it were an old nightmare. Painful experiences are just like bad dreams—they fade and lose their punch with time."

***

In Moira's Berkeley Hills home, Mick Jagger's satanic voice sidled through the lyrics to "Time Waits for One" like some twisted twentieth century John Donne. When Moira finally realized the telephone was ringing, she struggled to extricate her tall frame from her loom bench and turn down the CD player before dashing to the phone. If this was one more complication with the show, she didn't know what she would do.

But it was Evvie, just beginning to leave a message. "Moira, it's good news. Estrogen-receptive and—."

The phone screeched like a strangled parrot as Moira contended with the answering machine. "Wait, wait. I'm here. Let me turn this damned thing off." She fumbled with the phone. "There, that's better. Bless you for calling, darling. I hated having to leave LA without knowing the final verdict. You say it's good news?"

"That's what Abrams said. The cancer's estrogen-receptive, hasn't spread to the nodes, and is so small and non-aggressive he doesn't even want to stage it."

"Meaning…?"

"Meaning he thinks I'm going to live. After radiation, of course—but no chemo. Unless it comes back, of course."

Moira brushed aside the last bit. "Darling, that's wonderful. How are you feeling? How's the breast?"

"You know, it's actually not that bad. It's sore, but nothing like last week. Abrams said it's healing just fine. The really good news is that, now that I'm not taking any more of that damned Darvocet, I can shit again."

Moira laughed. "At least you've got your priorities straight. Now we just have to make sure you get the best herbal and homeopathic defenses against that nasty radiation, and you'll be in the pink again. I'll Fed-Ex an overnight care package to you this afternoon."

"Moira, you don't have to do that."

54

"Silly girl, of course I do. You can't leave me hanging up here with nothing at all to contribute to your recovery. At least do me the favor of letting me feel useful." She wagged her finger at the receiver. "And don't just humor me by pretending to take what I send you. This stuff works. Britain's royal family has been homeopathic for decades, and you can tell they're all healthy as horses. Too bad most of them look like horses, too." Her eyes traveled to her massive cherrywood loom, where multichromatic shades of green, red, and yellow yarn cones were ready for warping off her large cone rack. "I'm working on a surprise for you. I'll bring it with me when I come back down again…Evvie, darling, maybe I should just drop everything and come back now. Who cares about a bloody art show? And this radiation business …You might need—"

"For God's sake, Moira. This cancer has already been too much of a disruption in everyone's lives. Now that I know that I'm up against something relatively innocuous, I'm going to be fine."

"Well, take care of yourself, darling. Keep thinking positive. Try imagining your white blood cells as hardy little warriors that attack the bad cancer cells. Who was that doctor who came up with it? Simon, Simon …" Moira panicked. "Oh dear, I can't remember his name, but you must know who I mean. Why don't you do some of that creative visualization invented by Simon the Pieman, or whatever the hell his name is?"

"You must be thinking of Carl Simonton. But, you know, he didn't invent the concept by a long shot. Ideas about the nature of the body-mind connection go back as far as Hermes. And I suppose I should look into it."

"Yes, do, darling. I'll sleep so much better knowing you're covering all your bases. Relaxation is the key, isn't it? Don't let yourself get uptight about anything for a while. I'm going to send you vibes of staying *loosey-goosey*." She paused. "Good heavens, I must be having an attack of early Alzheimer's; I'm going all nursery rhyme-ish today. You'd think a woman who weaves to the Stones would still have a few brain cells left."

Evvie tittered politely, but Moira heard the strain in her voice.

Moira gazed up at her loom, momentarily distracted by its simple splendor. She'd been so lucky to find it last fall, just when her previous one was beginning to require too many repairs. This new one was particularly responsive to her preferred style of high-tension weaving.

But Evvie was signing off now.

"Goodbye, darling. We'll talk soon."

As soon as she hung up, Moira mentally kicked herself for the Simonton gaffe. She'd nearly blown it. Evvie certainly didn't need to know that she'd bumped into Simon Warwick last night, working as a clerk, of all things, at Cody's Books. She'd briefly toyed with the idea of telling Evvie what a loser he'd become, his once high-boned, ascetic face now jowly and baggy-eyed, dissipated by what had undoubtedly been too much alcohol and marijuana. The first time she'd met him, she'd thought his light blue eyes looked lackluster and shifty, but now they were like pale pools of self-pity.

Moira was pretty sure that Evvie still labored under the delusion that she'd kept a secret of her relationship with Simon all those years ago, a love affair that Miriam had blithely sundered with all the vanity and narcissism of a spoiled sixteen-year-old. Since Evvie rarely confided in her, Moira was never quite certain how the girl had managed to cope with all the complications that came afterwards.

But why rock that particular boat now? No, on the whole it was better to let the Simon thing lie. She just wished she could do something. For she had few illusions, and it was clear to her that Simon Warwick had a clamp on Evvie's heart as sure as that insidious disease had snuck up inside her breast. It was a shame that cancer had hit her at this point in her life, when the pool of seriously eligible men was like an increasingly drying-up well.

***

After hanging up with Moira, Evvie knew she should call her father to give him the news, but she found herself putting it off. She'd already told Miriam, catching her via cell phone in the cereal aisle at Gelson's.

Beady. That was who she wanted to call now. She managed to reach her just as her friend was pulling past the private gates of a potential backer for her new project. Beady brushed aside Evvie's concerns about delaying her meeting and whooped like a schoolgirl.

"Listen, Ev, now that we know you're going to survive this thing, would it be too weird for me to throw myself a little birthday party?"

"Your birthday! Beady, how could I forget?"

"Oh, please. With what you've been going through? Besides, at my age, it's not like I want anybody counting. No, it's just an excuse to go a little crazy before this thing heats up. And it'll give everybody a chance to meet Ezra. You think you'll be up for something in a couple of weeks? I don't want to push it, but I can't imagine having a party without you."

"Oh, absolutely. The doctor said I could go back to work tomorrow if I wanted. Thank God, I'll be able to relieve poor Maggie. I think the Millstone is driving her out of her mind. Do you need any help?"

"Uh uh. Just bring your fine ass. You think Miriam'll be able to make it?"

"Are you kidding? Have you ever known her to miss out on a chance to dress up and look ravishing?"

Whoopee, Evvie thought sourly, as she put down the phone. *I can't wait.*

She proceeded to check just about everyone else off her list in the next half hour, but it was only after Miriam returned—unloading bags full of snack foods for Ben, popcorn and Diet Cokes for herself, and fresh fruit and vegetables for Evvie—that she gritted her teeth and dialed her father's number.

"Hi, Dad, it's me. Do you have a minute?"

"Yes, but make it quick, will you? They're doing a retrospective on KCET on the early days of television, and I'm trying to tape it for later, if I can just get the damned machine to work. They're profiling Jack Paar. You probably don't know him. He was one of the earliest hosts of *The Tonight Show*. But, unlike Mr. Leno, he was a giant, an intellectual. He crusaded against Batista's dictatorship in Cuba. Of course, between the right wing and the Catholic Church, he caught a hell of a lot of flak for it."

"Uh huh. I won't keep you long, Dad. I just wanted to let you know ... I went to see Abrams today."

"What'd you say?"

"I got the verdict from Dr. Abrams."

"Of course. What's the matter with me? Wait a minute. Let me turn off the sound."

She sighed.

"Okay, now tell me."

"It looks pretty good. The tumor was estrogen-receptive, really small. He thinks that, after radiation, I'm going to be cured."

"What are the statistics?"

She looked up at the ceiling. "Five per cent chance of a recurrence in the same breast, ten per cent of any breast cancer again."

"Not bad. A strong girl like you, you should fall on the right side of the bell curve. No reason to think you'll be in that ten per cent."

She had to get off the phone. Now. "Well, don't let me keep you from your show."

"Sure, sure." He paused. "And Evelyn?" Her heart lifted. "You might want to turn on channel three. I think you'll find this program very interesting."

As she hung up the phone, Miriam came around the corner, a bowl of fruit in her hands. "Want an apple?"

"No, thanks."

"What's wrong?"

"I just got off the phone with Dad."

"God damn it. Did he go all pessimistic on you?"

"Well, no. Not really. Not at all. At least, I don't think so."

Miriam laughed. "Well, that's certainly clear." She put a hand on Evvie's arm. "Listen, you're probably just exhausted with relief that the numbers are on your side. Why don't you lie down for a while? I'll order us something sinful from Jerry's. What do you think—cheesecake? There's nothing in the world a little cheesecake can't cure." She paused. "I'll have to diet afterwards, but what the hell? You only live once."

Evvie stared at her. Was it possible they weren't actually sisters? Maybe their mother had grown up near a power plant, or perhaps she'd consumed too much Strontium 90 with her cereal. How else explain the genetic wobble that had popped two such different species of daughters into the world?

As for her chances, she was glad everyone else was so fucking cheery about them. What made them so sure she wasn't going to be one of the luckless ten per cent?

***

Ben was the last one in the family to hear the news. When he finally got home that night, it was just after eleven. He pulled the front door shut as silently as possible and tiptoed down the hall. But just as he was about to pass his mom's room, she poked her head out the door, her hair like fingers of flame. Her eyes looked sleepy enough, but her tone was sharp. "Where have you been?"

"With a friend."

She was right next to him now, slipping her arms into the sleeves of her turquoise satin robe. "Who?" She smelled like roses and toothpaste. He backed away, as if he'd be sucked right into her body if he let her get too close. Again, she hissed, "Who?"

"Come on, Mom. A friend. I'm tired. I've got school tomorrow."

She grabbed his arm and pulled him back. "That's the point, isn't it? Do you want to fuck up your grades by fucking around? You think Harvard or Yale won't mind if you let your grade point drop your senior year?"

He stood silently. He'd be damned if he'd let her spoil this night. *Oh, Tash!*

"It would have been nice if you'd gotten home in time to congratulate your aunt."

"What for?"

"The doctor told her he's sure she'll be cured. A little radiation and some medicine, and she'll be cancer-free."

He was so relieved he almost hugged his mom. Instead, he let the warmth in his chest sprout into a broad smile. "God, that's great."

"But she'll still need help with dinner and stuff. And remember, I've got to go out of town in a couple of weeks. Don't go assuming Evvie feels normal yet."

Once he managed to break away from his mom and get into bed, he simmered over her words. Either she thought he was stupid or she was an idiot herself. Did she really think he'd assume anybody could feel normal when they were getting treated for cancer?

But, as much as Ben loved his aunt, his mind ineluctably strayed to what had gone on earlier that evening. Like silk, Tash's skin against his. Their trembling bodies wet with desire. The sleek dance of her hair across his belly. And her beautiful, teasing lips around his dick. He could almost feel them now.

He slid his hand under the covers, then froze as he heard footsteps outside his door. Was it his mom or his aunt? He held his breath until whoever it was had moved away.

So much for his hard-on. He closed his eyes and rolled over but realized soon enough that sleep wasn't going to come easily tonight.

The thing was, whenever he was with Tash, this weird feeling came over him, composed in equal parts of power and helplessness. When he'd become such a stranger to himself, how could he hope that his mom and Evvie would ever understand?

One thing was for sure, though. If either one of them got wind of the kinds of things he and Tash were planning, there'd be no end to the hell he'd have to pay.

Ten

ON THE NIGHT of Beady's party, Miriam recklessly wove in and out of traffic lanes toward her friend's quiet Westwood neighborhood, convinced that all the drivers of Los Angeles had gotten into their cars during the past hour and were exchanging places like dancers in some vast *do-si-do*.

It was one of those heavenly spring evenings that in most other parts of the country could only occur at the very height of summer. Hot Santa Ana winds had kicked up, bathing the air in the sweet scents of gardenia and night-blooming jasmine. Miriam had to pick her way around a straggling rout of snails that were drawn like drunken holidaymakers to the buttercups and pansies lining the path to Beady's front door.

The house was a 1920s Westwood hacienda, with a welcoming courtyard splashed with colorful Mexican tiles. Its wide-open windows were lit with a golden glow, and a loud bass beat blasted out from them, along with the sounds of exuberant voices and laughter. Anxious not be left out of things, Miriam quickened her pace, cursing the fact that packing for her working trip to San Francisco tomorrow morning and getting her father fed had made her late for the party. She swept a hand through her hair, tugged at her red leather miniskirt, and lifted a hand to the wrought-iron lion's head knocker. But then she stopped. No one would hear her knock over this racket.

She felt a momentary stab of envy. This was the kind of home she'd love to own herself, but given the work schedules that she and

Evvie maintained, the demands of a house and garden were utterly impractical. Beady was lucky. Her own bouts of hard work were often broken up by months of leisure, and when she wasn't wielding her own green thumb, her ancient *grand-mère* was only too happy to pick up the slack, prodding a fortunately willing Tony to do her heavy work for her.

Pressing the doorbell several times in quick succession, she sighed. Beady was lucky in that way, too. Tony, who'd known for years that he wanted to be a landscape architect, was so much more focused than her own son, who was gifted as hell, but passionate about nothing.

The door flung open, and Miriam stepped back involuntarily. The slender figure of an unfamiliar male stood framed inside the arched doorway.

She leapt to cover her sudden nervousness with an accomplished grin, an outstretched hand, and a casual "Hi, I'm Beady's best friend Miriam. I don't think we've met before." Despite the casual pose, she could feel wetness spring up between her thighs. The man's milky complexion looked like it had never been touched by a razor, his almond-shaped eyes were nearly turquoise, and his lower lip curled down just slightly in a boyish pout. He couldn't be more than twenty-five or six, and he was at least an inch or two shorter than she was, but he had the confident air of an older man.

"Paul Welles," he murmured, giving her a mysterious smile. He took her arm and led her into Beady's living room. Miriam could sense other people following her into the house. Beady materialized at her side, and Miriam grabbed hold of her as if she were a lifesaver, so wobbly had her legs become.

"It looks like you two have met," Beady said, a shade too dryly for Miriam's taste.

Paul seemed oblivious to her sarcasm. He put two long fingers to his lips and raised an eyebrow. "Beady, why have you kept Miriam such a secret? Now I *definitely* don't regret moving out here."

Miriam reluctantly dragged her eyes away from this astounding creature to politely feign interest in her friend's response.

But Beady was saying something she shouldn't. "I didn't expect Miriam to arrive alone, since she's seeing someone." She nodded at Miriam. "Where's Evvie?"

Miriam flushed. "She decided she needed to preserve her energy for a field trip she's taking her seniors on tomorrow. As for James, he's history." Miriam flicked a quick look at Paul before adding, "Didn't I tell you he's staying in London for good?"

Beady merely shook her head, scanning the swelling crowd inside her living room. Miriam became aware of the sheer tumult of the party, people shouting over the music and some of them dancing in tight clusters as Marvin Gaye lamented that he'd heard it through the grapevine.

"I'm still working on your present," Miriam apologized.

"*Mm.* If you're making it by hand, I know it's going to be something special." She turned to Paul. "Miriam's a costume designer and an unbelievable seamstress. She's really got flair."

"That much is obvious."

Before Beady moved on, she briefly leaned in toward Miriam, putting a hand on her arm and whispering into her ear. "Tell Evvie I'm sorry she had to miss the party. And Miriam? He's a nice boy, so try not to eat him alive." Then she faded into the crowd.

Miriam promised herself she'd give Beady hell for that one, but for now she was content to toss her fiery mane over her shoulder as she demurely accepted Paul Welles's offer to get her a glass of champagne.

As he moved neatly through the unruly crowd and stepped up into Beady's fresco-walled dining room, she couldn't help but remark that, besides having a face like an angel, Paul Welles had a perfectly sweet little ass.

✳✳✳

Poking around Miriam's bedroom, Evvie wondered if she should have pushed herself to go to the party after all.

She'd fallen asleep readily enough. It had to have been really early, because the last thing she remembered was the minute hand of her clock passing its shorter sister at the numeral eight like some hypnotist's metronomic wand. But little more than an hour later, she'd awakened to a horrible crawling sensation all over her body, her bed sheets so drenched with sweat that she'd worried she'd wet the bed.

The infamous menopausal night sweats had struck at last. "Dumb fuck," she muttered. She'd been basking in the delusion that she could go off hormone replacement cold turkey without some sort of estrogen withdrawal. But what about these ceaselessly roaming itchies?

She scrounged through Miriam's sewing drawers until she found the magnifying glass she'd been looking for, then hurried into her bedroom, where she fruitlessly scrutinized her rumpled sheets. Her bedclothes gave off a moist, animal smell.

Fleeing to the more brightly lit bathroom, she wrestled out of her PJs. It felt like there were insects partying on her limbs. She scrutinized her arms and legs, but could see nothing but a familiar assortment of moles and veins on the surface of her skin. But what did she expect? The fuckers were probably microscopic.

Or, worse yet, what if this weren't an infestation of bugs at all, but some kind of weird, crawly cancer of the skin?

She ran a hand through her hair. Sweat bathed her scalp. She stepped toward the bathroom window and, with an aggressive heave of her left arm, pushed it open. The scent of lavender leapt into the room like a personal insult, a reminder that pleasure still existed in the world for those who were at ease enough to claim it.

As she turned, she caught a glimpse of her head in the mirror. Her hair was sticking straight up in the air. She looked like a female version of Don King. In spite of herself, she laughed out loud.

Hell with it. Her best friend's birthday party had to be a damn sight more important than this pity party of one. She swung open the shower door and jumped in, letting the warm jets override all other sensations. It was the right thing to do. She felt her skin calming down, and her muscles began to un-clench.

When she stepped out of the shower and began toweling herself off, she saw that she'd been in there long enough to completely steam up the mirror. If she didn't want to arrive sporting a messy frizz, she'd have to blow dry her hair. But so what? Wasn't Miriam always saying it was *de rigueur* to arrive fashionably late?

***

After James's impatience, Miriam was doubly appreciative of what a good listener Paul Welles seemed to be. "Anyway, you can't believe how awful it's been."

Paul gave her a sympathetic smile. "Come on, let's sit over here. You definitely need a little TLC."

Miriam dropped into the cushy embrace of Beady's plush chenille sofa, wordlessly registering Paul's tender caressing of her neck as he settled in next to her. She stole a glance at him as he carefully worked out the knots. She couldn't believe how cute and perfectly doll-like he was, with his compact little body and impeccable manners.

But suddenly Paul took his hand away, and the next thing she knew he was straining up from the sofa, reaching to shake hands with a dark-haired man whom Beady had led over.

"I want you two to meet Ezra Rosenberg," Beady was saying. Miriam shot the man an appraising look. His face was just short of handsome. Just then she heard the front door slam and was astonished to see Evvie pop her head around the corner.

"Anybody home?"

Beady let out a whoop of delight and rushed away to wrap her arms around Evvie. Miriam noticed the gleam of interest in Ezra's eyes as he, too, observed the women's warm embrace.

"Girl, as my *Grand-mère* would say with a little too much enthusiasm, you look good enough to eat. *Mm, hmm,* that's a hell of a get up for somebody as ancient as you and me. Turn around now, let me see the back of this thing." Beady gave Evvie a gentle shove to start her twirling around so she could see the low-backed coral dress that, Miriam had to admit, complemented Evvie's dark hair and olive skin. Responding to the admiration like a twelve-year-old, Evvie smiled shyly back over her shoulder as she obediently spun her skirt in a wide flare. Then she stopped short, eyes widening in embarrassment, as she noticed Ezra Rosenberg staring appreciatively at her.

Beady laughed and dragged her over to him. "Now don't go all tongue-tied on me. I was so disappointed when Miriam said you weren't coming. I've been dying for Ezra to meet everybody. It's just in the nick of time. We got a call a few hours ago. If Ezra and I can get our shit together to fly to London this week, we have a good chance of interviewing some mucky mucks from NATO. Anyway, Ezra, here's Evvie. We'll need to pick her brain for our psychological slant. She's my dearest, deepest friend."

Miriam shot Beady a look of pure venom.

When Ezra reached out a hand, he inadvertently grazed Evvie's wrist with his fingernail. An involuntary "ow" escaped her lips. "Never mind." She looked mortified. "Please, believe me, it's nothing."

Miriam was at her side in an instant. She put an arm over her shoulder. "It's understandable. You're just a little extra sensitive since your breast cancer."

Miriam had the decency to blush in the dead silence that greeted her words.

It was Paul who saved her. He gently pulled her hand away from Evvie's arm and laced his fingers through hers, talking fast. "Beady's really stoked. I understand you're the originator of this project. What was it she said you were going to call it? *Their Fathers' Sins?*"

Ezra had actually stepped back a few paces at Miriam's words, his face a rictus of distress. Now he responded with alacrity. "The title was her idea, but yeah, I guess you could say I was the one who got the ball rolling."

"What grabbed you about the subject in the first place? I know it's an important issue, but with all the work I understand you do, why this one in particular?"

Beady shuddered. She raised her eye at Ezra, then shrugged. "Back in a mo—"

Ezra chewed his lip and squinted off into the distance. Miriam was too busy berating herself to concentrate on what was going on. What in the world had gotten hold of her?

"If you really want to know, it's a hell of a story. But I'm warning you, it's pretty intense."

Miriam settled back down next to Paul on the sofa. Ezra went after a couple of empty folding chairs across the room, putting one down for Evvie and taking a seat in the other.

"The war in Kosovo had flooded Albania with refugees. It'd been a shitty winter in every way. Cold enough to freeze the waxed paper that UN crews call toilet paper to your ass if you were unlucky enough to have to use one of the temporary camp's makeshift outhouses."

Their laughter forestalled his impulse to excuse his coarse language, but he didn't let them linger in their hilarity too long.

"Anyway, I guess I might have been the first one to notice her. She was a few hundred feet away, but it didn't take the other camera crews too long to pick up on it. Somehow, she'd strayed away from the barn where they were keeping the kids who'd gotten separated from their families." He added grimly under his breath, "Or whose families were dead."

Though Ezra was speaking quite softly, something about the energy that was generating from this part of the room was pulling some of the other guests away from their partying. By twos and threes, they began to straggle toward Miriam and her companions, settling cross-legged onto the floor.

"She looked to be about five years old. Later, I found out she had just turned seven. The kind of skinny little underfed kid whose eyes look as big as their faces. Hers were black, like midnight. Of course, she was filthy. They all were. Hell, whatever water the rescue workers came up with was barely enough for drinking and cooking.

"I figure it was my fault the rest of the guys took such an interest. Before I knew it, they'd dumped their cigarettes and their crappy paper cups of coffee and were all running closer to get a better shot, maybe get in first and win her over and let her be their meal ticket to the big time. Oh yeah, everybody in the field's looking for a Pulitzer shot. And a pretty kid like that, standing alone and lost on a muddy field as if she were the last child left on earth, under a sky that looked like it was about to unleash the hounds of hell ... I ran, too. I could tell they were scaring the shit out of her. She just kept backing up and they kept coming, like a pack of hungry wolves. Finally, she stopped and sort of cringed. Next thing, I see a stream of pee trickling down those skinny little legs."

Miriam was there with him. The rest of the living room was, too.

The little girl remained mute as Ezra dropped his own expensive camera onto the mucky ground, leaving his buddy Tom Delaney to stand over it and block the other photographers with a ferocious expression on his normally cherubic Irish face. Ezra scooped the hunted child into his arms, shielding her head with his splayed fingers and her body with his heavy, olive-green field jacket, and ran with her until they reached the closest building, which he circled until they were out of view.

Setting her down as gently as he could against the rough-textured, gray brick structure, he felt around inside his jacket pocket for a hand-kerchief to wipe the urine from her spindly legs. As he knelt down and reached with the cloth toward the little girl's calves, her face took on a sudden, inexplicably feral look. She nodded once, pulled down her soaking panties, jerkily stepped out of them, then dropped onto the sodden ground, spreading her legs into a V-shape as she held her arms rigidly down the sides of her boyish torso, her eyes screwed shut.

Miriam realized that Paul had let go of her hand and was staring disbelievingly at Ezra.

Ezra's voice was tight. "I'm such a dumb ass, it took me a few seconds to register what she was doing. God forgive me. Letting her lie on that shitty piece of earth like that for even a few seconds was a few seconds too long."

In spite of the fact that the whole room was silently willing Ezra to stop, he went on. The little girl lay like a corpse, resigned to the inevitable, even as Ezra sank to his knees, wrenching off his jacket to fling over her. It took him a while to realize that he must be terrifying the child, hugging her tightly as he sobbed convulsively over her sweat-ily tangled little head.

"Even then, she didn't utter a word. Just looked at me uncompre-hendingly as I carried her over to the truck to get her some chocolate and a can of Coke. Little did I know that one of the other photogra-phers went back around to where we'd been. Saw her panties on the ground, I suppose." He clenched his fists. "Little creep actually gave me the 'nudge nudge, wink wink' the next time I saw him. I flattened him."

Ezra glanced at Evvie, who'd gone deathly pale, her left hand on her chest and her right pressing hard against her mouth. Silent tears streamed down her cheeks.

To Miriam's astonishment, he took both of Evvie's hands be-tween his own and held them lightly. "Forgive me. Now look what I've done. Goddamned bull in a China shop. Should've started out by tell-ing you that it looks like she's going to be okay. It's a miracle, what those UNESCO relief people do. Set up camps. Give them safe, clean quarters. Good food to fatten them up again. Tons of play therapy, and a whole lot of love. Sweet, selfless love." He squeezed Evvie's hands reassuringly before letting them go. The rest of the party, only too relieved that the story had reached a happy conclusion, began trickling away.

A sour-sounding burp escaped Ezra's lips. He reached into his trouser pocket, peeled a Tums out of its wrapper, and popped it into his mouth. "Sorry. My gut reminds me that I'm not so macho that it doesn't get to me. You'll be happy to know that little Lennie has been placed in a caring home. A childless Italian couple. It's perfect. The mother's roots are Albanian. Thanks to them, Lennie will likely turn out to be one of the lucky ones. Or as lucky as surviving hell can get." His eyes lit up. "Here." He reached into his pocket.

Miriam thought, *Jesus, this guy must have an ulcer or something.*

But this time, he extracted a creased piece of paper. "Lennie insisted that her adoptive mother Altagracia include this with her last letter. I like to carry it with me. My reminder." He unfolded it for Evvie, who nodded, beaming, then turned it around so that Miriam and Paul could see it.

Miriam couldn't tell what the fuss was about. Ben must've made a million crude crayon pictures like this one when he was a kid.

Lennie's efforts depicted a smiling child sandwiched between two adults, a sickly green smudge shooting yellow rays down toward the three of them. Miriam didn't have a clue what that was supposed to be, so it was particularly annoying when Evvie said, "I love the touch of the sun wearing your field jacket. I envy you."

A flush spread across Ezra's broad cheekbones, and he shot Evvie a grateful look. "Thank you. Hardly anybody gets it. You can see why it's worth it, despite all the grief. My family thinks I'm nuts to do the work I do."

Miriam leaned forward. Was this guy married? It suddenly felt crucial to find out.

"Family?" she said. She sensed Paul flashing her a look and she tried for an expression of harmless curiosity.

"Yeah, every damn one of them," Ezra responded. "To be fair, my sisters think that, even though it's cool that I get to travel a lot, the work's ridiculously underpaid for the risk involved. But my parents nearly die with worry if somebody flies from here to San Francisco, so they can't even imagine what would justify going to places that the major airlines don't even serve. Oh, the trials of being the only son of a Jewish mama and poppa. They think you take your life in your hands every time you walk out the door. So, you can imagine what they think of covering things like war." Ezra shrugged. "Ghetto psychology. You'd think having family killed in the Holocaust would've given them a respect for humanitarian efforts. I don't know what gives with Jews. Only interested in themselves and their own."

Miriam was getting a little bored with the direction this was taking, but Evvie jumped in, eyes flashing. "Wait a minute. That's not fair. Our father—"

But suddenly Beady appeared, chuckling as she precariously set a tray bearing four glasses of white wine onto the floor. "Our Father who art in heaven, hallowed be His name." Catching the distress on Evvie's face, she said, "I'm sorry, baby. Y'know I love poking fun at your daddy, but, truly, he's one of my secret heroes. People put down communists like they're the devil, but it's no small thing to have been a white man crusading for racial justice long before it was considered cool. Ezra, I don't think I mentioned that Evvie and Miriam's father is *the* Michael Kerr. Truly, the world'll be a lesser place when a man of his integrity goes."

Ezra raised his eyebrows at Evvie. "No shit? Your dad's Michael Kerr? Well, I stand corrected. I have a big quarrel with the communist bit—I've seen too much of what it's left in its wake across Eastern Europe. But your father is legendary. I hate to say this, but I didn't realize he was still alive. He must be getting up there."

Miriam wasn't going to put up with being ignored for one more second. "Oh, with any luck, he'll outlive us all. I couldn't bear any more sickroom stuff, at least any time soon. It's so depressing." As she saw them all stare blankly at her, she realized she'd done it again.

Beady just had to rub it in. "Honey, you may get an Academy Award for costuming someday, but the gift for tact seems to have totally passed you by."

Eleven

BY THE TIME Evvie rolled lethargically out of bed the next morning, Miriam was nervously chewing her lip at the curb in front of the Southwest Airlines departure terminal. Impeccably clad in black Prada jeans and a fitted sleeveless black turtleneck, she paced back and forth like a pent-up panther while a heavily lidded, pockmarked LAX skycap painstakingly ticketed her five costume trunks.

Miriam swore under her breath. What kind of cosmic joke was it that the very day after meeting Paul Welles, Bob Billings would need her on location in Berkeley? As it was, she wasn't exactly thrilled about working on *Psycho-delic*, Bob's dubious new comedy about an ex-hippie-turned-mental-asylum-director. But Bob's two leads were box office gold, and her agent had insisted that costuming for *Psycho-delic* couldn't help but improve her visibility. Which would be fine with her, if she hadn't just met Paul.

Paul was amazing. Oh, not amazing like Ezra Rosenberg, but she wasn't sure she was up for *that* kind of amazing. Paul was do-able. She'd felt their sexual energies vibrating together as soon as they set eyes on one another. But she wasn't totally confident that she was more than a casual blip on his radar screen. It was crucial that she see him again before he got snagged by some younger girl who'd only want him for his looks.

Anyone else with the kind of hangover Miriam was suffering would have been doomed to an unhappy lethargy, but even the excess of wine she'd consumed the previous night after her series of social gaffes was no match for her metabolism. Her irrepressible hyperactivity merely added to the agony of being last in line to board and, therefore, forced to endure one of the backwards-facing sardine seats with which Southwest maximized its profits.

It was so annoying to be reduced to a cheap coach ticket. She hadn't yet had time to establish with Bob Billings the kind of subtle sexual rapport to win perks like business class and a second ticket for one of her assistants to handle the checking in and out of all her cumbersome luggage. Let alone a booking at a halfway decent hotel.

Which was why Moira was standing at the gate in Oakland waiting for her, prepared to take her back to her own elegant home in the Berkeley Hills.

Moira was good enough to choose a roundabout route that bypassed Telegraph Avenue. Miriam's stepmother knew from previous visits that Miriam had no appetite for what the Avenue had become— a charmless version of London's Portobello Road, with cheap, hand wrought jewelry and ugly bongs on sale outside hodge-podge storefronts. After what she'd already been through, the last thing Miriam needed was to be confronted by one of the street's ubiquitous drugged-out beggars, stinking to high heaven and emboldened into obnoxious aggressiveness by post-Free Speech Movement laissez faire.

Moira seemed to sense that something was up. Once they'd deposited Miriam's gear in her spacious spare bedroom, she insisted on taking her out for a champagne brunch at Chez Panisse.

Moira being one of Alice Waters' few happily spoiled regulars, they were quickly installed at one of the restaurant's quietest tables. Miriam accepted her champagne goblet with alacrity, only too happy to let the hair of the dog mellow her frazzled nerve ends.

"I needed this!"

Moira cocked a perfectly plucked eyebrow. "Somehow, I get the feeling it isn't just the flight."

Miriam leaned forward confidingly. "Well, if you must know … Beady's birthday party was last night. You know what a great hostess she is. Yummy food, fabulous music, terrific people …"

"Did Evvie come with you?"

"No, she showed up later, but then she left pretty early. Had to get a good night's sleep for something she's doing with her seniors today. Anyway, the thing is, there's this guy who just moved here a few months ago. He does art direction for commercials. That's how Beady met him. His name's Paul Welles. He's small, like a dancer. Moves like one, too. Imagine Baryshnikov, but even prettier. But definitely not gay. He asked for my number. Trying to fall asleep after meeting some-one so appealing, well, forget it."

"Does this mean that James is definitely out of the picture?"

Miriam smiled sheepishly. "I guess he is now. But you know what? I've got to use the loo." Miriam endured a seemingly endless sequence of flushings and running faucets while she waited in the cramped area outside the ladies' room. When a tiny elderly woman finally toddled out, reaching behind to tug down her floral skirt, Miriam leapt past her, hastily locking the door and plucking her cell phone from her purse to see if Paul had tried to reach her while she was in the air.

Nothing. Just a message from Ben saying he'd be spending the night at one of his surfing buddy's so they could hit the beach at the crack of dawn. She felt a flicker of concern that Evvie would be on her own all evening, stuck with arranging for their dad's dinner, but what the hell. If her sister could handle Beady's party, she must be feeling pretty good again. Still, Miriam promised herself she'd read Ben the riot act as soon as she got home.

When she returned to the table, Moira gave her a knowing look. "Any messages?"

Miriam gave her a gentle bop on the head before sitting down. "God dammit, do you always have to be such a mind reader?" She slouched in her chair and began playing with the salt cellar. "But, since you ask, no. He'd better call soon, or I'll have a nervous breakdown."

"Oh, for heaven's sake. It's only been … what? … twelve hours? Give the man a chance. I'd lay odds that he calls before the day is through." Moira's expression sobered. "Now, before we get any fur-ther, tell me about Evvie. How is she doing?" But Miriam was lost in thought, still fiddling with the saltshaker. "Yoo-hoo." Moira pointed. "Now look what you've done. Spilled salt, bad luck. You've got to throw some over your shoulder and make a wish."

Miriam scooped her hair off her shoulder before tossing a pinch of salt over it, intoning solemnly, "Make Paul Welles like me as much as I like him."

"Oh, God. Don't."

"What's the matter?"

"I don't know. It just seems a little … If you get a wish right now, don't you think it should be for your sister? I have to tell you, I'm worried sick."

"You're not having some sixth sense, are you? I mean, the doctors all say she's going to be okay."

"No, it's not like that. It's just that every time I talk to her, she sounds … lost. Like she isn't really there. I suppose it's understandable. Can you imagine what it's like to have part of your breast cut out before you've even found a man?"

"Oh, come on. You're assuming she's reacting as you or I would. Evvie doesn't have an ounce of vanity to her." Miriam shrugged. "Personally, I don't think she cares much about having a man in her life. You know how much she thrives on relationships with family and friends. And with work." She laughed. "All those dramas with her old people. Sure, she's a little tired now, but once she gets back in her groove, she'll be fine."

They both fell silent. Miriam, whose mind automatically returned to the glory of Paul Welles' perfect body, imagined it twining with hers in a rhythmic flow. She failed to notice Moira studying her with a troubled frown.

***

While her stepmother fretted over Evvie's long-term destiny and her sister fretted over her chances with Paul Welles, Evvie was contending with more immediate concerns. In one of those infrequent intervals in the relentless flow of traffic between the LA basin and the San Fernando Valley, the private bus she was riding hurtled maniacally down the lone southbound lane of Laurel Canyon Boulevard. Exchanging an alarmed look with her assistant Maggie Rimes, Evvie staggered up the aisle to admonish their skinhead driver to slow down.

She'd been pleased when this particular vehicle had arrived at the retirement home to ferry the group of seniors on their long-awaited field trip to LA's Original Farmers Market. The bus was specially equipped for the elderly, with wide aisles, high-backed seats, and easily accessed storage alcoves for canes and walker frames. But now she feared its young driver was about to kill them all.

She lurched up behind him and rapped his shoulder, wondering if the skin under his flimsy shirt bore some nasty antisemitic tattoo. But the crooked grin he gave her as he applied the brakes was lascivious rather than prejudiced. She caught herself raking her hand through her hair in his rearview mirror and was disgusted to realize that she was actually a little flattered.

She felt guilty for judging him when, after parking next to the inevitable line of tourist busses with passengers hailing primarily from the South and the Midwest, the driver went to considerable trouble to make sure everyone piled out of the bus in one piece onto the Farmers Market's newly truncated parking lot. Easing Sarah Weitzmann down the last step, Evvie looked around in astonishment. The famous Clock Tower was still there. Right now, it had a colorful banner strung across it announcing the yearly Country Jamboree. But half of the mostly-covered outdoor market that she'd known as a child had already been razed for the planned new development of department stores and movie theaters that would soon engulf the cluster of sweetly aged, Colonial-style, white clapboard buildings like a band of Indians circling a wagon train. Evvie's cheeks flushed with indignation. "Do you believe it? Only in LA would they treat a sixty-seven-year-old landmark like an expendable piece of crap!"

Maggie shook her head in commiseration. There weren't too many Angelenos who hadn't gleefully wandered the maze of cramped food stalls, offering everything from spicy barbecued beef and jambalaya to roasted nuts and old-fashioned creamy ice cream in big waffle cones. Evvie knew she wasn't alone in getting a kick out of the outdoor produce stands, where old-time movie stars and sitcom regulars picked out perfect ripe mangoes and papayas, ogled by big-bellied families from the celebrity-deprived regions of the country.

The Market's advertising slogan, "Meet Me at 3rd and Fairfax," was hokey, but that was exactly what some of her seniors had actually done with great regularity when they were her age. The Fairfax area was crowded with so many Eastern European immigrants that its residents had long ago dubbed it the Borscht Belt. Scores of Jewish housewives still culled the stalls for the finest vegetables and herbs to season their tempting *Shabbat* dinners, while their sons and daughters in the entertainment industry made deals and connections at the patio tables outside Charlie's Coffee Shop when the weather was decent and scarfed down huge breakfasts at Du-Par's when it rained. Evvie took perverse pleasure in the fact that the same spot of real estate where Walt Disney was said to have drawn up his plans for Disneyland and where James Dean had supposedly eaten his last breakfast was also home to Farmers Market Poultry, whose Actors Club once provided discounts on chicken to performers who were "between engagements."

Evvie knew that her father sometimes met Dick Shea here to critique each other's pages. She had no idea if they were working on anything right now. Her dad wasn't the sort of man who volunteered such things, and questions about his personal life were about as welcome as a cat in an aviary.

"Oh my!" Sarah Weitzman was pointing excitedly with her free hand, and Evvie had to laugh. Emerging from the little aisle outside of Du-Par's, right next to a small roped-in pen replete with haystack and a couple of pigs and roosters, were two unusually handsome young men—probably this season's recipients of the Actor's Club chicken discount—decked out in clean, well-cut jeans and bright-colored vests over their white shirts. They wore hopelessly old-fashioned-looking straw hats that screamed, "Yup, we're country, alright." They were endeavoring to share a match to light their cigarettes, but the rims of their hats kept bouncing against each other, making them do a little clownish *do-si-do* trying to light up.

Now Bill Kreplitt was tugging at her sleeve. She jumped, and at her other side Sarah Weitzmann giggled like a six-year-old as Bill yelled right into her ear that he had to use the toilet. The poor man was deaf as a post.

Maggie Rimes was a peach. She immediately organized the seniors into a tight line and began inching them at a pace that even Millie Stone and her walker could manage toward the restrooms at the other end of the Market.

Bill was having a hard time trusting that they were, in fact, moving as fast as their assorted infirmities permitted. As they shuffled past Gill's Old Fashioned Ice Cream, the Ultimate Nut and Candy

Company, and innumerable little gift nooks, he kept clutching his crotch and moaning, "I've got to pee, when can I go pee?" Since he was sandwiched in the middle of the line between Millie Stone and Elsie Took, and she herself was stuck at the back helping Sarah Weitzman, Evvie had to restrain herself from yelling at him at the top of her lungs to just shut up. But it was Elsie Took who saved her from becoming a total psycho bitch. As they approached Bryan's Barbecue, Elsie decided to try to bum a cigarette from a pot-bellied tourist wearing a Bush/Cheney cap.

Elsie had the dubious distinction of resembling an older female version of Alfred E. Neuman. Her short gray haircut was a perfect foil for her stuck-out ears, and she had a loony wide grin that accompanied her braying ex-smoker's laugh. She was almost as determined to resume her suicidal nicotine habit as she was to defy everyone else's opinion that she needed to use a walker. Her legs were like little sticks. Elsie was apt to try to cadge a cigarette from any smoker in sight.

Evvie stuck her fingers in the corners of her mouth and whistled just as soon as she saw Elsie stagger out of line. Maggie got the message just as the old woman bounced off Bush/Cheney's belly and teetered dangerously on her pins. Maggie grabbed her, and—in a move that rivaled Kobe Bryant—made a quick pivot, finessing Elsie around a crunch of Japanese tourists who'd suddenly flooded the aisle between the restrooms and Sheltam's Newsstand. Evvie hurriedly grabbed Bill and pointed him toward the mouth of the Men's Room, giving him a gentle shove and smiling apologetically at the small crowd of Asian men who nodded politely as they gave him right of way. Maggie, who'd managed to usher all five of the women into the ladies' room, was shaking with laughter. She sputtered, "Now remind me, will you, whose idea was this? Just fire me if it was mine."

"Not until we're back on the other side of the hill. I need you too much now." She glanced at the long line of men outside the restroom, muttering, "I'd better wait for Bill. I just hope nobody murders him before he comes out again."

Maggie was struggling to stuff her hair back into her bun. "Well, okay, but don't go anywhere without me. Bill may be a handful, but five is worse than one, especially when one of them's the Millstone."

The day ended up going far better than its inauspicious beginning would have suggested. Evvie became momentarily alarmed when the whole group decided they just had to have some of Bryan's barbecue, having been tantalized by its heavenly aroma the whole time they were in line to go to the toilet. But she and Maggie managed to seat everybody at one long table for their lunch, and they convinced the staff at Bryan's to pour free samples of their hearty barbecue sauce over mounds of mashed potatoes, so that nobody had to get their false teeth snagged on spareribs just to satisfy their craving for a little spice in their lives. They only had to make two more trips to the restroom before leaving and everybody got to pet the pigs on the way out. Unfortunately, Evvie had run out of Handi Wipes long before Millie Stone decided to slop the pig snot on her fingers across Evvie's sleeve, obviously figuring that was preferable to soiling her own.

As she and Maggie escorted the flagging seniors across the parking lot, it took her a few seconds to register that someone was shouting her name.

Her face lit up. It was Beady, rushing toward her with Ezra Rosenberg on her heels. Maggie and the line of old people halted, and they watched with interest as Beady grabbed Evvie in a tight hug.

"Girl, this is amazing. What are you doing here? We're just coming to get some of that amazing jambalaya."

Evvie was hyperaware of Ezra. His Hawaiian print shirt and slightly beakish nose put her in mind of a tropical bird, but when he shook his head at Elsie Took's blunt request for a cigarette, the genuine kindness in his eyes made him look almost handsome.

But now Bill Kreplitt was pawing Evvie's arm. "What's she saying? I'm tired. I want to go home."

She put a hand on Bill's shoulder and raised her voice for him. "I know, Bill. Of course, you do. Don't worry, we'll be on that bus in no time." She shrugged at Beady. "Sweetie, I'm afraid we're at the tail end of a long day. These guys are pooped."

Bill looked around suspiciously, sniffing the air. He shouted at Elsie, "Did she say somebody pooped?"

Evvie turned away, stifling a laugh. Her eyes met Ezra's. He was barely keeping it together himself.

She saw Bill's hand inching down toward his crotch. Dear God, let it be just an itch.

"Listen, I wish I could stay and talk, but, as you can see, I …" Christ, how stiff she sounded. She felt herself blush under Ezra's amused gaze.

Ezra murmured to Beady, "We really should let these folks get on their way. But maybe we can get together for lunch or something when we get back into town."

Beady gave Evvie's arm a squeeze. "Definitely. We'll have to arrange something as soon as we return."

Evvie reached forward to shake Ezra's outstretched hand, then noticed the pig snot on her sleeve and hastily drew it back.

He stared at her in confusion, but Beady was already pulling him away. "Honey, I'll call you before I take off. I love you, girl. And we'll definitely make that plan."

Uh huh, Evvie thought, minutes later, hunkering down in her seat at the back of the bus. *I'm sure Ezra Rosenberg's just dying to have a reprise with Beady's socially inept friend.* What a fool she'd been to imagine that Ezra Rosenberg had seemed a little interested last night. He'd merely felt sorry for her. He was that kind of man.

And what in the world was she doing entertaining those kinds of fantasies, anyway? She was about to undergo radiation, for God's sake.

She told herself to give it a rest, but she couldn't help but skew around in her seat as their driver was pulling out of the parking lot. Beady and Ezra were nowhere in sight. A slight wind had kicked up, and the Country Jamboree banner flared and flapped against the Clock Tower.

Facing forward again, she let her eyes travel over the gray and white heads leaning revealingly sideways towards their seatmates. Like babies, they were sweetest when they slept. The whole crew would probably dream their way back over the hill. She closed her eyes. She was pretty exhausted herself. But it wasn't just that. As dear as they were, most of her charges wouldn't even remember this outing by the time they'd finished tonight's dinner.

She couldn't help but envy Beady that her efforts were tangible, captured on film for the whole world to see, while she herself was like some modern-day Sisyphus, pouring her energies into a series of perpetually leaking sieves.

Twelve

EVVIE MANAGED TO keep herself preoccupied with work for the next several weeks, deftly dodging the insidious fear that she might not live as long as the seniors she served.

But as her radiation consultation appointment approached, her pretense of normalcy flagged. When the day finally dawned, mostly overcast with an occasional tease of sun, she found herself staring haplessly at her nude body in the full-length bathroom mirror, an oversized towel bunched at her feet like a beached white whale.

And me? she wondered, her thumb rubbing her breast at a point just above her incision. The two-inch smudge of blue dye from the lymph node sampling made her feel like a USDA-stamped cut of meat.

It was hardly comforting that, just a few days before, on the occasion of her post-surgical follow-up visit, Dr. Manning had muttered a little defensively that the blue mark looked as pronounced as it did the day after the operation.

She restrained herself from commenting that he'd mentioned nothing about a permanent stain when he'd first proposed the Sentinel Node procedure, even though he'd carefully described how the traditional method of biopsying the lymph nodes involved removing so many nodes that the patient often developed lymphodema —she thought of it as Elephant Man's arm—where your affected arm blew up permanently in response to some common injury on your arm or hand. Something as small as a cat scratch, or slinging a heavy purse on your shoulder, or even flying on a plane could trigger a lymphodemic reaction.

He'd said they'd come up with new method of shooting blue dye into the area where the malignancy had been in the breast. The dye would naturally flow to the precise nodes that the cancer would have traveled to, if indeed there had been a metastasis, so only those nodes needed to be removed for biopsy. That would leave enough lymph nodes in her armpit to successfully fight off infections. By the time he got to that point in his pitch, she was flooded by memories of her mother sobbing as she drained her painfully bloated arm every evening. She'd agreed to the sentinel node biopsy with a hasty scrawl of her name on the surgical release form.

She had to admit that between the old-fashioned method and the new, it still seemed that Dr. Manning had pushed for the best option. But this blue swirl, unresponsive to soap and creams and angry rubbing with a washcloth, made her breast look like the pictures of the earth that the first astronauts had taken—a big blue marble. Except her particular marble was a war zone.

Her eyes flicked up and down the body in the mirror, fixating on the curves of her hips and thighs. She was probably the only person in the world who put on weight when they got cancer. Another bonus. It wasn't as if she were eating like a pig. Her hormones were bouncing around like crazy these days, wreaking havoc on her metabolism.

She wrapped the towel around herself and stuck her feet into a pair of fluffy white slippers before moving toward the door. But before she could reach for the knob, it began opening of its own accord. She jumped back in alarm.

Miriam's face peered around. "I'm sorry. I didn't mean to scare you." She looked like she'd just thrown on whatever was closest to hand. Her brown sweater was creased, and her royal blue loafers looked too dressy for the faded blue jeans she wore. "Are you sure you don't want me to come with you?"

Evvie tightened the towel around her midriff. "No, it'll be fine. If going back to work didn't faze me, with fifty *alter cockers* simultaneously whining about how could I abandon them so long, a little radiation consultation at the Cancer Center should be a piece of cake." She saw her sister blanch at the C-word and took pity on her. "Listen, they said

I won't even get measured and tattooed until next week. How about if you come with me then?" Miriam shot her a guilty look. "Oh, right. You'll be working. Listen, it really doesn't matter. I'm a big girl."

"Well, if you're sure ..."

"Believe me, if I didn't think I could handle it, I'd let you know like a shot."

***

It was the kind of morning that usually made Ben wish he could just stay in bed. Even on bright days, he wasn't the easiest of risers, vulnerable to his mom's ragging on him when the extra-loud alarm clock she'd bought him last Christmas failed to get him up. Add funky weather to the mix and you could bet money on him being late for homeroom, which seemed pointless to him anyway. Listening to Miss Hermione Jackson, a battle-scarred veteran of the teaching wars, calling the roll and reading off a list of announcements in a bored drone nearly put him to sleep all over again.

But today was different. He had plans with Tash, made even easier than usual thanks to Tony's mom having a film financing meeting in San Francisco. Beady would be leaving the house for LAX at noon, but Tony and Opal couldn't take advantage of the opportunity since they had an English test. Tony had offered Ben the key if he wanted it, and he definitely wanted it.

Tash had suggested they grab some breakfast at Jerry's Deli, then hang out for a while at the Virgin Megastore. She wanted to listen to some cuts by a new British band she'd been hearing about and get the Joan Osborne CD she'd been wanting to buy forever, the one with "What If God Was One of Us?" on it. She was psycho about that song. By that time, they could safely go back to Tony's house and fool around. Ben grinned as he stuffed his wallet into his back jeans pocket. He grabbed a couple of books from a pile on his desk—he didn't bother to notice which ones—and lurched around his unkempt room, swearing, until he located his car keys under a bunched heap of yesterday's clothes.

His aunt was just coming out of her bedroom when he emerged. He faintly registered that she looked a little distracted as she stood on

83

her toes to give him a quick peck on the cheek. "Have you had break-fast yet?" she said over her shoulder on her way to the kitchen.

He thought fast while he followed her. "Gotta pick up a copy of *West Side Story* before homeroom. Tryouts are next week." It was only half a lie. The script for the school play was already in his locker; he'd picked it up with Tash—who was auditioning for the role of Maria—yesterday after school.

His aunt smiled broadly, and for a moment her face seemed to lose the pallor he'd gotten used to since her surgery. "I'm glad you're going to try out for it. They'll love you." She spread her arms. "The Jets and the Sharks. I saw it when I was a kid. Great songs. But it packs a hell of a message, doesn't it?"

The more she talked, the guiltier he felt. "Yeah, it's a cool play. Totally relevant. I mean, it's not like the gang thing has gotten any bet-ter."

"What's this about gangs?" His mom had materialized behind him. "Not at Uni, I hope."

"Oh c'mon, Mom, don't go there."

"What kind of thing is that to say?"

Evvie intervened, her voice edgy. "Mir, you sound like it's his fault. Of course, there are gangs at Uni. You think we're living on an island? Ben's not a baby. He's a city kid. He knows what to steer clear of."

Ben knew she was prompting him. "Yeah, Mom, don't worry. They pretty much keep to themselves unless you go out of your way to provoke them. I mean, it's not like East LA, where you can't wear red or blue or anything." His Mom's eyes were wide, and the freckles across her nose were standing out more than usual. "It's just like"—he reached for a way to say it—"you know who hangs with who, and you treat the brothers bused in from the hood with a little extra re-spect."

"Respect!" His mom's eyes were fiery.

Evvie broke in. "Ben's right. Many of them are just insecure kids at heart. A little respect goes a long way to disarm adolescent bravado. That's why you made the right choice to keep Ben in public school. You've got to appreciate that you've got a streetwise son." She forced a laugh and shrugged at his mother. "It's not Kansas anymore, Toto honey. Hell, it wasn't even Kansas when you and I were young."

His mom opened her mouth to respond, then seemed to reconsider, darting a glance at her watch.

Evvie exclaimed, "Oh my God, you're right. It's not like I've got all the time in the world."

Ben didn't know what she was talking about, but he was quick to take advantage of the distraction. He edged into the hall, saying, "Mom, believe me, I'm careful as hell. Don't worry." He threw his words over his shoulder. "I gotta go, or I'm screwed."

Before either of them could reply, he was out the door.

By the time he had Tash buckled into his ancient Beamer and they were turning from Doheny onto Beverly Boulevard, he'd transformed his uncomfortable moment into farce. Tash giggled helplessly at his ditzy falsetto version of his mom's naiveté. "Gangs? How could there be violence in Westwood? Why, even that respected sports hero O.J. Simpson used to live nearby!"

Tash playfully punched him in the shoulder. "Stop, Ben. I'm going to pee in my pants."

He felt like a king as he made a hasty U-turn into the valet spot in front of Jerry's Deli. It briefly occurred to him that everyone he knew hung out at this particular Jerry's rather than the new one in Westwood Village because the Village had pretty much died after an Asian UCLA coed had been killed in the crossfire of two rival gangs.

But he didn't want to think about that now. As he entered the gaudily lit delicatessen, Tash was grabbing him around the waist, and the smells of smoked fish and hash browns and bacon were blasting his nostrils, making him realize he was hungry as hell.

***

Evvie hurried single-mindedly towards the glass doors of the Cancer Center, until a bell-like voice startled her.

"I'll bet it's your first time."

The child was staring up at her from a concrete bench beside the entrance. She swung her skinny legs back and forth under the bench. A pink pinafore flaring around her knobby knees revealed the kinds of bruises Evvie remembered from her own childhood, but this girl's head was completely bald, and she had an ominous, powdery pallor to her skin.

The child grinned up at her, revealing a couple of missing teeth. Her blue eyes glistened with lively interest, and a spray of pale freckles danced across her snub nose. She couldn't have been more than five or six years old.

Before Evvie could respond, a tight-lipped woman swept towards them, her face as bleached and dry as her shoulder length hair. "Temple MacBride, you have no idea what the lady's here for. She could be a visitor, and, besides, it's not good manners to speak out of turn."

Evvie responded protectively, "Oh no, it's fine," but young Temple broke in with calm assurance.

"She's not a visitor, Ma. She's a patient." Temple turned to Evvie. "Are you here for radiation or chemotherapy?" Evvie couldn't believe that a child so young could even wrap her lips around such words.

"Radiation."

The kid's legs were swinging a mile a minute now. "Oh, good. Me, too." She glanced at her mother. "I'm all done with my chemotherapy, aren't I, Ma?"

The woman gave an abrupt nod and turned away.

"I get my radiation now every morning at eight o'clock. If you come at the same time, we can talk." She leaned toward Evvie confidingly. "I can tell you all about what goes on here. Did you know the treatment rooms are all under the ground?"

Evvie found herself fighting for breath. The child reached up and put her hand around Evvie's wrist. Her skin felt papery-thin, but her grip was amazingly strong. "Don't worry. They make people better here. They're nice."

The sound of a vehicle pulling up and cutting its motor caused all three of them to look around. A beefy driver emerged from a dusty white van. He went around to the passenger's side and slid open the heavy door, then hustled to the back of the van, pulling down the rear door and yanking a ramp into position so that he could let out a gray-faced old man slumped awkwardly in a wheelchair. Out of the side door emerged a big, cat-eyed woman with deep brown skin. She looked to be in her fifties, but the Fates had dealt none too kindly with her.

Her nearly threadbare and heavily stained purple dress was missing a button where it stretched across the bosomy, if crooked shelf over-hanging her belly. Coiled ringlets fell over her forehead and across her high cheekbones as she gave an infectious laugh.

Her Southern accent was so thick that Evvie had to strain to understand her. "My poor bones are getting too old for all this climbing in and out." She cast a polite glance at Temple's mother. "How do, Miz MacBride." As Temple's mother smiled thinly back, the woman stretched her big hands toward Temple. A frayed cloth purse with a plastic strap dangled precariously from the crook of one of her elbows. "Ain't you gonna give me no sugar?"

Temple rushed into her warm embrace.

"Are you new, hon?" Evvie gave a nervous nod. "It ain't so bad, you know. I'm almost finished myself." She let go of young Temple, who snuggled against her thick thighs. She swept a hand across her chest. "Cancer of my left breast." As she saw the look of recognition in Evvie's eyes, she said, "*Tsk, tsk.* You too? Catch it early? Good, good. That's the best."

The woman held out a hand, and Evvie watched in dismay as her purse slid down her arm and onto the ground, spilling an assortment of keys, a couple of pencils, a lipstick tube, small change, and an over-stuffed black wallet. "Shoot," she muttered, scrambling to pick up her things. Evvie and Temple knelt to help her. Only Mrs. MacBride remained standing, surveying the parking lot with a bitter expression. Once they'd all straightened, the woman once again extended her hand to Evvie. "That's all right then. I'm Ida Mae Washington."

Evvie shook her hand. "Evvie Kerr."

"You going in or out right now?"

"In," said Evvie, then she gasped. She glanced quickly at her watch. "Oh my God, I'm late."

Instantly, Ida Mae had hold of her arm and was pulling her toward the entrance. "Well, come on then, woman. I'll show you the way." Then she muttered so indistinctly that it took Evvie a few seconds to figure out what she was saying. "Though, truth be told, around here it's hurry up and wait most of the time." At the door, Ida Mae turned to wave back at the little girl. "See you tomorrow, little fish stick. Y'all take care, Miz MacBride."

Temple was grinning back, but her mother still looked distracted, sweeping one hand through her hair as she signaled to the valet with the other.

Temple called out, "Remember, eight o'clock's my time. Don't forget. I'll be waiting for you."

"She's a sweet child," Ida Mae said as they entered the sterile-looking lobby. "Too bad it don't look too good for her, poor little thing."

Evvie shot her a horrified look, but a woman behind the counter, wearing one of those precision squared-off haircuts that spoke volumes, was trying to get her attention. "Your name? Ah, yes. Evelyn Kerr. We've been waiting for you." She shoved a folder into Evvie's hands. "Here's your paperwork. Elevator's on your left. You want the basement." As Evvie moved obediently toward the elevator, where Ida Mae was pushing a button and gesturing for her to hurry up, the woman at the counter barked at her. "Oh, and welcome to the Cancer Center. Don't forget to get validated by me before you leave."

***

If Evvie worried that Miss Stick-up-the-Butt at the information desk was the best she could expect from the Cancer Center staff, Dr. Chloe McPherson made her reconsider. The tall, curly-haired doctor strode into the examining room, where Evvie sat shivering on a papered table, and gave her a firm handshake. "Evelyn, it's a pleasure to meet you and to have the opportunity to make you well again." Her examination was brisk, but her tone was reassuring. "We work as a team. The first thing we do is measure you for your radiation treatments. It's painless, but we do ask you to lie still for a long time while we make sure we get an exact measurement of your breast and the area where the tumor was. Then we tattoo you—oh, just a pencil dot, you'll barely feel it—in the precise places where the technician will aim the radiation beams during your treatments. Each visit, you'll be radiated directly where the tumor was and then we'll direct a more diffuse beam across the whole breast, in case any vagrant cells might be lurking.

"I'm recommending radiation for thirty-seven days, five days a week. Most of the time, you'll be dealing with the technicians, and I can promise you they're a wonderful bunch." She pulled Evvie's gown back over her shoulder. "Ooh, you're cold, aren't you? I just can't get them to keep these examining rooms warm enough. Now, over the course of radiation, you'll experience a few side effects, but they're really not too bad. Toward the end, you may be a little more tired, but most people are able to continue working just fine. Dr. Abrams has probably told you there's a small risk of lymphodema and pneumonitis, but, believe me, especially since you had a negative sentinel node procedure, the first is unlikely and the latter quite rare."

She flipped through Evvie's paperwork. "No heavy lifting on your job? Great, you'll definitely be okay to keep working. Your breast will begin to show signs of what I think of as a bad sunburn toward the end, as well as getting a little thicker-skinned. It may shrink or become larger than your left breast. We recommend a cotton bra during radiation, so your skin can breathe, and towards the end we have some healing gel you can use. Your technician can tell you which types of deodorant to avoid, since some can interfere with your treatment."

Dr. McPherson looked up and tilted her head. "You have beautiful hair. Do you blow it dry?" Oh, no. No one had warned her that radiation would make her lose her hair. "You might want to think about cutting it a little. Radiation has a tendency to stiffen the affected arm, and my patients tell me that blow-drying can get downright uncomfortable. Of course, you could just let it do its own thing. Most men think we're nuts, anyway—curly headed women straightening their hair and vice versa." Her laugh was surprisingly girlish, but Evvie felt incapable of joining in. "Anyway, it's up to you. I'm sure that all of this is way too much to remember, but we'll be going over it many times, and you can call me any time if you have questions. Is there anything you want to ask now or would like me to know?"

Evvie took a deep breath and murmured, "No." She didn't think Dr. McPherson needed to be told that her head felt like it was spinning like the kid in *The Exorcist*—with no compassionate priest in sight to talk her down.

***

Just across the street from Cedars-Sinai Cancer Center, the over-worked wait staff at Jerry's Deli was just beginning to collect its breath as the breakfast rush began to subside. A few of them—including the full-breasted young Russian who'd served French toast and black coffee to Tash and a three-egg omelet, hash browns, buttered sourdough toast, a side of bacon, two glasses of orange juice, and coffee with cream and sugar to Ben—were out smoking in the rear parking lot. Huddling together and sharing their plans for the upcoming weekend, they greedily inhaled their nicotine before commencing the fevered preparation for the lunch crowd that would pour in from Cedars, nearby shops, and the stylish Pacific Design Center up on Melrose. Tania Klyatchkov was nervously new here, having quit her cashier's job at a local Russian-owned car wash when the owner's son Dmitri followed her into the ladies' restroom and put his aggressive hands on her breasts. It was understandable that she'd forgotten to inquire whether the two lovebirds at table four wanted their check before she took her break.

Ben scanned the main dining room for their waitress's face. Giving up, he regarded Tash, who was squinting into a little mirrored lipstick case she'd retrieved from her Kate Spade bag, expertly dabbing at her lips with a wand of plum-colored lipstick. Her black hair moved like a silken curtain across her neck as she checked her lips, her V-necked sweater just hinting at the delights of her small, but perfectly shaped breasts.

He reached over to touch her cheek. She spanked his wrist. "Bad boy. I'm not done yet." She put her head to one side, saying in a baby voice. "Aren't I worth waiting for?"

Ben looked away, embarrassed by the intensity of his desire. The sun had finally come out, and the glare from a car window across the street caught his eye. The car was parked in front of a small modern building standing near one of the looming Cedars-Sinai Hospital towers, and the driver's door was open wide. A valet guy was running toward a blue Honda that had pulled up right behind it.

Ben jerked. Wasn't that his aunt Evvie's Lexus in front of the Honda? And wait—wasn't that Evvie, leaning against the hood of her car? He stood up, thrusting his chair behind him and then righting it as it nearly fell over. "Oh, God," he muttered, flopping back into his seat. "That's what she meant this morning."

"What is it?"

"I forgot. My aunt Evvie told me last weekend. I just saw her across the street."

Tash glanced out the window and saw the Cancer Center sign. Her expression darkened.

But then a long, black-skirted torso moved in front of them, blocking their view. "Well, this is a first. Tash Lem and Ben Kerr. I didn't know you were going out. Naughty, naughty. Didn't figure you two as the class-cutting type."

Flushing, Tash responded with an equivalent archness. "I wouldn't talk, Anna. At least we were in our beds asleep last night, which you obviously weren't." Tash wasn't being psychic. Anna Sumter was dressed for clubbing, her black stiletto heels emphasizing her model's body, her blond hair swept up in an artful chignon, and a full application of war paint on her face. "Who're *you* here with?"

Anna leaned towards them and whispered in a confidential tone, "Maybe you've heard of him. Thad Larsen? He's the hottest club promoter in town. Listen, he's in the bathroom, but don't say a thing about Uni when he comes out. Everybody at the Viper Room thinks I'm twenty-one, and Thad would drop me in a second if he found out I'm not."

When Anna's friend Thad showed up a moment later, Ben realized how right she was. He looked twice Anna's sixteen years, with dark circles under his eyes and age lines beginning to deepen the grooves parenthesizing his ultra-hip soul patch. His black leather coat barely concealed how snakishly skinny he was.

"Thad, I want you to meet some college friends of mine, Tash and Ben."

"Pleasure." His handshake was barely a touch of a few fingers before he reached for a napkin on the table. "May I?" He honked into it a couple of times, then threw Anna a mysterious grin. "Wanna go?"

Anna chucked him under the chin, giggling. "Okay, rude person." She spread her hands. "What am I going to do with him?" Nonetheless, she threw Tash a victorious smile over her shoulder as they walked away.

Ben scowled. "What the fuck was that all about?"

"I don't know, but how old do you think he is?" Tash hadn't taken her eyes off the departing couple. "If it were me trying to pull off that lie about college, it'd be like there were neon letters on my forehead, spelling out, 'Don't believe a word she's saying.' I swear, it's like some people are just born under a lucky sign."

Ben glanced back across the street. Evvie's Lexus was gone. But the sad fact was that it wasn't his aunt who'd gotten his heart beating so fast.

No, that was down to Tash. And the wistful look he'd seen on her face when she'd watched Anna leave the deli, arm in arm with Thad fucking Larsen.

Thirteen

HER HEART BEATING a mile a minute, Evvie had to forcibly drag her feet along the yellow directional line that led from the Cancer Center's main basement reception area to the radiation treatment wing. On her way, she passed a series of open doors revealing clerical staff in small cubicles munching on doughnuts, shuffling papers, peering into computer screens. The odd person looked up and flashed her a perfunctory smile.

It seemed like everything down here operated on some weird natural law of slow motion, as if the closer you got to the earth's heavy core, the more everything moved like molasses. It seemed to take forever for the young Latina at the other end of the hall to meet up with her, gently pushing to one side her chrome cartload of blue plastic pouches labeled "Warning: Blood Products." The girl had the kind of shiny black straight hair that was the envy of every frizzy haired Jewish girl Evvie knew. "Do you know where you're going?" she asked.

Evvie brushed aside the existential ramifications of the question as she mumbled, "Thanks, yes I do." Having had her breast measured, mapped, and tattooed by Chloe McPherson just last week, she knew at least a bit of the drill. Then, too, she'd been put off by the impersonal waiting area filled with rows of gray seats, some of them facing a droning television set mounted high above the reception desk.

She felt absurdly grateful when Russell, the radiation scheduler, looked up at her with a warm expression on his wide brown face. "Hi, Evelyn, how are you this morning?" She seized on the fact that he'd remembered her name as a good sign.

Reluctantly, she retrieved a hospital gown from a gray laminated shelf to Russell's right. The gowns were stacked around a used-gown disposal hole that reminded her of those awkward latrines in cheap French hotels, where the challenge of getting your feet into the little indentations on each side of the smelly maw was nothing compared to the terror of falling in. She really didn't fancy letting her fingers touch the used gowns sticking out of it. But who was she kidding? Did she really think other people's cancer cooties were worse than her own?

Clutching the gown to her breast, she shuffled into one of the cramped partitioned dressing rooms, where she removed her cream silk blouse and the new all-cotton bra she'd been instructed to buy so that her breast could breathe. She wondered whether the building's designers had left mirrors out of these dressing rooms on purpose, to spare the patients' seeing their own anxious faces as they prepared to be nuked.

She pushed aside the sliding screen and quickly made for the closest seat. Several male patients looked up. She avoided their eyes as she scanned the room, hoping to find Ida Mae, Temple, or even Sally Mac-Bride. She could really use a familiar face right now. She found two. On the suspended TV screen, the *Today Show's* Katie Couric was interviewing frequent guest commentator on women's health issues, Dr. Judith Reichman.

For a brief moment, Evvie forgot where she was. *The Today Show* was one of her secret addictions. Before discovering the joys of jogging at West Hollywood Park, she used to get up at the crack of dawn to establish herself as channel czar of the condo's exercise room before any of her neighbors more partial to *Good Morning America* arrived.

Katie had just asked Dr. Reichman about the relationship between estrogen and breast cancer when Evvie heard her name called over the loudspeaker.

She stood up, looking around blindly until she spotted a short, plump woman with curly, gray-streaked hair, whose suntanned face was wreathed in a welcoming grin. The woman quickly covered the distance between them. "Evelyn? I'm delighted to meet you. I'm Helen." She laughed. "Similar names, you and me. Except everybody calls me Hell for short. What about you?"

As she talked—so familiarly, so casually—she guided Evvie toward a set of open double doors. "Don't let it scare you. The machine looks big and makes a weird racket, but I promise you, nothing hurts, and the whole thing lasts just a few minutes." A steel structure, about the size of a baby elephant, dominated the middle of the room.

Helen began adjusting movable parts of the machine. "Now, if you'll just bear with me, I'll get this set up for you." She strained to shift a dome-like part of the machinery away from the white-papered treatment table. "Sometimes it's a little tricky to get this into just the right position. Now if you'll just take the gown off your one shoulder. No, that's the left. You're probably still half asleep. Been up since five myself. Had to check on a sick horse at the stables before heading out here. I'm a volunteer groom for three of 'em. They're my babies, along with a couple of pugs at home."

Helen placed her foot on a floor pedal, and the table began to descend. She reached out a hand to help Evvie climb up. "Easy does it, we're setting precious goods down here."

Evvie lay back and listened as the radiation machine was switched on.

"Okay, I'll be right outside. Just hold nice and still for me."

She automatically closed her eyes, prompted by some crazy notion that by doing so she could keep the radiation out of everywhere but where it needed to go. It was a strange sound that the machine made, eerily melodic, less like a medical gizmo than a foghorn. After all the surprisingly comforting prattle of the earthy Helen—whom Evvie was beginning to think merited the moniker Heaven rather than Hell—Evvie had the odd sensation of being cradled on some vast ship cutting its way through long-forgotten waters.

It stopped. Helen's voice sailed in from the hallway. "Now hold still a little more. It'll move around and seem like it's going to touch your face, but it won't."

As if on cue, Evvie could sense movement above her, almost like someone breathing over her face. She kept her eyes closed, mentally crossing her fingers that Helen knew what she was doing. Sure enough, the movement ceased without anything touching her, and once again, sound— this time a little lower-pitched—bathed the room.

A half hour ago Evvie wouldn't have believed it, but when Helen arrived back at her side— lowering the table, helping her to sit up and insisting she wait a few seconds to orient herself before stepping off— Evvie found herself wanting to linger, get Helen to talk about her horses or pugs, anything to keep her there with her in that womb of a room. But Helen was gently ushering her toward the door.

"I'll see you soon, same time tomorrow." Then she did something astonishing. She started belting out in a hearty alto the old cowboy song, "Happy Trails."

As Evvie turned the corner, somebody guffawed. Once she reached Reception, she realized it was Russell, twisted around in his swivel chair. "Oh, spare us. Roy Rogers and Dale Evans? Your choice of music's just showing your age, my dear." High-spirited whoops of laughter burst from the room behind him.

Evvie shook her head in wonder. This was where they treated people with cancer? She had the feeling she was going to get a lot more than radiation therapy here.

***

The next morning, it was much easier for Evvie to bring herself to the Cancer Center. When she entered the crowded radiation wing, she spied young Temple at the far end of the room. The child ran over and led Evvie back to a low-slung coffee table, where a Barbie coloring book and a Crayola box lay beside a pile of pamphlets bearing the title "Radiation and You."

Evvie looked around for Temple's mother, but Mrs. MacBride was nowhere in sight. "Don't worry 'bout Ma. She's just talking to my doctor." Good heavens, the child was psychic. "Do you want to color with me? I've saved you a seat." Evvie's eyes darted to the dressing cubicles lining one side of the room. Temple clapped a hand to her forehead, giggling. "I forgot. You have to put on your gown. But will you color with me, after? We'll have lots of time. My ma said one of the machines broke. That's why they're so slow today."

The child was obviously right. People were lined up against every available wall, a few of them frowning at their watches in annoyance, but most looking merely dispirited. To make it worse, the TV was on the fritz; every couple of seconds it seemed to suffer some kind of electric shock that dismembered the figure of Al Roker with lightning lines of static.

When she went to sign in, Russell barely flicked his eyes up at her before shooting out of his chair to hold a whispering confab with a harried-looking nurse. Evvie nearly tripped over somebody's foot as she turned to get her gown. Even that area was a mess. The clean gowns had been flung haphazardly onto a pile without even being properly folded. She darted a glance at her watch. She'd let them know at the Home that she might occasionally be late these next seven weeks, but she was due to lead a meeting for the nursing staff at ten this morning about new procedures in charting clients' incontinence.

She approached Temple as soon as she exited the dressing cubicle. "Do you want to see my favorite?"

As Evvie bent down to look at the coloring book, she caught a glimpse of her own cleavage. She tugged her gown more tightly over her chest before settling behind the kneeling child. She could sense the other people seated around the perimeters of this table watching her. She didn't even want to think about what had inflated the head of the man in the wheelchair across from her into a ghastly pink balloon. "Mm?"

"You see how nice she looks?" Barbie was entering a dance studio with a towel slung jauntily over her shoulders. "I made the slippers pink, just like mine. See? Ma said she's gonna have to get me a new pair, that's how much I'm growing. She says me getting bigger is a really good sign." Temple issued such a loud and gleeful whinny that the dour-faced woman next to Wheelchair Man issued an acid, "Shh!"

Startled, Temple looked up. She rose and walked toward the vacant-faced man, putting a hand on his wide knee. "I'm sorry, Mister. Ma says I need to be quiet here, but I forget." Her gaze fastened on his abnormally enlarged head. "Does it hurt?"

The man started moving his mouth around like a ruminating cow, and his lips shone with spittle as he pushed a series of incoherent grunts out of his mouth. He fell silent again, then slowly hauled his hand off his lap and gestured clumsily at Temple's ballet shoes. Amazed, Evvie saw that the eyes in his otherwise expressionless face shone with a kind of transcendent joy.

His companion regarded the man with considerable surprise. She turned to her neighbor, whispering, "If I didn't see it, I wouldn't believe it. He's been like a vegetable for weeks." She dipped a hand into her jacket pocket. "Here, little girl, want a candy? Do you like fruit-flavored?"

Temple accepted a handful with a thank you. She offered one to Evvie as she settled back down at her feet, humming as she resumed her coloring. Evvie looked around the room again. Several people had brought books with them and were reading intently. She saw an attractive young man at the next coffee table peel an orange, then she realized that a big bowl of oranges and bananas sat in the middle of the table at the center of the room. A few people were obviously impatient and annoyed, and several disheartened-looking souls seemed to be flagging, but many of the room's occupants were talking and laughing together. Why hadn't she noticed them before?

She slid down to the floor and picked up a vermilion-hued crayon. Temple nodded in approval when she said, "I think Barbie might like a backup pair of ballet shoes. What do you think—is this a good color?"

Just as she began making soft parallel strokes inside the outlines of Barbie's slippers, Ida Mae Washington hove into view like a giant steamer. A bulkily filled trash bag was clasped to her ample bosom, and her faded cloth purse bounced from her elbow like an inferior sidekick. The purse hung open, wide mawed, but she'd clearly made an effort to mend its yellowed plastic strap with whorls of Scotch tape. Undaunted, she crossed the threshold of the radiation waiting area, calling out loudly, "If y'all like figs, I'm your woman, 'cause my tree decided to do its thing a little early this year after my nephew D'Shawn went and took an axe to it."

She dumped her load onto the nearest table, a flood of figs pouring out. "Course I told him what he could do with his axe when I caught him at it. When you're looking the Grim Reaper a little too close in the eye yourself, ain't nobody gonna cut down no tree in your own backyard." She plucked one of the dispatched figs from the table and held it up for collective inspection. "He said the tree is sick. Now does this look like a sick fig to you?"

Evvie waited for the room to signal disapproval of her flamboyance, but it seemed that nearly everyone was regarding Ida Mae with easy affection. The woman with the fruit candies got up and joined the line of people reaching for their share of Ida Mae's harvest, all of them politely ignoring the baring of a fair number of skimpily gowned buttocks. At Temple's urging, Evvie got up.

Ida Mae welcomed Temple into her opened arms. "That's my sugar." When it was Evvie's turn, the woman smiled knowingly. "Looks like the child's got a friend."

It was only after Mrs. MacBride—looking like a wilted yellow daisy—came and fetched her daughter for her treatment that Ida Mae was able to fill Evvie in on the girl's story. It turned out that friends were at a premium for Temple. She and her divorced mother had been sent here from Missouri thanks to a series of ambitious fundraisers by their church and its affiliates, since Cedars offered a particularly promising experimental treatment protocol for Temple's rare form of cancer. But the costs were exorbitant, and Temple's mother came to the City of Angels with barely enough funds to pay for one full trial of chemo and radiation. She'd settled with her daughter in a dirt-cheap motel on Pico Boulevard frequented primarily by illegal immigrants from Mexico and El Salvador.

"We're all that little fish stick's got right now, us and her mama, who you can see is just about fried through herself. Helen told me that if this radiation trial don't work, there's not too much Miz MacBride can do about it, 'cause she's just about out of money already. The insurance her ex pays for doesn't cover experimental procedures like this, so she'll just have to go back and go through the motions of the standard stuff they got to offer in Missouri.

"Myself, I'm nearly cured, they tell me. About to graduate from radiation next week." She reached for a fig and bit into it, unselfconsciously sucking a little juice before chewing. "An' I do appreciate all they been doing for me, but"—she leaned forward to whisper in Evvie's ear, and Evvie could feel little squirts of fig juice mist her jaw—"I'd give all the healing over to that little girl, if I could. Why should all us folks who've had a full life—husbands, children, an' all—be kept alive when a little child like that might be taken by the Lord?"

Fourteen

IT'S THE RARE American woman who doesn't exhibit some sort of kinship with sisters across the globe who lengthen their necks with rows of binding necklaces, fashion weaves with straw and goat hair, or etch their skin in elaborate scarification. It took Evvie several weeks to realize that Chloe McPherson hadn't been kidding about the hair issue, and by then it was nearly too late. Wrapping a lock of hair around her fattest round brush was easy enough, but keeping it taut at a ninety-degree angle to her head had become impossible. She'd been going to work for weeks now with a beret stuck on her head, wayward curls exploding rebelliously below the headband.

Now she sat on a pedestal in an unfamiliar salon, watching a wide mirror reflect a face shamelessly exposed in laughing abandon. B.C., if a camera had caught her in such an unflattering pose, she would have ripped up the photo. But at this moment, she couldn't care less that her nose looked big and blotchy next to her crinkled eyes and that, thanks to her recent weight gain, the hint of a second chin was threatening to sprout beneath the one she'd been born with.

She'd been dragged inside this ivy clad building on Melrose Place by Beady, who'd insisted that if she was so hell-bent on cutting her beautiful dark hair short for the first time since childhood, the renowned Peter Hale of the Fragonard Hair Salon was the one to do the job. It was evidently a miracle akin to Jesus walking on water that Peter had an opening this month, some rock and roll diva's last minute cancellation just fitting into a break in Beady's shooting schedule.

Beady had been going to Peter for years. She said he was the only one she'd ever found who could cope with her wild, blond fuzz. Her actual words had been, "Girl, most hairdressers in the hood are so eaten up with envy for my platinum hair that they want to shape it into a helmet fro, and the rest of them want me to go all the way in the white direction by straightening the shit out of it. As for white folks, most of them freak out as soon as they try to brush this mop out, as if they think a woman with a lifetime's worth of big frizz can't take a little pulling on her scalp. Peter, on the other hand, is so self-absorbed that it doesn't even occur to him that the person whose head he's brushing feels anything at all." With a hand on her hip and a glint in her eye, Beady had added, "But, honey, I don't go to him for sympathy. He's simply the best, and that's the truth."

Misinterpreting the doubt written across Evvie's face, Beady had wagged a finger at her. "Listen, I know how much you detest the LA scene, but you don't choose your hairdresser for his character. Let's be real. I personally don't give a shit if that world renowned surgeon of yours beats his wife, ignores his kids, and salutes a picture of Pat Buchanan before he goes to bed, as long as he's done right by your sweet body. It's the same difference when it comes to Peter."

Evvie couldn't come up with a good enough argument, not unless she was prepared to confess to Beady that it wasn't her values that kept her from places like Fragonard, but how gross and out of it she felt when she ventured into the land of the young, thin, and trendy.

Now, as the dishy Peter cut a decisive five-inch swatch of wet black hair from the side of her head, Beady laughed. "Girl, you look like somebody just goosed you." Evvie burst into a fit of anxious giggling.

Peter merely smiled, holding his sheers aloft like a silver-winged bird until Evvie's hysteria spent itself. She grabbed a tissue from the counter in front of her and blew her nose, stealing a quick glance at him in the mirror. He was like a gay Sting. The same mantic eyes and self-possessed mouth. A line of magazine cuttings on the wall attested to the fact that he'd doctored several Academy Award winners' tresses. She was a little nervous that he seemed to be spending more time looking in the mirror at his own stylishly short, bleached blond head than at her ridiculously lopsided dark mane, but she figured that if he'd satisfied Sharon Stone, he probably wouldn't do too badly by her.

After seeing a dozen people that morning who were bald from chemotherapy, she'd been tempted to just ask Peter to shave her head. When she'd voiced that fantasy to Beady, her friend had merely shot her a look and said, "Oh, please, do me a favor and cut the crap."

It was easy for Beady to say. Look at her. Dressed in pale yellow linen overalls and a *cafe-au-lait* T-shirt, she looked like a tempting chocolate ice cream cone.

But now the ice cream cone was speaking, her delectable head cocked to one side. "I wonder how you'd look with it blond."

As if on cue, Peter put a hand on his narrow hip. "Amazing. Do you know I was thinking the very same thing?" Squinting in serious assessment, he started fussing with the shortened curls on the right of Evvie's head.

Evvie held up her hands in alarm. "Don't even think about it." Peter let go of her hair and raised an eyebrow. "I mean, this is already a big adjustment." She skewed around in the revolving chair to face Beady. "Can you imagine what my dad would say?"

"Honey." Peter spun her chair back around and put his handsome face just inches from her own. "Didn't Beady tell me you're a *therapist?* And you're still worrying what your daddy thinks?" He turned to Beady and hooked his forefinger into the apron of her Dianne Merrick outfit, tugging it playfully as he affected a deep Southern drawl. "If I lived my life by what my parents wanted, I'd be a farmer back in Kentucky, wearing a pair of mud-streaked overalls a lot less stylish than these. With a gap-toothed wife named Effie Jane and a couple of pimply, overweight kids addicted to McDonald's and heavy metal."

Evvie tittered until an image crossed her mind of what her father was like when he was especially outraged. She appealed to Beady. "Help me out here. You know what he's like."

"I have to admit it. There *is* something about Michael Kerr that puts the fear of God into you. You worry that he'll rain down some plague on you if you go against what he thinks is right."

"You'd better not let him hear you mention his name in the same sentence as the word 'God.'"

Peter looked confused.

"Never mind," said Evvie. "Trust me, you don't want to know. It's too complicated."

"Oh no, it's not. Evvie's dad used to be a communist. I mean, the real thing. Card-carrying."

Evvie's heart thudded. Though Peter's expression seemed harmlessly inquisitive, she wondered what he was thinking. Growing up just on the heels of McCarthyism, you learned early on that there were some things you never talked about in public. Your parents' membership in the Party headed the list, even if they *had* quit after the revelations about Stalin's atrocities. Early stories about the Rosenberg children being orphaned after their parents' unjust execution as communist spies had filled her with terror about what might happen to her, too, if the world knew what her parents believed in.

As it was, her mom had died much too young anyway.

The name Rosenberg stimulated yet another disquieting image—her awkward conversation with Ezra Rosenberg in the Farmers Market parking lot. Beady seemed to be totally oblivious of how Ezra had managed to be tied up every time she tried to get the three of them together. It was no surprise to Evvie.

"Do you really think I could get away with blond hair? I mean, maybe I should look at some hair magazines or something before making a hasty decision."

Peter turned to rummage through a pile of glossy magazines on a table beside a modernistic beehive hair dryer, while Beady knelt on the floor next to him, adding her own editorial commentary.

Evvie stared at herself in the wide mirror. The hair on her left side hung in loose damp ringlets; the hair on the right, cut almost as high as her cheekbone, was already drying into frizzy little sausages. She held up her hand lengthwise, covering the longer scalloped locks on the left, and tried imagining what she'd look like with all of it short and blond. She felt like Pandora right after she'd opened her wretched box.

As Peter rose up, exultantly waving a magazine photo of a beautiful blond model, she said a silent prayer that the Fates would be merciful to her for what she was about to do.

***

Ben was the only one home when Evvie returned with her fashionably tousled blond haircut. She spied him from the hallway, stretched out on the longer of the two living room sofas, staring sightlessly out the window.

When she entered the room, his shock actually lifted him onto his feet. "Aunt Evvie! What've you done?"

She winced and put a hand to her head. "Is it awful?"

"No, I'm sorry, it's not. It's just…it doesn't look like you."

"I know. Do you think I should dye it back?"

"I guess not. Not unless you want to." He failed to notice her hurt expression.

"What's wrong?"

What did she have, some kind of radar? "Nothing. I guess I'm just wasted from midterms." He made his excuses and fled to the bedroom, taking a couple of deep breaths before picking up the phone.

He had to find out what was going on with Tash. It had scared the shit out of him to see her crumple like a rag doll at this afternoon's *Westside Story* rehearsal. Oh, sure, she'd scrambled right up again, but still. He cursed himself for being so slow to notice her recent weight loss. What if she had one of those eating disorders the girls at school were always going on about? It could be. She'd started hanging out with Anna Sumter's crowd, and he swore every one of those girls was as skinny as Ally McBeal.

What was bugging him most, though, was how evasive Tash had been after rehearsal, refusing his offer to drive her home with some lame excuse about having to talk to Sam Troop, her history teacher, about some pop quiz she'd fucked up on. Tash didn't fuck up on anything academic.

He punched in her number and waited for what seemed like forever. He heard trance music vibrating in the background when she finally answered.

"Hey," he said, nervously rubbing his thumb along the side of the phone.

"Hey." Uh-oh. She sure didn't sound overjoyed to hear him.

"I, ah, just wondered how it went with Troop."

"What?"

"Troop. You said you had to talk to him after rehearsal."

"Oh … yeah. It was okay. It's not like I'm gonna fail or anything." Her laughter seemed forced.

"Are you okay? I mean, it was scary how you just fell …"

"God, how embarrassing was that?"

"No … I didn't mean it like that. It's just that you seem kind of checked out lately."

"Did you call to rag on me?"

"Baby, I'm not ragging on you. I just think something's different." He took a breath. "Are we okay? I mean, you and me?"

"Of course, we are. Why wouldn't we be?"

"Tash, you know I really care about you. If you're having a hard time, I want to know."

"Shit, Ben, you sound like I'm dying. Everything's cool. We're cool, I'm cool, you're cool."

"Okay, okay. Listen, I know you're going on that family trip this weekend, but what do you wanna do next Saturday? We could hang with Tony and Opal." He grinned and lowered his voice. "His mom's going out of the country for a month. We'll have a whole bedroom to ourselves any time we want."

She was taking a hell of a long time to respond. "I kind of made plans to hang out at Anna's … Nicole and Tammy are going, too."

"Girls' night out?"

"I guess you could call it that."

For a brief moment, Ben was distracted by the memory of his aunt's spiky blond curls. He'd always balked when his friends resorted to the male mantra that women were all nuts, but when even Evvie showed signs of succumbing to the crowd, he had to wonder.

But Tash's impatient breathing brought him up short. He made his voice purposefully casual. "You've gotten pretty tight with Anna, haven't you? Don't you think she's kind of out there?"

She giggled. "Yeah, I guess you could say she's kinda wild. But she's fun."

"More fun than me?"

"Please. You know it's not like that."

"What kind of fun is she?"

"You want to come, too? Satisfy your jealous soul? Just don't say I didn't warn you. You never know what'll happen with a bunch of crazy girls!"

No, he didn't. But that wasn't going to stop him. He was just grateful that Tash wasn't looking to dump him. At least he hoped she wasn't. If he lost her, he didn't know what he'd do.

***

Ben was so preoccupied with his anxieties about Tash that he'd forgotten it was his grandfather's birthday. Evvie hadn't. Living eyeball-to-eyeball with her own mortality these days, she was more than aware that turning eighty-six was nothing to sneeze at.

Which was why, she suspected, her father hadn't objected when she'd suggested that she and Miriam and Ben bring some dinner over to celebrate. She'd had to do a bit of persuading of her sister, though. Miriam was in a funk over some fight with Paul Welles, and Evvie had to haul out the big guns of Jewish guilt to remind her that, while boyfriends come and go—anyway, Miriam's certainly seemed to—they had only one father, and who knew how long he'd be around? Personally, Evvie wasn't quite convinced that Michael Kerr wouldn't live forever, but that wasn't anything she'd care to say aloud.

The backseat of Miriam's Jaguar wasn't the most comfortable place to sit, especially when you were constrained by a new, slinky black skirt that had somehow, over the course of a couple of days, grown too tight. And being surrounded by the makings of a four-course gourmet meal didn't help. She'd had to cede the passenger seat to Ben, unable to compete with the demands of his long legs.

She shifted the wooden salad bowl in her lap, careful not to crush the prettily wrapped parcel next to her. It was her major coup of the decade, an original edition of *The Grapes of Wrath* that she'd managed to track down through an antiquarian book service. She couldn't wait to give it to her father. Michael had been quoted in innumerable magazine interviews citing Steinbeck as his favorite American writer since Poe.

She caught a glimpse of herself in Miriam's rearview mirror. Her short, blond locks bounced whenever she moved her head. She shuddered to think what her father would have to say about her hair. When she'd broached this birthday plan a week ago, she hadn't reckoned on the personal makeover she'd blundered into at Fragonard.

When they pulled up to the curb on Wonderland Avenue, Ben was the first to tumble out of the car. He rushed around to relieve Evvie of the salad bowl. She gave him a big smile as he helped her up to the curb. "*Oomph!* I've got a serious case of old-lady-itis." It was true, she'd begun to notice that her knees went stiff whenever she sat in one position for more than fifteen minutes. "Don't look so alarmed, baby, it's just that your auntie's not a spring chicken anymore." Not that she herself wasn't spooked. Breast cancer, itchy night sweats, arthritic knees. Barely forty, and she was already coming apart at the seams.

But then she had to laugh. Soleil's nonagenarian mother Delphine, known to Beady's friends simply as Grann, was squinting at them from her front yard. While Soleil had moved back to the *tantes* and *oncles* in New Orleans, and Beady had purchased a lovely Westwood home for herself and Tony, Grann had insisted on holding the fort on Wonderland Avenue, refusing to abandon her beautiful garden.

Beady liked to say her *grand-mère* could grow greenery from barbed wire. When the three generations of Blanchette females moved next door to the Kerrs, Grann had created an eclectic Eden around their new home with seeds she'd pilfered from a host of renowned gardens, not the least of them a millionaire's mansion in the Virgin Islands and Churchill's exquisite grounds at Chartwell. Grann was showing her age now, trundling toward them cautiously, trowel in hand, blinking as if she couldn't make out exactly whom she was approaching in the dusky light. Evvie warmly clasped her clawlike hand, whose fingernails were so encrusted with dirt that they looked like the root system of a tiny hedge.

"Why, Evvie, it *is* you. It's a treat for sure to see you up and around and looking so well. I've been asking after you to Beady, but, girl, she didn't say anything about your hair!"

"Do you think it looks terrible?"

Grann carefully scratched her nose with the tip of her trowel, leaving a little mole of dirt behind. "Girl, you couldn't look bad if you tried. No, the blond hair suits you. You look just like that actress in *Never on a Sunday*. What was her name? *C'est insupportable*, an old woman's memory."

"Melina Mercouri?" Miriam interjected.

Ben approached now, bestowing a kiss on the old woman's forehead. "Hi, Grann. I hate to be a traitor to my family, but you're the prettiest one of all."

Grann just chuckled, but her ancient, wrinkly face—brown as the earth she tilled—was wreathed in a winsome grin.

"I remember Melina Mercouri, Grann," said Miriam. "Beady took me to a couple of her films." She inspected her sister's face. "It would never have occurred to me, but now that you mention it, I can definitely see the resemblance."

Evvie was feeling both flattered and confused. The name sounded vaguely familiar, but she couldn't place the face. She kissed the old woman's forehead. "It's so good to see you, Grann, but we should probably get a move on. It's my dad's eighty-sixth birthday."

"Eighty-six you say? *Mon Dieu*, now that's a marvel. And still such a good-looking man. Wish him happy birthday for me." She grinned slyly. "Tell him if he can figure out how to shave a couple decades off the two of us, I'll put my best satin sheets on my bed for him, yes, I will."

They caught Michael peeking out the window when they let themselves in. He came toward them, rubbing his hands together, eyes glowing. "Ah, my family." He patted Ben on the back and gave Evvie a quick peck on the cheek. "You feeling okay? Good, good." Not a word about her hair.

Evvie stared at him. She hadn't even answered his question. But he was already turning to her sister, who reported Grann's offer. He laughed. "Can you imagine what a beauty she must have been? With those sloe eyes and tawny skin? A Jean Toomer kind of woman. Did you ever read *Cane*?" Before Miriam could respond, he stepped back and raked his eyes over her white sleeveless dress, embellished by a single silver band encircling her slender upper arm. "Speaking of beauty, what did I ever do to deserve such a lovely daughter as this?"

Evvie simmered all the way through their first course, but her father was completely oblivious. He pushed away his unfinished salad and turned to Ben. "Any closer to narrowing down what you want to study?"

"Not yet, but my advisors keep saying we should take lots of different classes. Most colleges don't make you declare a major until you're a junior. But it doesn't make it any easier when Tony and some other friends of mine already know exactly what they want to do. Grandpa, did you always know you were going to be a writer?"

"Hell no. Before I met your grandmother, I had two ambitions: becoming a journeyman plumber and advancing the socialist cause."

Miriam made a face. "God, a plumber. I can't believe a man like you setting your sights so low."

"Miriam, I can overlook your lack of interest in the kind of world we live in, but I can't abide a lack of respect for people who labor with their hands. People like plumbers make life a breeze for the rest of us. Not that I was any good at it myself." He chuckled. "I'll bet I never told you kids about my last day as an apprentice. Pass me the bread will you, Ben?" He tore off a hunk and held it aloft, clearing his throat.

Evvie traded looks with her sister and nephew. In resigned unison, they settled back in their chairs.

"I might have handled the whole thing better if hadn't been the end of a backbreaking day replacing a cracked bathtub in the Bronx. Who knows? But when the call came in from my dispatcher Ernie Crabbe, I was desperately navigating my brothers' rattletrap truck home on streets slick with sleet. Remember, how I told you, Ben, that an old childhood case of rickets kept me from joining my brothers in the fight to smash the Nazis?" Ben nodded obediently.

"Anyway, Ernie's voice crackled and spat with static, but I got the message, alright. 'Kerr,' he says, 'this miserable war has eaten up every one of our journeymen. I just got a call from some guy named Holt. Manages a fur shop on Fifth Avenue. You're the only free man I've got, but if you screw this up, I'll make sure you get canned.'

"It sounded like a simple job. Toilet flushing sluggishly. I figured the pipes were plugged with ladies' pads.

"But when I get there, the guy at the door barely bothers to hide his disgust at my soiled uniform. He tells me he's in a hurry, but makes me spend five minutes wiping my boots before leading me to the storage room at the back. I walk in and see wall-to-wall racks of fur coats and jackets. All I can think is that my sister had left for work that morning wearing a couple of layers of flimsy sweaters under her cheap cloth coat.

"Holt points toward the small bathroom off the storage room, mumbling something about not wanting to miss the opening of a new play. He locks the connecting door to the showroom, says all I have to do is pull the alley door closed behind me when I'm done. The automatic lock will take care of the rest.

"I can barely maneuver in that cramped bathroom. The pipe is so frozen that I can't wrench it open at any of the joints. I realize I've got to cut into the line to get my snake inside."

Evvie stared down at her uneaten salad. Ben and Miriam looked as uncomfortable as she felt, but her father's voice had the telltale pitch of suppressed mirth.

"I had no reason to suspect that the pipe's contents had frozen unevenly and that someone in the flat above the shop would flush their toilet at the precise moment I broke into the line. Before I know it"— Michael was laughing so hard, they had to lean forward to make out his words—"slushy shit is spewing everywhere. I'm paralyzed. Raw sewage is exploding across the walls of the bathroom and right through the doorway onto the furs. I clasp both hands over the end of the pipe, but it's no use—it's like trying to control a loose-bowelled elephant.

"I can see the furs turning into dripping brown monsters. I consider pulling the bathroom door shut behind me to protect the merchandise, but then I imagine Holt finding me the next morning, buried alive in excrement. There's nothing for it but to let go of the pipe and make a run for it, gobs of shit flinging themselves at my back as I yank open the alley door."

"Stop. It hurts." Evvie was clutching her side in uncontrolled laughter. Miriam and Ben looked as if they were about to piss themselves.

But just as quickly as he'd seduced them into hysteria, her father shifted gears. His voice turned sepulchral. "As soon as the shop door swung shut behind me, I realized that I'd left my tools inside. My sister had worked like a dog for a year to help me pay for those tools."

Evvie felt guilty for having laughed, but Miriam, dabbing at her smeared make-up with the edge of her napkin, wasn't having any of it. "That was a shame, but it was just as well, wasn't it? You were obviously not meant to be a plumber. The last thing I'd ever buy is a real fur, but what you ended up making as a writer gave Evvie and me pretty much everything we wanted, didn't it, Ev?"

"I don't think that was Dad's point, Miriam. I—"

It was only then that he actually took her in. His face went from pale olive to purple. "Good God, woman, what have you done to your hair?"

Miriam, the traitor, immediately rose up and left the room, claiming a sudden desire to fetch some butter for her bread.

Evvie desperately threw out, "Don't blame me. It was Beady's idea. She insisted on taking me to her hairdresser the day before she and Ezra left."

Looking at her as if she'd just passed some particularly odious wind, Michael muttered, "Who's Ezra?"

Miriam tiptoed back in, butterless. "He's Beady's new love interest. *Veddy* interesting. If he wasn't already taken, I think I might give him a whirl myself. They're doing a documentary on kids in civil wars or something." She caught her pointy little tongue between her teeth like a cat. "You're not the only man in the world with a mission. He told us this awful story about some little girl getting raped."

Evvie felt like she'd been punched in the gut. Why hadn't Beady told her she was going out with Ezra? She was sufficiently distracted that she failed to notice her father staring glassily at her sister.

Ben tried to save the day. "I think Aunt Evvie's hair looks great. Grann says she looks just like Melina Mercouri."

Evvie exploded, "Oh, for Christ's sake. Who the hell is Melina Mercouri?"

Her father looked like he was about to have apoplexy. "Who's Melina Mercouri? One of the great women of our time? Married to Jules Dassin?" He flung the words at her like a curse. "That one ring any bells?"

Ben put on such a guilelessly curious face that she wondered how many times he might have conned *her*. "Grandpa, I've never heard of them. Who are they?"

Thank God, her father took the bait, shifting right into oratorical mode. "Melina was a gifted actress, nominated for an Oscar for *Never on a Sunday*. Beautiful as a goddess, yes, but a woman of substance, a woman of vision. She fought in the Greek resistance against a rightwing junta that was supported by our CIA. She had to flee into exile, but when Papandreou took the reins of government, she became his Minister of Culture. I met her husband Jules years before in the YCL." Michael looked pensive—lost, Evvie speculated, in an earlier season of his life.

Evvie took in the perfection of her father's dining table, its intricately carved legs turned gracefully beneath an Irish linen tablecloth. These water glasses were crystal, and the salad plates had been handcrafted in Italy. As for Michael himself, even at eighty-six, with his still-full head of silver hair and his dark, soulful eyes, he looked handsome and distinguished. For someone who'd had rickets as a kid, he was having a hell of a run of grace and abundance now.

"Jules started out as an actor in Yiddish theater before becoming a writer. Ever hear of *The Naked City*? He did tremendously well." A cloud crossed Michael's face. "Then along came an American Hitler named Joe McCarthy, who attracted a bunch of other little Hitlers—sonsabitches like Ed Dmytryk, Elia Kazan—like a human shit magnet. I know you know about the blacklist, Ben. I was lucky enough to enter the industry just as it was starting to ease up, but before then Jules had to leave the US and struggle like hell to build a career abroad. He did it, though. His *Rififi* won for best picture at Cannes."

"Is he still alive?"

"Yep. Just like your granddad. One of those old war horses fated to outlive his contemporaries."

"Melina Mercouri, too?"

"Oh, no, she died a long time ago. Cancer. But that's not what's important. What's important is that the two of them had great integrity. They made a dent in world affairs."

Right. And there you had it. At least she didn't have to worry about the hair issue anymore.

Fifteen

EVVIE WAS AT least partially wrong. Her hair was the first thing to pop into Michael's mind when he woke the next morning. He couldn't understand what kind of lunacy would make her want to color it blond when she'd been blessed with her mother's shiny black waves.

He cracked open an eye and saw the yellow legal pad he'd angrily flung onto his bedside table the previous night. What did it matter that Dick's idea was a winner, when he himself was too old and clumsy to do justice to it?

Groaning, he sat up and propped his pillow against the headboard. While he'd been through many mattresses since her death, this four-poster bed was the same one he'd purchased with Riva all those years ago. It was stately and elegant, just like this bedroom, which bore no resemblance whatsoever to the tiny corner where he'd slept as a child. Back then, his makeshift cot had shared cramped quarters with a sooty old stove and a small, wood-plank "dining" table that did double-duty as a desk for his older brothers, who used it to study the Torah. That type of arrangement was more common than not in the humble Jewish enclave of Kodnya, whose name couldn't be found on most maps of Russia even before the Nazis leveled the village.

Had there been a street in Kodnya, it would hardly have occurred to anyone living there to name it Wonderland Avenue. No, a name like that had to be earned by bedrooms like this one, with its mahogany desk as wide as a small boat, a pair of glass-fronted legal bookcases stuffed with hardback treatises on history and philosophy, and a walk-in closet the size of his first home.

On a sudden impulse, Michael stumbled out of bed and approached his closet, where he shoved aside a cluster of hanging suits encased in plastic bags to reveal his first wife's old pine keepsake chest, hidden behind boots and shoes on the floor. Arthritic knees screaming, he slid the chest across the carpet to the middle of the room.

He breathed heavily, staring at its intricate lock until, moved by some ancient memory, he shuffled toward a leather jewelry box on his dresser. Sure enough, he found a shapely antique key resting beneath an assortment of rarely worn cufflinks.

He rolled the key in his hand. The heat of his palm warmed and moistened it, reminding him of the long-ago feel of Riva's skin, especially in that sacred place, his favorite, the stretch of inner thigh just before it angled toward the wild jungle of her prickly, black pubic hair. He liked to look up at her half-closed eyes while he stroked that particular plain of silken skin, so tantalizingly close to her center. The power to reduce her to such pleasure made him feel like a king.

As he dropped down beside the chest, a repetitive tapping pulled his attention to his bedroom window. A lone crow, perched on Delphine's roof, was busily pecking at one of the Spanish tiles, where potato vine tendrils twisted and twined. As if sensing Michael's anguished gaze, the bird cocked an imperious head in his direction. *Quoth the Raven "Nevermore."* With a startling flap of its shiny wings, it took ungainly flight past green fingers of the privet bush dividing the two properties.

Michael tried shifting his position and swore. Age was a thief. His body no longer belonged to him. Somehow, he managed to sit with one leg parallel to the chest and the other bent awkwardly so that he could attack the lock and push back the lid, his upper lip pearled with perspiration.

The creamy satin pouch was still on top, where he'd placed it twenty-five years ago. With trembling hands he extracted its sole content, a lock of ebony hair, still shiny and alive-looking. He held it up to his nose and sniffed, but Riva's scent was long gone. With careful fingers, he inserted the hair back into its pouch and tucked it into the bosom of Riva's folded, lacy Mexican wedding dress.

116

As he started to lower the lid, a bulky, tissue-wrapped package in the corner caught his eye. His breath caught for a moment at the memory of watching Riva wrap his father's gray and black fringed *tallis* and gold-embroidered *yarmulke* in these folds of tissue paper. After his sister Rose had dropped dead in the middle of a raucous street march in aid of unionizing New York City janitors, it had fallen to Riva to dismantle Rose's third floor walk-up apartment. Riva had discovered his father Abraham's prayer shawl and velvet skullcap stowed secretively beneath Rose's frugal underclothes.

When his wife brought these sole remnants of Abraham's life back to their home, she'd wrapped them around pungent, polished blocks of the finest cedar, placing the package in her keepsake chest for safe-keeping. *Foolish woman*, he'd thought at the time.

Now Michael unwrapped the parcel and rose, clutching the *tallis* and *yarmulke* to his chest. He collapsed with them onto his bed, the fringe of the *tallis* tickling his unshaven cheek. The face of his father appeared before him.

Abraham Kirschon had been an oak of a man. His hardheaded devotion to his forefathers' religion precluded any sympathy for Michael's refusal to say his prayers after what happened to Golda Starekova. Most of the men in the village had been at least a little besotted with Golda, but for young Michael she'd been the one bright flower winking from the center of Kodnya's hard soil. But Abraham gave no quarter to grief. He'd tried to beat religion, or at least obedience, into his youngest son.

The old man would never forgive him if he knew that his great-grandson hadn't become a bar mitzvah and that his granddaughters had no concept of lighting the candles or keeping a kosher home. But he would undoubtedly have been captivated by Miriam, as vivacious as Golda herself. The girl had been a spitfire from the very beginning. Nothing, not even the death of her own mother, had gotten her down. Even now, her spirit was green and youthful.

Michael absent-mindedly jabbed at his lip with the scratchy edge of the *yarmulke's* gold braiding. Maybe Miriam was staying young a little too long. What if she never managed to settle down with one man— what would happen to her and Benjamin? He was too old-fashioned to believe that a family could be solid without a man at its helm.

Michael had made sure that, once he was gone, his three loved ones would inherit the assets of his house and, Lenin forgive him, a secret stock portfolio that at least avoided the worst offenders of the military-industrial complex, but he longed to see his daughters looked after by men of their own.

Both of them. After all, he had some reason to hope that, in spite of Miriam's fickleness, her guiding star of self-interest would lead her into some successful man's conjugal bed. But Evelyn? Being a spinster was tragic for a woman of such substance, whose compassionate dark eyes were so like Riva's he could barely stand to look at her.

Michael pushed a hand through his silver hair. There'd been nothing in Marx or Engels to give him guidance in raising two girls. If anything, his politics seemed to have alienated him even more from them. Miriam couldn't care less about the fate of the world, and Evelyn, seeing only those parts of communism that had been clumsy and brutal, seemed to think he was some kind of political Neanderthal.

But neither one had any inkling of the harshness of life in Czarist Russia, particularly once the war disrupted farming in his native Ukraine. Despite his mother's insistence upon giving her youngest son extra bites of woody potato and a full half of the family's one rationed egg each week, the ache of hunger made sleep impossible. His belly had begun to bloat, and his legs were bowed from rickets. Infants and old people were dropping like flies.

And then one day a small but splendid band of men rode into his village on horseback, waving red flags and distributing baskets of food to Jew and Christian alike. After spending a few hours listening to their stories of wresting power from the hands of tyrants, he'd watched them ride out again, hunks of yeasty bread in each of his hands and a mouth full of the sweetest apple he'd ever tasted.

Michael buried his head in his pillow. What had happened? He'd outlived his first love for twenty-four years and the USSR for nearly a decade. The righteous anti-Nazi Serbs had become the fascists of Europe, the Soviet Union's nuclear arsenal was being sold off to black market bidders, his eldest daughter was fighting the disease that killed her mother, and he …? He was a pathetic old man who didn't know how to tell his ailing daughter that he loved her.

Michael wiped his eyes and sat up, his jaw working with sudden resolve. He reached a hand toward the telephone beside his bed.

***

Evvie had slept especially poorly the previous night, wrestling rage and a relentless attack of the itchies, so she very nearly let the answering machine pick up the call. But then she worried it might be Ben. When she heard her father's voice, she wished she'd gone with her first impulse.

Nonetheless, she forced a modicum of warmth into her tone. "Oh hi, Dad. Did you have a good time last night?"

"Yes, yes. Listen, Evelyn, don't let me forget, the next time you come over there're a few belongings of your grandfather's I want you to have. They're just accumulating dust in my closet."

"What things, Dad?"

"Oh, a *tallis* and a *yarmulke*." He gave an uneasy laugh. "Religious relics, but maybe you can find some kind of use for them."

"Dad, that's sweet, but I'm not really into Judaism."

"Evelyn, I didn't call for an argument."

You could have fooled me. "Maybe you should give them to Ben."

"Nah, he wouldn't know what to do with them. And I certainly don't need them. They're just adding to the general clutter."

She barely had time to murmur a faint thank you before he rang off. Great. What was she supposed to do with a *tallis* and *yarmulke*? How many times had she told him that organized religion left her cold?

As she lay her head back down on the pillow, she had to admit to herself that that wasn't strictly true. But her father had no way of knowing how she'd secretly prayed to Baby Jesus as a child.

It had taken an older girl in the neighborhood to introduce her to the notion of an infant who could save the world with the innocence of his love. When Evvie was just approaching puberty, sixteen-year-old Sherry Nielsen had spent her after-school hours gathering the younger girls on their block into the converted garage adjoining her family's Hollywood Hills home, where half the time she led them in prayers to Baby Jesus, and the other half she had them all remove their blouses so she could "massage" their flat little chests. To this day,

Evvie always felt a little flare of sexual arousal whenever she heard someone begin the prayer, "Now I lay me down to sleep ..."

She mouthed the rest of the words, curious to see if she could remember them. "I pray the Lord my soul to keep; if I should die before I wake, I pray the Lord my soul to take." What kind of a thing was that to teach children? Though as time passed it became a pretty good fit, what with having to tuck herself into bed at night to the sounds of her mother puking her guts out in the bathroom down the hall. As the retching grew increasingly violent, she'd whisper her ritualized add-ons even more frantically: "God bless Mommy and Daddy and Miriam and Uncle Max and Auntie Rosie and Cousin Naomi and all the poor and suffering people in the world. And please, God, I promise I'll be very, very good, just don't let anybody I love die." Only then could she shut her eyes and, with one hand cradled in the moist, private place between her legs, fall asleep.

It occurred to her now that it was probably thanks to that early wedding of prayer and sexual excitement that she'd fallen so hard for Simon. From their very first encounter at Tower Records, his fingers brushing hers as they both reached for the same Dylan album, he looked—with his lean ascetic frame and shoulder-length blond hair curtaining his translucent hazel eyes—like a counter-culture Jesus. And afterwards, the two of them hip-to-hip, chain smoking and drinking bitter black coffee at Barney's Beanery, Simon's casual references to William Blake and *The Kama Sutra* made him seem like a cross between the Messiah and the Hindu god of love. He'd only added fuel to the fantasy when he brought her back to his studio apartment on Rose Avenue. Stroking the big thighs that she'd always despaired of before encircling her full, round breasts with his slender hands, he'd whispered that she was the perfect Shakti to his Shiva.

Evvie groaned and curled into a fetal position, her hands curved protectively over her chest. What was it they said, that if you get too close to the gods, you're sure to pay?

Sliding toward sleep, she barely broke the rhythm of her languid breathing as a fog lifted her out of her body to observe her bandages slowly dissolve before her eyes.

She tried rousing herself. This was getting to be a habit. But despite her efforts, little Michael crept out from the arched wound above her nipple, this time looking a little the worse for wear. He seemed intent on getting her to follow him, crooking his index finger back and forth before turning on his heels and leading the way across a vast field, where tall purplish and tan reeds waved in unison with the wind.

He halted at the edge of a winding narrow river, where a group of thirty or forty people were huddled together. They had an air of suppressed excitement. Was this some kind of game?

But just as she was getting into it, the scene turned sour. Not too far from where Michael and his companions hunched together, scores of stately reeds were falling in ragged heaps.

It came to her that this was Easter time in Old Mother Russia. Peasant women in Easter dresses spilled from a tiny village church as if on fire, heavily ornate crosses jouncing on their breasts as they ran. Their men mounted horses and rode toward the riverside, determined to avenge the murder of God's only Son.

Little Michael and his companions, hearing them coming, strained to hide their offending *yarmulkes* and scarf-topped heads under the screen of the tall reeds. They communicated with anxious eye gestures. Mothers covered their babies' mouths until they nearly ceased to breathe.

No one had to place a hand over little Michael's mouth. It was clamped in a tight line. His dark eyes widened as the riders' scythes mowed down swathes of reeds, seeking the Christ-killers' necks. With every swoosh of a crescent-shaped blade, a broad clump of reeds fell with a great sloughing sigh, jolting little Michael's body like a powerful electric current. People on either side of him were passing out in fright.

Ultimately, though, the Fates were kind. The frustrated horsemen gave up, cursing as they rode off, and Evvie felt a surge of victory and delight. But the villagers weren't celebrating. They rose slowly, dusting themselves off, barely trusting to talk to each other in more than a whisper. Little Michael darted away.

A big wind came up, whistling louder than the murderous scythes. Michael ran like someone possessed.

It was rough going. He had to navigate past tricky spots where reeds thickened as they met the earth, but he hardly faltered and finally managed to break free into a clearing. It was then that Evvie saw what his village had become. The air was heavy with smoke. Nearly every hut had been set on fire. Blood was everywhere. Split-open carcasses of freshly slaughtered goats and chickens littered the ground. Little Michael zigzagged deftly around them, halting only when he arrived in front of the redheaded girl's home.

The body of her ginger cat obstructed the entrance. A sickly grin smeared its glass-eyed face, and from its rent belly, entrails spilled like twisted turds.

Fists at his sides, young Michael hesitated briefly before stepping over the creature to go inside. An ancient-looking woman lay on the pile of blankets in the corner. Only her face was visible. A brightly colored patchwork coverlet was tucked right up to her chin. Deep wrinkles scored her nut-brown face, and her mouth was open as if she were about to speak, but her eyes stared, unblinking, at the ceiling. She would never again see the much younger female who lay beside her, her flung-out hand nearly touching the old woman's sunken cheek. Nor would the younger one ever again see her.

Something had sucked the air out of this place. Little Michael knelt and stroked the teenager's red hair, still clinging close to her scalp from having been bound by a gaily patterned headscarf. The scarf had been yanked down from those vibrant locks to the neck and twisted tightly, cutting into the skin below the bloated blue face with its tongue hanging out like a dark snake.

The teenager's green and yellow flowered skirt was rucked up by her waist. Little Michael tried to tug it back down over her knees, but it was impossible. Her legs were spread widely, like a wishbone ready to be cracked in two, and blood pooled sickeningly beneath her hips. The little boy held up his fingers and studied them, as if he didn't know how they'd gotten so red.

He rose then and walked, unseeing, toward the low doorway. His brown eyes were without expression, his young body absolutely erect, his face set—hard and old before its time—like an immovable stone.

Evvie sat bolt upright in her bed, assaulted by waves of nausea.

"Jesus!" she moaned. What if that wasn't just a nightmare?

She shuddered. All her life, she'd been vaguely aware that her father nursed a romantic fascination for women who'd died. She'd always assumed it was because of her mother, but what if it went much back further than that?

She reached for the phone, then quickly replaced it in its cradle. How could she know so little of her own father? Even if it turned out that these dreams and visions of hers were more psychic than psychotic, who was she to open old wounds? Besides, whatever would she say?

She felt disgusted with herself for her resistance to her father's offer of the *tallis* and *yarmulke*. Admittedly, he was pretty cryptic about why he wanted her to have them, but even so, couldn't she have managed to welcome his generous gesture with a little grace?

Sixteen

A FINE MIST was falling over London and its surrounding boroughs by the time Beady and Ezra cleared Heathrow customs. The roadways were jammed, and Beady could have sworn that their cab traced an infinity sign several times between Buckingham Palace and Trafalgar Square before breaking free for Knightsbridge.

They got hung up again outside the Sloane Square tube station. Beady fastened curious eyes on a group of adolescent boys whose creamy complexions and closely shorn hair marked them as natives. A gaggle of Eurotrash smoked at little tables fronting a Parisian-styled bistro, while a trio of Arab women moved past them in harmony, everything about them cloaked in black robes but their haunting, kohl-lined eyes. As their cabbie finally managed to turn the corner, she saw a dreadlocked kid wave a copy of *The Big Issue* at a well-dressed young woman pushing an expensive pram.

Beady gave Ezra an appreciative grin as they mounted the stairs of his friend Tom Delaney's graceful Victorian townhouse, its brick exterior adorned with white wood trim, shiny black railings, and window boxes filled with lively red geraniums and pink and white impatiens. Ezra had been thoughtful enough to schedule a few days of recovery from jet lag before they traveled to the first of three refugee camps where they planned to shoot additional footage for *Their Fathers' Sins*. Since Tom, like his best friend Ezra, spent nine-tenths of his time on disaster gigs across the planet, his well-appointed flat in Lower

Sloane Gardens was a particularly welcome stopover for peripatetic journalists and news photographers.

While Ezra carted his suitcases toward a bedroom down the hall, Beady gratefully dropped her bags onto the exquisite Persian carpet of Tom's master bedroom. She re-tied her headband and freshened her lipstick in front of the dresser mirror and grinned at herself in approval. Even though she and Ezra had agreed not to complicate what was becoming a comfortable friendship, she didn't mind tantalizing him a little with what he was missing.

When she wandered back into the living room, she discovered that Ezra, an addictive newshound, had already turned on Tom's small TV. A sober-faced news announcer was describing in typically subdued BBC tones another escalation of violence in the Gaza Strip, with the Palestinians now firing mortars into Gaza City, as well as at Jewish settlements in the strip. Ezra swore and turned his back on the TV. "Jesus, this fucking *intifada*! In 1987, it was rocks and Molotov cocktails. After all the peace talks, this is where we've come?"

"It's not like the other side hasn't upped the ante. The Israelis're using gun ships and tanks and mortars of their own. And hey, don't aim that thing at me!"

Ezra had a razor in his hand. From the looks of the dark shadow on his cheeks and chin, he was the kind of man who needed to shave twice a day. "Sorry. I just go nuts whenever I hear they've notched up the hostilities again—I don't care which side it is. You think it's just because I'm Jewish?"

Beady replied archly, "Honey, I wouldn't blame you if you were a little biased. If this were South Africa or anywhere else where it's been Black against white, there's no doubt in my mind where I'd stand."

"But aren't you just as white as you are African American?"

"About as white as those half-Jewish Christians who got gassed by Hitler."

"Point taken. Do you mind?" She nodded, and he flicked off the TV. "We'll be getting enough of this kind of crap up close and personal in a day or two. Flying parches the shit out of me. I've got a terrible thirst. How about you?"

As she and Ezra drifted into the kitchen in the *folie a deux* that an old-fashioned English *cuppa* might cure their jetlag, Beady had to laugh.

Tom's flat might be situated in the pricey land of Sloane Rangers, just a hop and skip from the demure little shops once frequented by Princess Di, but its kitchen was a decidedly downscale British affair—separate cold and hot water taps that refused to pour in unison, diminutive dishwasher, tiny fridge, and an even tinier washing machine that would take a good two hours to process its paltry load. Wordlessly, she pointed to the washer.

"Yeah, it's nuts, isn't it? But you realize, don't you, that compared to where we're heading, this place is a palace?"

"I'm trying to prepare myself. I keep remembering what the Buddhists say. 'Life is suffering.' The older I get, the more I think they're right."

Beady paused, transported back to Evvie's living room a couple of nights earlier, when her friend had confided that her body was itching all over, especially at night. Evvie said that her oncologist had speculated it was her own version of hot flashes. Jesus—the cancer wasn't enough?

She suspected that, in some mysterious way, what was tormenting Evvie wasn't purely physical, but she daren't voice that, lest it sound like she was suggesting that Evvie had brought on her own discomfort. There was nothing more treacherous these days than the New Age tendency to blame the victim. No, Beady had a hunch it had more to do with Evvie's inner world becoming increasingly Balkanized between how she'd always lived and what this new, post-cancer reality would demand of her.

Ezra retrieved a couple of Wallace and Gromit mugs from Tom's cabinet and stood patiently at the sink, holding an electric Russell Hobbs kettle open for the grudging trickle of water from the tap. "What's wrong?"

"Am I that transparent? All that talk about unfairness made me think about Evvie."

Ezra frowned. "How's she doing?"

"Okay, I guess. I actually thought that if we got her a really great hairdo, it would cheer her up. As if going blond makes a difference when you're fighting cancer."

Ezra turned away, fussing in a drawer before extracting a couple of spoons. "You think she's going to make it through this?"

"Her doctors all swear she's going to be out and out cured."

Ezra faced her, and for a moment she thought she detected moisture in his eyes. "Surely that's wonderful news."

"Yeah, but what if they don't know what they're talking about? I'm not exactly a big believer in modern medicine."

He raised an eyebrow. "Listen, these days physicians are running so scared on the malpractice front, they don't stick their necks out until they're pretty damned sure." He paused. "You two are really tight, aren't you?"

"She's been my best friend forever. Talk about tight, we actually got our periods on the same day." She laughed. "Sorry. I'm not exactly the queen of delicacy. Actually, we were a threesome as kids. I'm right between Evvie and her sister Miriam in age. My *grand-mère* always said *le bon dieu* was on our side when we moved next door to the Kerrs. He was certainly on mine. Evvie must've inherited her father's sense of justice. Argued the pants off every kid who made fun of my kinky hair. And when Soleil—that's my evil mama—ragged on me, which she did most of the time, Evvie would tell me that just because I had a bitch of a mother didn't mean I wasn't the nicest person she knew. Even as a kid, she was a little psychologist, trying to figure out how somebody like Soleil could get so mean when they were raised by a woman as sweet as my *grand-mère*. She decided it was because Soleil was envious of my green eyes and light hair, which was a pretty sophisticated concept for a little kid."

Ezra scratched his chin thoughtfully. "She seems like the kind of woman who'd be in a committed relationship."

"And what kind of woman is that?"

"Now, now. It's perfectly obvious you could wrangle five marriage proposals by dinnertime, if you cared to. C'mon, you know what I mean."

"Well, yeah … between you and me, Evvie never got over the first no-count sonofabitch she fell in love with." She bit her lip. "God—sound familiar? I don't know what's the matter with our generation. It's like we're all suffering from some emotional immune deficiency syndrome. So fucking fragile that the first time we get hurt, we set up impenetrable walls to stop some other hurt soul from breaking through."

128

Ezra paused for a moment, as if considering whether Beady's theory applied to him. "Don't worry. As soon as you set foot inside a refugee camp, you'll forget about the pathetic state of your love life." He laughed, but Beady thought it rang rather hollowly. She watched in silence as he pulled a tin of Fortnum and Mason's Royal Blend from Tom Delaney's cupboard and plugged in the kettle for tea.

Seventeen

EVVIE'S CONFESSION TO Beady about her itchies was the product of sheer desperation. The habit of stoicism is a hard one to break.

Which was why it took her until the end of her third week of radiation before she found herself trying to describe to her sister and nephew how amazing she found her mornings at the Radiation Center.

Sitting opposite the two of them at the dinner table, she nervously pushed a trio of overcooked peas around her plate. "You can't believe what it was like watching a man with a head blown up like a pig's bladder light up like neon over a bald-headed little girl. I know it sounds weird, but there's something surprisingly sweet about the place."

She had the feeling that neither one of them was getting it. Ben, at least, looked like he was trying to pay attention, but his mind was obviously a million miles away. When they'd finished their dried-out roast chicken and soggy potato pancakes, he got up without a word and raced to his room. Miriam, who had to bite her lip to restrain herself from yelling at him about slamming his door, wasn't any better. She kept mumbling how sorry she was that they were eating so late, it all being the fault of Jerry's for taking a lifetime to deliver their dinner.

It was true. By the time Ben had returned from ferrying Michael's portion to their dad's house, it had been nearly nine o'clock, but Evvie hardly cared. She felt like she could just look at a piece of food these days and put on another five pounds. Besides, though she didn't have the guts to tell Miriam, it would've tempted her so much more to have some home-cooked food every once in awhile, even if it were a grilled cheese sandwich or some *matzo brei* and jam. She sighed and watched a tense-looking Miriam dig her cell phone out of her purse and edge into the hall. Evidently, some new drama was brewing between her sister and Paul Welles.

If it weren't for the existence of Ben, Evvie would write off all of Miriam's affairs as exercises in sheer futility. There was such a sameness about them, their initial manic charge aborted with regularity by her relentlessly fickle sister. *Nothing though*—a nasty, unbidden voice reminded her—*as abortive as what happened with you and Simon.*

Dr. Jose Alarcon's cold, dark eyes met hers, just as they had when the anesthesia wore off at the tail end of her abortion. She pushed away the memory of him, but couldn't help but feel ashamed of having gone to a cash-only abortion clinic in East LA to—as Simon had put it at the time—"take care of things."

Still living at home back then, she hadn't dared let her father find out she'd gotten pregnant. Which was why she'd let Simon cart her off to that unfamiliar part of town in his beat-up VW van, her face a goopy mess from her tears. She should have realized there was a reason why Simon knew about Dr. Alarcon's clinic. He'd undoubtedly been there before.

Evvie wandered past Miriam's closed door to her own bedroom and sprawled across her duvet without turning on the light. God, how long had she bled after her abortion? Three weeks, a month? How many nights had she carefully folded up her bloody Kotex pads and smuggled them out to the trash? Enough that she'd finally had to toss the purse she'd carted them in. The smell of rusty iron that wafted out of it every time she snapped it open made her sick.

What wouldn't she give at this point in her life to smell that woman's blood smell again?

In her worst moments she worried that her early menopause had been down to a botched procedure. Some nasty inner sadist loved to interrogate her relentlessly—if she was going to get rid of her baby, why not at least have the guts to tell her father and have the damn thing done right? She'd failed at the most basic of responsibilities—to take care of her own body. And she was still paying for it.

The front door slammed. It must be Ben going out. He'd mumbled something at dinner about having a date tonight, but it was odd that he'd left without bothering to say goodbye.

She forced herself to get up. Passing Miriam's bedroom, she could hear her sister scattering epithets like ashes. Poor Paul. Evvie hurried into the service porch, where she lifted an apron off a hook. Struggling to fit her hands into a pair of yellow rubber gloves she'd found under the sink, she marveled at their cleaning lady Carmella's tiny hands, bemoaning her own wide, peasant ones.

It wasn't until she was drying the last of the dishes that her sister flew into the kitchen. "That son of a bitch!"

Evvie carefully hung the sodden dishtowel over the oven handle before responding. She was beyond exhausted. She figured she had the itchies to thank for that. She was having them all the time now. She'd even started to dream about them—the Jews of old Russia scratching themselves like monkeys while they hid in the rushes from the Cossacks' sabers.

"What's wrong?"

"Paul is really getting up my ass. He says I should have remembered to call him when I was out of town. Do you believe it? You know what it's like on a shoot!" *Did she?* "For Christ's sake, I rarely get to sleep before midnight, and then up at five to make sure the costumes are all ready and nothing needs mending. And something always does. Is it my fault if Bob wanted me at his side every night while he drank himself into oblivion? It's not like he's cute or anything. He looks a shitload older than the thirty-five years he answers to, but I need to work. And this is the best gig I've gotten for ages. You know how much fun I've had designing all those hippy-dippy outfits. I'm hardly going to say no to joining him for a couple of glasses of wine if it keeps me on his good side. And then Paul gives me shit about it? Little fucking Napoleon! Do you believe it? He can't manage to give a thought to anyone but himself. He's so immature! You'd think he was younger than Ben."

Who did Miriam think she was kidding? At the rate she was going, she *would* end up with somebody younger than Ben. "Speaking of Ben, did you notice he seemed a little nervous at dinner?"

Miriam shot her an annoyed glance. She clearly hadn't finished with Paul yet. "Who cares? You know teenagers. They think their little growing pains are world-shaking. Whatever he's going through, he'll have forgotten about it a week from now."

Jesus, couldn't she manage, just once, to think about anyone beside herself? Evvie decided that she'd better stay awake in case Ben needed to talk when he came home. It was inevitably her, and not his mom, he confided in when something was troubling him.

She just needed to lie down and close her eyes for a second. The day had felt so long.

But the moment she stretched out on her bed, she was down for the count.

***

As Tash slid into the Beamer's passenger seat, Ben couldn't help but note her air of suppressed excitement. He tried to ease his nerves by leaning over and getting a whiff of her familiar scent.

"What's wrong?" she said.

"Oh, nothing. It's just … Are you wearing a new perfume?"

"Yeah, it's a mix of ylang-ylang and patchouli. Anna turned me on to it. Don't you like it?"

"Sure."

She shot him a look full of misgiving, then shrugged and turned on the radio. A BBC reporter was solemnly itemizing the damage caused by the latest suicide bombing in Israel. Tash made a face and changed the station to KROQ.

When Ben pulled up in front of Anna's parents' California Craftsman bungalow, Tash jumped out of the car before he could rush around and open the door for her. He followed her up the concrete walkway, which pulsed under his feet with the throbbing bass of house music.

Nicole Engstrom flung open the door, and music blasted out at them. Ben had spoken with Nicole a few times at school, and he hadn't been particularly impressed. She was one of Anna Sumter's groupies, a small cadre of pretty, but insecure girls who arrayed themselves around the self-assured Anna like Rose Bowl Princesses fawning over their Queen. He knew that Anna was smart, and her golden hair and classic features were delectable eye candy, but she had a way of always knowing a little more about whatever you were talking about than you did, or at least making you think so, and he couldn't imagine why a girl like Tash would waste her time hanging out with her.

Nicole was doing her own sizing-up. "Oh my God, Tash," she screamed, "you're wearing those pants. Agnès B, right? Tammy and I saw them last week, but they didn't have them in my size. I sure wish I had a real figure like you." Nicole's jeans rode low on her narrow hips. She wore the briefest of tank tops, lavender with tiny roses on the straps, and her mosquito bite nipples were clearly visible on her flat chest. Her short, peroxided hair stood up electrically, and her blue eyes lit everywhere but on his. "It's so dope, you won't believe it. Tammy just called from Damiano's—she's not off till ten, poor baby. They've just delivered an order to Mark Wahlberg at the Four Seasons! I mean, isn't that amazing? You know, he hit on Anna the last time she was at the Viper Room. God, it's like *Six Degrees of Separation*."

Nicole took Tash's elbow and pulled her into a living room hazy with cigarettes and incense. She rushed over to the stereo to turn the music down, giggling. "Shit, you guys, I didn't realize how loud it was till I went outside. We could get busted."

Ben followed stoically, slowing when he saw Anna, cross-legged on the floor behind a black lacquered coffee table. Her good looks were considerably dimmed by little screws of bloody toilet paper projecting from her nostrils. She was sliding an American Express platinum card across an Oasis jewel box to sculpt a neat line of white powder.

"Gotta take a little break myself. Fucking nosebleed again. But we'll catch you two up. I scored a particularly amazing eight-ball in honor of a visit from the outrageously handsome Ben Kerr. Did I ever tell you, Ben, that I've had the hots for you ever since ninth grade?" She rubbed some of the coke on her gums and made a ferocious face. "Yes!" She rolled up a twenty-dollar bill and handed it to Ben.

His eyes slid nervously in Tash's direction. She took pity on him and grabbed the bill. "Ladies first." She deftly snorted a line, then rubbed her nose, which went instantly pink and runny. He had to look away from her. Something in her eyes scared him.

135

While Anna prepared to cut another line, Nicole was moving around the room like a frenetic grasshopper, tidying everywhere she lit. Within minutes, the living room had been transformed into something out of the *Stepford Wives*. Except, of course, for the coffee table.

Anna looked up at him with a shit-eating grin. She'd shaped the letter 'B' in powder with a razor blade. Tash passed the rolled-up bill to Ben. He could feel all three pairs of eyes on him. He went down on his knees and took a deep snort.

The change in the room was instantaneous. He had a weird chemical taste in his mouth, his jaws were clenching like a vise, but he felt extraordinary, like a film had been lifted from his eyes. Everything was clearer, finer, and connected in ways he'd never realized.

Nicole giggled, and Tash gave him a knowing look. Anna pulled the pieces of toilet paper from her nose and flung them onto the coffee table. "Dude, did you see how he just zambonied that shit up? I think you were putting us on, Tash. Ben's an aardvark."

"Yeah," murmured Nicole, simultaneously dumping the contents of two ashtrays into a Gelson's bag. "I think you're right. The dude has definitely hoovered before."

Of course, he hadn't, but he couldn't imagine why not. This was the bomb. Three absolutely gorgeous girls were looking at him as if he were God, and they just might be right. He was on top of the world, and the world was fucking amazing.

Eighteen

IT WAS BARELY past 8 a.m. when Beady and Ezra arrived at the refugee camp in Albania. A lone songbird signaled the new day on a barren vista broken only by three large, communal tents surrounded by barbed wire. An exhausted-looking boy not much older than her own Tony, dressed in military fatigues, let Beady and Ezra through the gate. A line of similarly attired boys, rifles slung from their hunched shoulders, wordlessly smoked cigarettes as they leaned against the closest of the tents. Even at a distance of several hundred feet, Beady could see the boys' cigarette smoke spiraling above their helmeted heads in the crisply freezing air. What might have been a few locals were beginning to set up tables nearby for what looked to be simple platters of bread, cheese, yogurt, and jam.

Given the preternatural stillness, Beady was hyper-aware of her new, heavy combat boots scuffing the ground, the folds of her nylon jacket singing against itself. The young peacekeepers registered their approach with wary eyes. They'd obviously had to deal with enough reporters, aid workers, and low-level political functionaries to smell that she and Ezra weren't worth standing at attention for. As Ezra flashed them his press badge and she herself held up their official papers, not one of the soldiers bothered to acknowledge their presence.

Ezra held the flap of the tent open for her, and she stepped inside. She had to stifle the impulse to step right out again. The stench was overwhelming. A stew of sweat, shit, and vomit. She scanned the interior of the tent, struggling to take it in. There were over a hundred people packed in here, and precious little served to demarcate one family group from another, save small piles of belongings. She was surprised by the variation in physiognomies, which ranged from dark eyed and olive-skinned to the kind of blond hair and freckles she'd always thought of as all-American. A chorus of babies cried from every corner of the tent, while their older siblings whimpered or sat quietly, staring at their bleak-faced parents the way kids in the US watched TV. There was a cacophony of tubercular-sounding coughing. She couldn't believe it, but a few lucky souls actually still slept, as if this whole thing were merely a nightmare. She stole a glance at Ezra. He, too, was sizing up the situation, but he appeared a lot calmer than she felt.

A girl who looked no more than sixteen appeared before them. Her wispy hair was escaping her bun every which way, and she wore a Red Cross armband on her worn leather jacket. Ezra passed her their papers. She squinted uncomprehendingly at them. "You're *Eengleesh?*"

Beady stepped forward. "Yes, we've come to make a film."

The girl frowned, and Ezra signaled to Beady that he'd take over. "*Nous devrions faire ici un film. Nous esperons qu'il aide. Est-ce qui'il y a quelqu'un ici qui peut traduire pour nous?*" His French was far better than her own.

The young Frenchwoman excused herself with a quick nod and returned shortly with an owlish guy wearing a white lab coat over his blue jeans.

He had a surprisingly deep voice, and his young face was serious, but expressive. Beady felt goose bumps spread over her scalp. He was going to make for a great interview.

"Hi, I'm Dr. Sam Barrows. But please call me Sam. I'm chief medic at this shithole. Giselle says you're here to try to get us some press."

Ezra handed him their papers. "Good to meet you. Ezra Rosenberg. And this is Beady Blanchette."

The man started. "Are you're kidding? I don't believe it. Didn't you do a documentary about a Free Clinic on the Lower East Side?"

"God, yes. I didn't think anyone saw it."

"We did. Did my residency there a year after you finished filming. They used your documentary to recruit a bunch of us from Beth Israel Med Center."

"I didn't think that film did anything but lose my distributor a lot of money. I hope to get a little more notice for this one." She looked around, stifling the impulse to cover her nose. "Lord knows, you guys need it."

"No shit," he said, returning the papers to Ezra, who stowed them back in his jacket and picked up his camera. Sam Barrows grinned sheepishly. "Guess if I'm going to be famous, I'd better stop swearing."

Beady noticed that an old woman in black was leading a sickly-looking little boy in their direction, both of them awkwardly stepping around the web of seated and reclining bodies lacing the tarp-covered ground. "Look, I know you must be swamped. I wonder if we could just tape you as you …" The woman and child were fast approaching, so Beady spoke hurriedly. "You don't speak Albanian, do you? I mean, if you could translate for the folks you're treating ..."

"Yeah, I do. Actually, the joke among us aid workers is that nobody speaks anyone else's language very well, but we're all weird enough to be fluent in Albanian. Mostly, because at least one of our parents came from this part of the world. For me, it's my mom." Beady was reassured to see that the camera was running. Ezra was the best kind of cameraman. He knew exactly when to shoot.

As the woman stepped forward, Beady saw that she had a fresh-looking vertical scar cutting across the middle of both lips. She let loose a flood of incomprehensible words. Sam, who clearly had to strain to understand her, put a hand on her shoulder and carried on a brief dialogue with her. "Her name is Irina. She thinks there's something the matter with the boy. I'm going to examine him first, and then I'm going to see if I can do anything for *her*."

They followed him as he led her and the child to a corner of the tent, where he began poking around a small metal cabinet, teetering haphazardly on three wheels and overflowing with medical supplies.

Sam spoke gently to the child. "*Si ju quajne?*"

Irina poked the boy in his skinny ribs a few times before he mustered a whispered response. "Pavli."

As Sam examined Pavli's frail body, the woman kept prattling away. Sam translated her explanation of what had happened to the boy. "They took the men in the village, including his father, out a little ways, made them dig a mass grave, then massacred them." He put his stethoscope to Pavli's chest, and the child took a couple of deep breaths for him. Irina kept talking a mile a minute as the doctor pulled the boy's shirt back down over his shivering torso and fished a thin wool blanket from a pile next to the cabinet to place over his shoulders. The child himself was expressionless. "*E kuptoj, e kuptoj*," Sam assured her.

"Sounds like his mother had a psychotic break. She was Irina's next-door neighbor. Irina came over with some food just when Pavli's mother was trying to smother her son in his bed with a pillow, and when Irina intervened, the mother pulled a knife out of her bosom and slit her lip for her efforts. Irina had to turn the knife on her to save herself and the child. The mother died in her arms."

Beady addressed her words to Sam, but she couldn't take her eyes off young Pavli. "Is he sick? Will he be okay?"

"He seems healthy enough to me, as healthy as they can be around here. A little malnourished, but that's not surprising. Whether he'll be okay or not—your guess is as good as mine."

"Don't you think somebody else should be…watching over him?"

Sam put away the thermometer. "I think she's the best one for him. She did save his life." Beady fell silent. Ezra gave her a quick, appraising look. "Why don't I meet you outside in a minute? I'll just get a couple of pick-up shots."

She hurriedly thanked Sam and promised to call his mother when they got back to the States. Then she staggered out of the tent and emptied her flight's worth of orange juice and Danish onto the ground.

Straightening, she passed a trembling hand over her mouth. She realized that the soldiers had kept their eyes politely averted. Who the hell was she to be judging them? And dear Jesus, how was she going to survive her own tour of duty of these hells on earth if she couldn't even stomach their smells?

"I *thought* it was getting a little rough for you." Ezra had materialized by her side. He reached into his pocket, then dabbed her chin with a handkerchief.

"How embarrassing."

He gave her a sad smile. "Pretty understandable, under the circumstances."

"I can't believe it. Did you see that child's eyes? And when I think of him being cared for by the woman who murdered his mother." She shuddered. "They call the glorified gang warfare at the root of all this misery e*thnic cleansing*?" Ezra was silent. "But you know what's really creeping me out?"

"What?"

"I've gotten in touch with what keeps this crap cycling and recycling, generation after generation. I swear, if I could get my hands on the fuckers who did this to Pavli, I'd be first in line to cut their goddamned throats."

Nineteen

ON THE MORNING of her twenty-first radiation session (*but who was counting?*), Evvie sat up in her bed and fumbled for her alarm clock. The heavy beat of Ben's footsteps forging up the hall and the distinctive *ker-thwack* of his bedroom door made her check the time again. How strange. He must have realized he'd forgotten something after setting out for school. Tall as an oak, he could still be as disorganized as a little boy.

Somehow, she managed to fumble into her sweat suit and drive—guided by a bat-like radar—to West Hollywood Park. She only really woke up after her first circuit of the dusty oval track, passing the other disciplined regulars without even a nod of recognition, as if there were some kind of code that decreed that you couldn't acknowledge people who weren't yet washed and made up and prepared to meet the world with public persona in place. Nonetheless, she felt close to them.

They say home is where the heart is, but she figured that intimacy was defined by who you woke up to, and she was waking these days to this weird bunch of stalwarts. The Persian-looking man who'd just passed her, his thick, black eyebrows nearly connecting over his nose like a giant caterpillar. The elderly *bubbie* who hobbled determinedly behind him on bowed, sausage-shaped legs, moving to one side to make room for the tanned sports bra wearing twenty-something who actually jumped rope as she ran.

She was always on the lookout for a new face to speculate about, which was why she took particular notice as an impeccably suited, white-haired man approached the park, carrying his black valise with erect dignity. On her second orbit around the track, she spotted him again, clad this time in a long white gown. He had an array of scissors and combs and powders neatly spread out on a bench, right next to an even older man, whose silver hair he was cutting with a studied air. She got distracted the next few rounds after a patently anorexic teenager zoomed by, her body looking as if it were crazily constructed from pick up sticks. Evvie debated whether she should say something, but was forced to admit that the girl would hardly welcome a stranger's intervention. She completed her final circuit just in time to see the open-air barber carefully stowing his equipment back in the briefcase and solemnly accept payment from his neatly shorn customer. She lifted her face to the sun and laughed aloud.

How weird was she, finding comfort in what most people would dismiss as merely bizarre? Like the pleasure she took in gabbing with the other patients at the Cancer Center, their superficial conversations laced with the tacit awareness of a shared Sword of Damocles suspended invisibly overhead.

She'd begun to keep quiet track of those comrades-in-arms. The newly diagnosed—fright oozing from their pores. Remission's fallen angels. She prayed that an absent face merely signified the end of treatment and not a life.

She herself moved in and out of analogous mental states—diagnostic panic, dread of recurrence, certainty of imminent death. When she realized how ephemeral the whole show was, she cursed the day she was born, but then she'd catch Ben slurping his cereal like a six-year-old, and she'd issue a silent, fervent prayer to God to let her live to see his children.

And it wasn't just Ben.

Her face hot now and dripping with sweat that was probably half exertion and half hot flash, Evvie spun off the track toward the parking lot. Yanking open her car door, she thought about Temple. Even the brittle Sally MacBride had recognized how much her daughter had formed a powerful attachment to Evvie. Sally had yielded without complaint to Temple's request for a "play date" once she and her daughter had had their outings to Sea World, Knott's Berry Farm, and

Disneyland. Evvie was all too aware of the fear that lay behind Sally's need to cram as much pleasure into her daughter's life as possible.

Evvie couldn't wait to give Temple her new Curious George doll this afternoon. Temple was crazy about the mischievous monkey, frequently clutching several of the books to her chest when she arrived at the Cancer Center, along with the ubiquitous Barbie coloring books. They'd fallen into a pattern of the little girl sliding onto Evvie's lap, the two of them making monkey faces as Evvie read to her until one of their names was called for radiation.

Radiation. Dear lord, what did it mean to have your life dependent on something that could kill you? Even if Temple defied the Fates and survived, what kind of shape would all this chemo and radiation leave her in?

As if on cue, Evvie's skin began to prickle. She scratched frantically at her belly, and then—as the crawling-ant sensation traveled—raked her fingernails across her ankle and along her outer thigh. "Oh, come on, God," she snarled, "can't you give me a little break here?"

She had a sudden image of a dark demiurge sloping around the world, severing families, torturing children, getting under her skin to wither hope and meaning. "Fuck you," she yelled. "Fuck you!"

She was far too preoccupied to notice the old sausage-legged lady waddling past her, shooting her a look of absolute compassion as she fingered the chain on her neck with its Hebrew *chai*.

***

Ben would have been stunned at his aunt's perception of him as child-like. These days, he felt more world-weary than his grandfather.

Protective of his girlfriend's image and reputation, he'd tried keeping his worries to himself, but when Tony had suggested cutting school that morning, Ben suspected it wasn't just to surf. Tony wasn't his best friend for nothing.

He did have to admit that it *was* a perfect day for surfing. Following an unseasonable three days of serious rain, the waves at Malibu were awesome, and when the two of them stretched their panting, goose-pimpled bodies beneath a sun that had begun to reassert its supremacy, the beach was still nearly deserted.

Ben stared vacantly in the direction of a cloud of midges that hovered over the wetsuits they'd thrown onto the sand beside their surfboards. Sensing movement beside him, he turned.

Tony was settling onto his side, digging his elbow into the ground and leaning his head on his palm. Iridescent drops of water poised at the tips of his spongy black hair. "So, dude, how're things going with Tash?"

Without warning, as if he'd been just waiting for this moment, tears coursed down Ben's face.

"Hey, man. Take it easy."

Ben couldn't believe it. The last time he'd cried in front of Tony, he'd been six years old and Tony had punched him in the nose for making fun of the way his *great-grand-mère* talked.

But Ben couldn't take anything easy right now. Whatever inflated majesty he'd felt getting high last month at Anna's had turned, on the way back down, to bleak despair. Now he described to Tony how he'd woken around five the following morning wrapped in a jumble of female limbs, not even wanting to think about how he'd gotten there. Somehow, he'd managed to extricate himself from the pretzel of bodies and get himself back home quietly enough to elude his mother's evil eye. It hadn't been the fear of his mom, though, that stopped him from doing coke again, but concern for Tash and what she was becoming. She was starting to sound more and more like Nicole and Tammy, gushing over Anna, getting skinnier and skinnier, forgoing studying for partying. Coke, pot, X. He hated what Tash was doing to herself, but he couldn't seem to stop himself from becoming her mournful hanger-on.

Ben swiped away his tears with an impatient flick of his hand. "I feel like some kind of pathetic trash man, cleaning up her messes, doing her homework for her, making sure she gets home before her mom wakes up the next morning. I'll be fucked if I know what else to do."

"Man, you need to cool it. She's on a bad ride, and if you don't watch out, she'll take you down with her. Opal's backed off from her ever since Tash decided that Anna Sumter was the best thing since sliced bread."

"You guys are getting pretty serious, aren't you?"

146

"Tight enough for her to be thinking about going to Greenwich with me, if I get accepted. I think she's the one."

Ben had felt pretty much the same about Tash, but these days the only thing Tash seemed to be serious about was partying.

"You've gotta chill from her, dude. This is your senior year. You can't be wasting your time with this shit. Cut her loose."

"I don't know." Maybe Tony was right. He didn't need to be stressing over this when his whole future was on the line.

But, then again, how fucked up would it be to just walk away when someone you cared about was falling apart?

***

"Olly olly oxen free!"

Evvie could barely catch her breath. How was it that a seriously sick little girl could run circles around a woman who jogged five times a week?

Temple ran at her legs at a hundred miles an hour, crowing as she wrapped her skinny arms around Evvie's thighs. "I win! Now it's your turn."

"Again? Oh, my God, you've got to be kidding! Don't you know I'm older than you? Besides, beating me four times in a row clearly makes you the all-time world champ." She knelt down and touched her finger to Temple's dimpled chin. "I think the winner deserves to be taken out for froyo. And they sell the best in the world at the Bigg Chill."

In unison, they looked over at Temple's mother. Sally MacBride slouched like a shadow against one of doors of the run-down apartment building, her thumb flicking ash from her cigarette away from the threshold.

"Can we ask my ma to come, too?"

An hour later, Evvie found herself inching around the side of a double bed that just about filled the MacBrides' tiny bedroom. A torn, ruffled curtain patterned with faded horses and riders hung unevenly from the dirty sliding glass window above the bed. Tucking a cotton coverlet over Temple, whose hand curled around her new Curious George doll, Evvie realized this was the first time she'd put a child to bed since Ben. As Temple's perfect, cupid's bow lips parted to release a gentle snore, Evvie had to refrain herself from licking her own fingers and rubbing away the child's frozen yogurt moustache. She tiptoed out of the room.

Sally MacBride lay on her side on the shabby living room sofa, clasping her knees to her chest. Her faded blond hair looked like dried wheat in the dim light of the room's sole standing lamp.

Evvie sat down gingerly at the other end of the sofa, and Sally pulled her feet tighter into her fetal curl.

"Oh, you don't have to …" Evvie squeezed herself against the sofa's hard arm.

"No, no. Always was a couch hog." Abruptly, Sally sat up and attempted to run a hand through her tangled hair. She smiled thinly. Gaunt hollows were scooped under her eyes. "Goin' to hell in a hand-basket." She looked at Evvie appraisingly. "Like your hair color. Do it yourself?"

"Actually, no. My best friend took me to a fancy salon. I never would have gone there myself. Walked in with longish dark hair and came out like this." She fingered her short locks. "Honestly, every time I look in the mirror, I think it's somebody else."

"Suits you. But I could see you as a redhead, too. You're one of those women who'd look good any which way."

Evvie stared at her in surprise.

"'Course you're lucky to keep your hair."

"Oh, God, I'm so sorry…"

"No offense taken. Guess I'm luckier than both of you." Sally sighed, then reached for the pack of Marlboro Lights on the chipped glass coffee table. She shot Evvie a sideways glance. "Wanna come outside with me? Know I shoulda stopped years ago. For all I know, I gave it to her, secondhand smoke and all." She shrugged. "Doctor Martinez says no, that couldn't have done it, not her kind of cancer, but …"

"I hear you. I keep wondering what I did to bring this on myself. I can only imagine what you, as a mother …"

"You know, then. How much you torture yourself with thoughts." Her fingers played with her unlit cigarette. "Anyway, only smoke outside now. Wanna join me?"

The night was surprisingly warm, given the brush of gloomy weather they'd been having. Sally MacBride lit her cigarette and threw her match onto the unswept concrete, swirling it around with the toe of her sneakered foot. They both looked down the walkway as a shaft of light sprung from an opening door a few apartments down and a blast of raucous *mariachi* music goosed the air. A blue-jeaned man, a thick belt underpinning his hefty beer belly and a wide-brimmed cowboy hat and Pancho Villa moustache hiding most of his dark, round face, stumbled out of the apartment. An invisible alto inside yelled some incomprehensible words in Spanish and ribald laughter could be heard above the loud music. The man, laughing himself, suddenly noticed Evvie and Sally watching him. He did a little drunken bow and tipped his hat as if he were royalty, then proceeded to stagger around the building. The door slammed shut, and Evvie could hear the sound of urine hitting the ground.

Evvie and Sally MacBride stared at each other, then broke into laughter. Sally flipped her cigarette butt onto the walkway and scratched the back of her head. "I'm gonna miss this place," she said.

Evvie looked up sharply.

"I'm down to my last two thousand. A couple more treatments and we're goin' back home." She crossed the fingers of both her hands and shook them defiantly at the night sky. "I just hope to God they work!"

"Sally, there must be something … I mean, I have a ridiculously large savings account that I've been wondering what to do with …"

"Large enough to cover a couple hundred thousand dollars' worth of a clinical trial?"

"But, my God, there's got to be some way ..."

"Yeah, an' I'm the Pope's granddaughter." Sally's face softened. "Look, I really appreciate it, but I've tried everything. I've had every social worker in LA working to keep Temple's treatment going. The hospital's gone a distance to meet me halfway, but they have hundreds of kids in this city with no insurance they're already being charitable to."

Evvie flushed. How often she'd dismissed her father's ideology out of hand, but on this one, he was absolutely right. American capitalism was still functioning in the Dark Ages when it came to health care. And what the fuck was the matter with her, anyway, looking down her nose at Sally MacBride just because she resembled one of those trailer-trash-types spilling their guts on Jenny Jones? Sally MacBride had voluntarily submitted to being poor and single in a city that waved its wealth in the face of the world like a gloating toreador. Living in a crappy old apartment building that was a couple of steps above the dog pound, she was nearly killing herself with worry over her little girl. Had *raised* that little girl to be the angel she was. Sally MacBride had done more to justify her presence on this planet than she herself ever had.

The fact is, any mother worth her salt has the better of me.

"Sally," she whispered, "if there's anything I *can* do, ever, promise you'll tell me."

Sally stared back at her, but it as was as if she were seeing through Evvie into some dark place that only she knew. "I keep thinking about what it says in Scripture. 'For just as the body without the spirit is dead, so faith without works is also dead.' On my first day of Bible school, my granny gave me a little ring. Oh, it was a cheap little thing. She didn't have much. But it meant a lot to me. My first ring. The next day my daddy took us to the State Fair. We stopped at some gas station so I could pee, and after we got to the Fair, I realized my ring was gone. My mama and daddy said I probably lost it in the sink at that station, and I did have a hazy recollection of taking it off so as not to get soap on it. I wanted to go back and get it, but my daddy just told me it was a lesson. I figured what he meant was that it was my punishment for the sin of not being careful enough about something that mattered to me."

She put her hand on Evvie's arm. "You see, the Bible was what we lived by. An' sure enough, when Temple got sick, it was church brothers and sisters who raised the money to send us out here. By now, I reckon every Evangelical congregation in the US is praying for us. I haven't had the heart to tell the folks back home that I've lost my faith in the Lord. I just can't see the Jesus I believed in doing this to my little girl. You can see it yourself. Her heart's as pure as a little bird's." Her grip on Evvie's arm tightened. "The only thing I can put any faith in anymore is works. I'll tell you what you can do for my girl. Just love her up like you've been doing. And after we leave, keep thinking about her. Promise me you won't forget. No matter what happens, tell me you won't forget."

Evvie became aware of a powerful signal of pain. Sally MacBride was gripping her right arm so hard that it was beginning to turn white. The fear of lymphodema rose up inside her like a bloated specter, but there was no way in hell she was going to ask Sally to let go.

Twenty

ONLY TOO EAGER to loosen herself from the tension of their latest taping, Beady leaned back against the sofa. The dulcet tones of Sade wove through Tom Delaney's smoke-filled living room. Tom had swung back into town from a rent-paying freelance fashion shoot in Moscow at one of those rare moments when London's version of a heat spell coincided with the presence in town of most of his old gang of Yale alumni. He'd taken advantage of the serendipity to host a celebratory gathering of the clan.

Beady's abundant yellow frizz was splayed across the back of Tom's sofa, her caramel fingers cradling a glass of Pinot Noir. The wine was excellent and particularly welcome after a week of pub ale that had pooched out her normally flat tummy a quarter inch or so. She studied this gathering of peripatetic men with considerable amusement.

In particular, she found it difficult to take her eyes off the complicated oral rituals of Fred Samuels, a short-ish tubby lighting man in transit between gigs in Kosovo and Northern Ireland. Beady decided that he had more shaggy hair in the eyebrows overhanging his beetle-black eyes than on his prematurely balding pate. He interspersed his frequent contributions to the conversation with hasty puffs on a series of Rothmans cigarettes and the consumption of fistfuls of curry-flavored potato chips—or, as the British called them, *crisps*. She couldn't quite figure out how he managed to orchestrate the subtle timing of when to speak, swallow, or inhale, but sticking stuff into his plump-lipped mouth certainly wasn't getting in the way of his incessant, clever chatter.

Associated Press cameraman Isaac Dorfmann, on a much-needed R&R from a prolonged stint documenting the ongoing hell of Hebron, mostly sat back in his floral chintz armchair and listened to Fred, nodding and laughing on cue at the pudgy man's caustic wit.

Aaron Deals, the disconcertingly good-looking EU correspondent for the *Washington Post*, seemed to be suffering an attack of the jitters and kept on getting up to inspect Tom's CDs, straighten the arresting collection of original art on the living room walls, and generally flit his tall and lean body around the room like some restless black dragonfly.

Ezra Rosenberg sat next to her on the sofa like a protective big brother, his bear-like body alert, as if his dog of a buddy Aaron—whom he'd already warned her about—was likely to jump her bones right there and then. Truth be told, she herself was disappointed to note that Aaron had so far barely given her a glance.

As for Tom Delaney, over the course of this past week she'd gotten to appreciate why he and Ezra were so tight. A thinning carrot-top from a large Catholic family outside of Boston, Tom still looked and sounded like the altar boy he'd once been, but his nose for injustice was as keen as Ezra's. They shared a kind of childlike earnestness and a taste for loony humor and sixties blues.

What Beady couldn't quite figure out, though, was the conversation maintained by this bright batch of guys. She was used to the company of documentarians, who couldn't shut up about their latest projects—herself, she had to admit, included. She was only too eager to flaunt Ezra's major coup in finagling them a damning interview with the head of NATO, the fruit of several days' worth of muscling his way up the channels here in London. But these guys barely said a word about their own gigs. Instead, their conversation was a cosmopolitan version of the kind of small talk you'd hear in a small Midwestern town where people cycled endlessly around what happened last night on some sitcom or the unpredictable vicissitudes of the weather. Ezra's friends yattered about the best brasseries in Paris, the virtues of Guinness over Bass Ale, which good-looking BBC reporter was fucking whom, and whether to order some takeout *tandoori* or draw straws for who'd fry up a traditional English breakfast in Tom's tiny kitchen.

When Beady mentioned the documentary she'd completed last year on the post-college lives of Berkeley's aging Free Speech Movement leaders, the sole comment had come from Fred, who'd merely murmured (albeit with an apologetic smile), "In the room the women come and go, talking of Mario Savio," and changed the topic to Ali G's appearance in the latest Madonna video.

She didn't mind any of it (except the part about cooking in Tom's kitchen, in case any of these men had some lurking fantasy that she'd be doing the little woman bit), and, indeed, found the badinage entertaining, but she wondered at their dedicated avoidance of anything serious.

When Sade's tour of a woman's heart gave way to an old Talking Heads number, Aaron suddenly approached the sofa and bent down to extract a little leather pouch from his briefcase. The case was leaning against the coffee table leg right next to Beady's feet, and before Ezra could even turn his gaze away from Tom, with whom he'd been comparing the relative merits of Manchester United and Arsenal, Aaron actually brushed her leg—accidentally? well, anyway, definitely excitingly—as he retrieved it.

"My man!" Tom exclaimed, as Aaron pushed aside several glasses, an empty wine bottle, and an ashtray full of crumpled Rothmans to shake the contents of his pouch onto the coffee table. Before Ezra could forestall him, Aaron was squeezing his fine ass down on her other side to roll a big fat joint. Only then, as he passed it to her, murmuring softly, "Ladies first," did he look right into her eyes like a hungry panther, and she suddenly realized that the whole marijuana business had been his way of getting next to her. Her eyes crinkled, and, taking a nice long toke, she didn't even bother to look up as Ezra rose, muttering disgustedly that, from the size of the stash, he might as well play Jeeves and scare them up a shitload of food.

The temperature in Tom's flat got hotter as the music got louder. Clever little Fred had gotten loose as a goose with all the dope and wine. He was slurring his words and working his ample eyebrows like a couple of cool-jerking caterpillars. And when Tom resurrected a long-lost Ike and Tina Turner CD, Fred popped out of his chair like a roly-poly jack-in-the-box to jiggle his little booty and bigger belly to

Proud Mary's big turning wheel. Within moments, they all jumped up to join him.

Beady had to admit that it was exhilarating to dance with five increasingly uninhibited men. She grinned when Tom, reverting to Irish type, brought out some choice whisky and turned up the CD player's volume as far as it would go. Beady had read in *The Guardian* just that morning that London's population was currently forty percent single young people, and she figured that was a damned good thing. No reasonably tolerant twenty or thirty-something would be likely to call Scotland Yard to bust them for the outrageous amount of noise they were making.

When Tina Turner gave way to "Whip It," they all roared. Fred stripped down to his jockey shorts, which revealed far more of his overhanging polar-white belly than she'd ever want to see, and the other men tossed off their shirts. Beady could hardly take her eyes off Aaron's undulating six-pack. Still, clothed or not—and she as sure as shit wasn't going to go native herself in this crowd—the flat was still steaming.

"Fuck it." Tom flung open the front door and propped it agape with an ashtray. As if it had been patiently waiting outside, a cat immediately sprang into the room, undeterred by the fevered dancing and raucous din.

"Oh, how sweet." Beady got down on her knees and crawled around drunken male feet toward the animal, attracted by its ebony fur and almond-shaped green eyes. She crooned, "Pretty kitty, pretty kitty, I won't hurt you." She needn't have bothered with the caution. This was one brave cat. It stood its ground until she got to it, then arched its back with uninhibited flirtatiousness when she ran a hand from its small head to its coiling question-mark tail. She scooped the compliant creature up and took it over to the couch, where it purred like a house afire on her shoulder.

Aaron was at her side in an instant. He leaned closer to whisper in her ear. "She's just like you, baby, black and sleek, and big eyes like some ocean I could just swim right into. I'd like to pet you, too, pretty baby."

Beady groaned. Why was it most intelligent men couldn't come up with better lines than any sleazeball at a Hollywood Boulevard bar?

She'd have to tell Evvie this one when she got back home. The cat put a paw on her nose, as if to remind her to keep petting it. "Okay, puss puss." She laughed helplessly up at Aaron and gestured toward Tom's open doorway. "This reminds me of when Silly Dog used to walk into my friends Evvie and Miriam's house." Aaron looked confused. She play-cuffed his ear. "Okay, I realize that was a complete non sequitur. There was this dog—I think he lived around the corner. His owners used to let him roam the neighborhood. That dog had the sweetest disposition in the world, but, honey, he was ugly! Had him a mottled black and brown coat, the kind of short dog fur that's a little rough to the touch, and a wide ass with a short cigar tail that he used to wag like a maniac when he was excited. I mean, he wagged his whole ass, not just the tail. He'd come into the Kerr's house when we were playing and race through all the rooms, nearly knocking everything down with that fat, wriggling ass of his. We called him Silly Dog, and we'd run after him till he worked his way through every single room and then back out of the house again." Beady realized that she had acquired a larger audience. Fred had plopped on the floor opposite—speaking of animals, sweating like a pig—and Ezra and Isaac were hovering over the coffee table. The room was quiet. Their DJ was fast asleep on a chair; Tom farted, and the rest of the men laughed. Tom awoke for a moment, mumbling, "Hey, not fair," then slumped back into dreamland.

Beady kept going, as much to rescue her host's dignity as anything else. "And then there was the chicken some neighbor's nanny kept in their backyard. Wandered in one morning, doing that ridiculous chicken strut, head edging forward, you know how they do. My friend Miriam was so scared that the chicken might crap in the house or lay an egg somewhere that she ran after it with a broom, but Evvie grabbed the broom away from her and spent an hour with that funky chicken in her lap, petting it and whispering to it till I swear she had it mesmerized, as though it had re-imprinted onto her like she was its second mother."

The next thing Beady knew, tears were running down her face. The cat had jumped out of her arms and was out the door like a shot, but Beady kept rocking back and forth, anyway.

Aaron looked like he didn't know what to make of her. This wasn't the kind of baby or the kind of rocking he'd been looking forward to. But Ezra knew just what to do. He kicked the other men out, all but Tom, who was totally comatose by now, snoring like a bull as he sprawled sideways across the chintz armchair.

"I'm sorry," Beady sniffed. "I'm not usually a melancholy drunk."

Ezra sat down next to her with a box of tissues. "Hey, don't worry about it. Frankly, I'm envious. My own wonder years were so drab and suburban I nearly died of boredom." He grinned. "No doubt why I thrive on shooting disaster and mayhem. Damn thing is, most of the people in my life worth knowing are doing the same thing. A night like tonight comes around just a couple of times a year."

She blew her nose loudly, then looked up at him. "Ezra, you don't ever talk about women. Wasn't there ever a someone who made you want to stay put?"

Ezra pulled another tissue from the box and held it up toward her face. "Do you mind? You've got a little mascara there." As he dabbed at her cheek, he said, "Just one, really. But it was never going to work." He sat back and studied his handiwork. "That's better."

"Why not? What happened?"

"Oh, it's not terribly interesting. I lived with Rebecca, off and on, for ten years, and for the last nine she never let me forget what a sacrifice it was to be with a man like me. We'd known each other forever—actually went to the same high school—and we had this easy familiarity. But the kinds of things I was encountering in my work, well … I should've realized much earlier that I'd never be able to give her what she needed. You know—nice house, couple of kids, a kind of saccharine predictability. That's just not my scene. Like the poet Philip Whalen, I seem to be called to stay aware of the wickedness of the world." He laughed ruefully. "She ended up with some hotshot lawyer. Bumped into them once at Century City. He treated her like shit. You know, one of those Neanderthals in a suit. Kept staring at some young blonde while we were talking, but Rebecca seemed oblivious, going on and on about their house in Westwood and which private schools they were sending their kids to. Guess I shouldn't blame her. What she was asking for wasn't much different from what most women want."

"Oh, please. I come from a long line of independent bitches, myself."

"Not too independent to give birth to a son. What about Tony's father?"

She laughed. "Miles? He was a poet like Whalen, except his job was to *keep* the world wicked, rather than stay aware of it. No, it was clear from the beginning he was just passing through. Trouble is, every woman I know seems hung up on some version of their father. Since I never knew mine, men with one foot out the door have this invisible magnet."

He gave her a sidelong look. "You realized I saved you from yourself tonight?"

Beady flushed. "Aw, come on. Push come to shove, I wouldn't really have gone to bed with Aaron."

He just looked at her. They both knew she was lying.

That night, she dreamed of the arthritic old storyteller in Wim Wenders's film, *Wings of Desire*, who wandered the postwar ruins of Berlin's Potsdamer Platz and wondered why there were so many heroic tales of war, while so little was sung and celebrated about peace. Except in her dream, the question he kept repeating in his thick German accent was, "Why are so many women left cold by the really good men of this world? What's so compelling about a man who's a dog?"

Twenty-one

MICHAEL KERR DIDN'T know if it was his dwelling on the past or the chopped liver he'd spread for himself on a score of Ritz crackers, but the acid indigestion that moved into the guest house of his belly several years ago was now threatening to invade the whole of his upper torso. He reached for another Tums, reproaching himself for his weakness, and tried to force his attention back to Dick Shea's notes on their childless couple, but it only increased his pain.

He wasn't quite sure what to do about his belly. Unlike most of his friends, he'd never been hospitalized, and his visits to the doctor over the years had been more a sop to his overanxious family than to any need of his own.

As for the other kind of pain, the more ephemeral agonies of what some people liked to call the spirit, he'd managed up until recently to keep its sources in check, thanks to the diligent twenty-four-hour guard shift maintained by his wary mind. But now, nearly eighty-three years after the Reds had ridden into Kodnya with food to fill his village's hungry bellies, that same stomach surged with acid over the unfairness of his oldest daughter's fate.

He'd always assumed his daughters lucky, never knowing the sharp edge of want that he had. But had it been lucky for Evelyn to have missed out on the blessing of motherhood—not just losing her mother at the age of sixteen, but failing to have a child of her own?

No revolution could cure what was ailing his daughter. No public policy could rectify such abuse. Yet, there was something about the way she met her fate with such unselfish equanimity that spoke of an uncannily strong and beautiful spirit. The thing was—some invisible barbed wire seemed to entangle him every time he imagined speaking to her of such things.

As if in recognition, his heart muscle contracted in a vise of dismay and shame. The pain seared all the way through his chest to his back and shoulders, then sent a feeler down his left arm. Big beads of sweat broke out across his brow, and he began to wonder if what he was feeling was merely gas or something far worse.

He stared blankly at Dick's pages and decided to give the Tums another half hour to work, but after ten long minutes, his fear got the better of him. Reaching across a pile of reference books that obscured the tissue-wrapped parcel he'd put aside for his eldest daughter months ago, he picked up the phone.

"Hello? Miriam? Don't get too alarmed. It's probably nothing, but I think we should probably get me looked at for a little pain I've got in my chest."

***

The following morning, an anxious Evvie snuck a glance at her dashboard clock as she sped toward Cedars. It must be some kind of a cosmic joke that she and her dad would be sharing the dubious status of patienthood at the same medical center at the same time.

She shot past a stunned pedestrian who'd already started through the crosswalk. Blushing furiously and mumbling an apology that the furious woman would never hear, she forced herself to slow down. She reminded herself of what Miriam had said. Not one of the ER doctors had even mentioned the words "heart attack" or "stroke." For all they knew her father's chest pains were only gas. But Evvie hadn't worked with the aged for nothing. She knew damned well that no insurance company in this brave new managed care world would have vetted the admission of her dad for "observation" if the doctors didn't suspect that something might be seriously wrong.

She ended up sharing the elevator with an unsmiling nurse's aide accompanying a tiny woman on a gurney whose face was waxen and yellow and whose gnarled index finger shook repetitively in Evvie's direction. Evvie looked away. Fuck John Donne. She didn't need this particular reminder that the bells were tolling for her, too. The sixth floor couldn't come fast enough. The door to Room 605 was slightly ajar. Evvie took a quick, nervous peek into her father's room before entering. He was alone. Miriam's guilt at waking Evvie so early had been offset by her reluctance to miss the last shooting day of the most difficult movie she'd worked on in years.

"What are you lurking there for, like a conniving Cossack?"

Evvie hastened to her father's bedside, her face crumpled in an apologetic grin. Michael had IV lines going into both arms, which looked paler than she remembered, his still relatively well-toned biceps barely covered by a familiar-patterned hospital gown.

"Did you bring me anything to read?" he barked.

She slammed the bag she'd packed for him onto a side chair. "You're welcome. It was no trouble at all."

He shot her a wounded look, and instantly she was filled with shame. She wanted to wrap her arms around him, but instead merely patted his shoulder. "How're you feeling? Have the doctors been to see you yet?"

"Why are you here, anyway? Miriam had no business asking you to bring my things. Something's the matter with Benjamin, he couldn't be bothered?"

"Dad, it was I who insisted. Ben wanted to come, but he has school today. He'll be here this afternoon. Besides, I wanted to see you. It was nothing at all to make a little detour here before I go for my—."

Suddenly, her father's face suffused with blood. "Go. You can't afford to miss your appointment. I don't know what's the matter with your sister. She doesn't know what's important?"

They stared at each other.

When she finally responded, Evvie's voice was high-pitched and childlike. "I can't leave until I find out what's going on with you." She looked toward the open doorway. "Has anyone said anything, I mean, about why …?"

His face closed up. Ah, this was more familiar. He was an ancient tortoise retracting into its horny hide. "It was nothing. The nurses will confirm it, if you don't believe me. A little stomach upset, and because

163

it was nighttime, I must've panicked. Superstitions are born from the night, you know, when the light of rationality gives way to the fears of the nursery." He smiled wickedly. "I think even your Freud would agree."

She started to move toward the doorway. "He's not my Freud. I've told you before, I think he was mostly full of shit." A little comforted by landing back on familiar territory—how many times had they argued this one?—she flung her retort over her shoulder. "Jung's much more my cup of tea. Takes the notion of God seriously, y'know."

She could hear him yelling into the hallway, "How a daughter of mine could even consider the notion of a God in this miserable unjustness of a universe ... What, you've had no evidence yourself lately that our fates are all a meaningless throw of the dice?"

She wanted to put her hands over her ears, anything to stop herself from considering that he might just be right, but she had to stop three alarmed looking nurses at the nearby nursing station from rushing to him. "Honestly, he'll wind himself down in a minute," she said dryly. "He just does it to aggravate me." It was only after they'd assured her that his condition was stable, that for the moment they knew nothing more than she did, and that they'd call her on her cell phone as soon as the staff cardiologist had made his rounds, that Evvie felt comfortable leaving him there.

She arrived at the Cancer Center building just a few minutes later. It took descending the elevator and coming face to face with Sally MacBride to remind her that she'd promised to bring Temple back to her condo that day to watch a videotape she'd managed to obtain of Disney's *The Aristocats*. It was Temple's last day of treatment at the Center, and Evvie had arranged for Maggie Rimes to cover for her while she spent some special time with her young friend. Sally and Temple were booked to fly back to Missouri that weekend.

Even as she greeted Sally MacBride, she wondered how in God's name she was going to pull this one off. All she wanted to do was run home and pull the covers over her head, but she couldn't possibly let Temple down. She squared her shoulders. "It's a big day, eh, Sally? Temple still in with Helen?"

The child emerged from the treatment area, surrounded by a small crowd of grown-ups and proudly clutching a ballerina doll clad in a sleek leotard, tufted tutu, and perfect little toe shoes. Helen lightly rested one hand atop Temple's smooth scalp and clasped in her other hand a page of parchment covered with calligraphed lettering. An emotional looking Russell walked with them, bearing a small gift bag with an arrangement of multicolored giant lollipops sticking out of it. Evvie and Sally went to meet the group.

"Ma! Hi, Evvie! This is just like a birthday party. Ma, look at my new doll! Can I bring her with me to watch *The Aristocats* if I promise to be careful? Helen says she's delicate."

Sally knelt down with her hands around her daughter's waist, letting Temple point out all the doll's special features.

Helen shoved the parchment document into Evvie's hands before hurrying away, sniffling, and someone else handed her a pen. Evvie looked at the paper. It said, "This certifies that Temple MacBride has completed her course of radiation with style. Good luck and best wishes." There were signatures all over it from the radiation wing staff. *Just like a high school yearbook*, Evvie thought, fiercely jabbing the end of the pen against her lip before adding her own signature, followed by a series of outsized hearts.

Temple loved the condo and obviously enjoyed having the run of a considerably larger living space after her months living on Pico Boulevard. Sally MacBride had declined to come along. She'd whispered to Evvie that she had reams of papers to fill out at the Cancer Center as part of her obligation to the medical trial Temple had been a part of.

Evvie allowed the child to inspect every room of the condo, and when they returned to the living room, she was stunned to see how strong Temple's skinny arms were as the child did a handstand on the living room carpet and even "walked" a few steps before gracefully returning her feet to the floor. When Temple finally settled down with Evvie in her four-poster bed to watch *The Aristocats*, the two of them managed to consume two giant lollipops and a huge bowl of popcorn between them. Evvie did have to stop the tape several times for Temple to pee. She noticed that the bathroom smelled weirdly chemical after Temple used the toilet. She hoped it was only some aftereffect of the chemo and not a bad sign.

Returning to the bed, Evvie found herself pulling the child closer to her as they cuddled, depositing little mini-kisses across her perspiring scalp. Despite the cloud cover of mortality overhanging them, Evvie realized how much her body was soaking up the sweetness of the physical contact. Had she not been this physically close with anyone since Ben was a little boy?

As the end credits began scrolling the screen, Evvie burst into words from its theme song, improvising, "Evvie Kerr, Temple MacBride, that's who wants to be a cat!"

Temple grinned up at her. Evvie slipped off the bed and began dancing goofily around the room, holding a scooped palm alongside her head for a cat's ear and wriggling her other hand behind her ass like a tail. Temple scrambled down to join her, and the two of them snaked through the condo, giggling, until they collapsed into a jumble of limbs on the floor.

Later, when she finally belted Temple into her Lexus for the drive home, the child skewed around to face her. "Evvie?"

"What is it, sweetie?"

"Did you ever have a cat?"

"You know, I never have. My sister's allergic to them."

"I had one. I called her Muffin because her fur was all creamy."

"*Mm*, she sounds beautiful."

"She was. She used to sleep under my covers every night, right next to me. One day, we let her out to play and she didn't come home. My ma found her later. She died."

Evvie fought for breath.

"Do you think cats go to heaven?"

Evvie hesitated, then said lightly, "Oh, I think they must, don't you?"

"Is it the same heaven that people go to?"

They stared at each other. "You know, I'm sure it's the same place."

"That's what I think, too."

***

Two days later, the MacBrides took off for Missouri. Evvie insisted on driving them to the airport, though Sally was just as insistent that she drop them off at the curb, rather than accompany them to the boarding area. Evvie couldn't get the image out of her head of Temple making the quickest swipe across her eyes before resolutely taking her mother's hand and turning away.

Returning home, Evvie opened the door to the condo, shouting, "Hello? Anybody home?" She was more disappointed than she cared to admit to find a note taped to her bedroom door from Miriam, telling her that she and Ben were both going out. Damn. If only Beady were back in town.

Two glasses of wine and several debates with herself later, she even tried calling Moira, but no luck there, either.

In spite of herself, Evvie found herself dialing her father's room at Cedars. They'd all been frustrated when he hadn't been released the day after his supposed gas attack, but none of them would dream of fighting his internist's wish to keep him under observation for a few more days "because of his age and out of an excess of caution."

When he answered the phone, sounding just slightly out of breath, an inner alarm went off, but she hardly knew what to say.

"Hi, Dad. How you doin'?"

"Not so good. They're driving me crazy. First, they say it's only gas. Now some specialist comes around, trailing a bunch of brown-nosing interns behind him, and he's got to show how smart he is by insisting on keeping me here a day or two longer, just so he can do a bunch of tests and make the hospital a little richer on my nickel."

Oh, shit. "When was this? What kind of tests?"

"They just left, and I have no idea. Angiograms, stress tests, CT scans, MRI's, fluid samples—I can't keep track of them anymore. The *momser* threw around words like pericarditis, aortic aneurysm, and congestive heart failure like a bingo caller. You'd think, with a man my age, they'd just let you live in peace till you croaked." As if he'd shocked even himself, her father's voice trembled a little. "Evelyn, did I tell you that Dick and I are collaborating on a screenplay?"

As weak as her father sounded, this had to be a good sign. "Dad, you sneaky Pete. I didn't know you were writing again." But he didn't answer. "Dad?"

167

"Evelyn, don't you think it's time you thought about settling down?"

"What?"

"After all you've been through, wouldn't you like to have someone to share your life with?"

She laughed nervously. "Dad, at my age, it's not as if there are a bunch of eligible bachelors growing on trees." She imagined Simon, suspended from a tree, then saw herself beside him, but *she* was upside down, like the Hanging Man in Beady's Tarot deck.

"What do you mean? I've got a pile of magazines on my desk with articles discussing how men and women of your generation are taking their time to find their partners."

She managed to get off the phone quickly, making him promise he wouldn't let anyone do anything without first calling her. But she felt troubled by more than his medical condition. This was the first time she could remember that he'd actually offered advice about her personal life. Too bad he didn't know what he was talking about.

***

Michael hung up the phone. He could barely breathe, the pain was so bad. He'd only managed to stop from crying out to her by reminding himself that it was merely acid reflux. Fretfully rubbing his midsection, he ran through a mental list of what he'd eaten that day. Cold whole wheat toast and non-fat cream cheese, a bowl of prunes, some kind of soggy white fish and overcooked steamed vegetables. How could bland hospital fare put such a fire in his gut?

But he wasn't a fool. Even if these pains were merely the wheezings and whistles of an ancient belly, he could smell his mortality lurking just around the corner. And he was filled with such an overpowering sense of urgency that he took refuge in a ritual he'd foregone nearly three quarters of a century ago. He closed his eyes and let his upper body find its way into a once-familiar rhythm. *Davening* like some ancient ancestor at the Wailing Wall, Michael Kerr silently prayed—not for himself, but for his daughter Evelyn, that she be given some sweetness to balance whatever calamities the Fates still had in store for her.

168

For, while the former was still in question, the latter was something he knew you could bet your life on.

Twenty-two

THE CRAZY QUILT of history books strewn across his bedroom floor bore witness to Ben's struggle to complete his paper on FDR for Frank Tuttle's Twentieth Century American History class. Radiohead's *No Surprises* filled the room like some ancient dirge as Ben stared at his computer screen. Roosevelt's words about fearing fear itself were a bunch of bullshit. When you were afraid, you were afraid. There was no choice about it. You might as well try to tell yourself you weren't hungry when you were starving to death.

The phone rang, and his hand automatically reached for it. As if he'd been waiting. As if something in him knew. Still, the desperation in Tash's voice raised the hairs on his arms.

"Ben, I'm at Anna's. Can you come over? It's really bad."

"Are you okay?"

"It's not me. It's Anna."

"Shit, she's OD'ed, hasn't she?"

"No, but she's bleeding everywhere, and her parents're out of town, and I don't know what to do." The pitch of her voice kept getting higher.

"Call 911. I'm coming, but you've got to call 911."

"Of course. 911." Her voice grew faint, as if she'd turned away from the phone to talk to someone else. "Why didn't we think of that?"

"I'm coming now." He hung up on her, dialed 911 himself, gave the operator Anna's address.

By the time he got there, the ambulance had arrived. There was a fire truck in front of the house, too, its engine running and its spinning red light illuminating the faces of neighborhood looky-loos.

Ben dashed up the walkway, only to be blocked at the front door by the outstretched arm of a frowning fireman. "Sorry, son. Can't let anybody in there."

"I've got to."

"Are you a relative?" But before Ben could answer, he saw two paramedics in the living room, pushing a gurney. The fireman pulled him aside as they hustled their burden out the door. Anna's face streaked past, looking gray and insensible.

Tash materialized at his side, smudges of blood on her cheek and her white blouse. She looked up at him with wide, terrified eyes. "They say she's going to be okay, but God ..."

He took her arm and led her away from the fireman, who stared at them speculatively. "What happened?"

"She had a miscarriage. I didn't even know she was pregnant. Remember that day at Jerry's? Turns out Thad Larsen knocked her up, then disappeared as soon as she told him. She started cramping before she and Tammy and Nicole went out tonight, but she was so high she didn't want to deal with it. When she started bleeding at some club, the bitches just dropped her off here so they could party some more. She was hemorrhaging when she called me. Ben, when I got here, Anna was screaming and there was blood everywhere." She scowled at the neighbors, still clustered in whispering groups on the sidewalk. She said, purposely loud enough for them to hear, "I can't believe nobody heard her." The ambulance door slammed shut, and Tash whirled around. "God, we've got to follow them." She started toward her car. Ben grabbed her. He led her to the Beamer and made her get in.

She buckled her seatbelt. "Go!" The ambulance was already turning the corner.

But he surprised both of them by taking her arm and roughly turning her to face him. "So, what's the deal? Are you going to destroy yourself, too? Fuck up your whole life?"

"Don't. You're hurting me." He let go, but he didn't take his eyes off her. Tears streaked her face. "Please. Not now. You can't imagine how scared I was ... Anna bleeding all over the place, freaking out, begging me to help her, but then pleading with me not to call anybody. What did she expect me to do? And now you, sitting there judging me." She flicked her tears off her cheeks and reached for the door handle. "Forget it. I should have known I was alone in this one. I'll deal with it myself."

"Damn it, Tash, stop! If you're so fucking alone, what am I doing here?" She didn't say anything, but she didn't get out of the car, either. He turned on the engine. "Did they say where they were taking her?"

"Cedars."

Of course, he thought bleakly, as he pulled away from the curb.

***

The next morning, blissfully unaware of Ben's crisis, Evvie and Miriam decided to share a leisurely breakfast before visiting their father. As they prepared a batch of homemade blueberry pancakes—Miriam pushing the ingredients around with a thick wooden spoon while Evvie measured and poured—Miriam began singing the words to "Don't Stop." Evvie felt a surge of admiration for her sister's talent for pleasure. But when the phone rang, they both jumped, exchanging a look of wordless alarm.

Miriam rushed to get the call. "Hello?" Then her voice went peaches and cream. "Well, *hello*. It's *you*. I thought it'd be my dad. Oh, he's been hospitalized for a few days, but he's okay. No, really … Anyway, what have you been up to? I was hoping you'd keep in touch." She flung her hair over her shoulder and put her chin in her hand, her elbow resting on the Sunday paper.

Evvie mouthed, "Paul?"

Miriam shook her head, giggling. "I didn't realize you guys were still in London. Bet Beady's snuggled up right next to you. … What? Aaron Deals? No, she didn't … But I thought you guys … Yes, it was a great party, wasn't it? Beady brings such *interesting* people together." Evvie watched, mesmerized, as her sister made circles with her foot. "Paul? He's fine. I guess. To tell you the truth, I'm not exactly sure when I'm going to see him again. Oh, you know how these things go. … Well, thank you. It was a pleasure to meet *you*, too." Then she frowned ever so slightly. "Yes. She's right here." With a look of reluctance, she passed Evvie the phone.

Puzzled, Evvie said, "Hello?"

Ezra Rosenberg was laughing. "Hi, Evvie." Miriam, just exiting the kitchen, failed to see the dirty look Evvie threw her. "Just wanted to connect before it gets crazy again. Beady and I are nearly finished here in London. I'll have a small window of time back in LA, and I was hoping you'd agree to have dinner with me."

Evvie's heart skipped a beat. "Dinner?"

"Yeah. We never got a chance at a real conversation, between the crowd at Beady's party, and then your group of old poop-smellers …" Evvie tensed. Was he laughing at her? "Anyway, what do you think?"

"Sure, I guess so …"

"I know you're probably pretty … busy these days. If dinner's too ambitious, maybe we could grab a cup of coffee." Evvie's lips felt like they were gummed together with molasses. "Hey, if the timing's not great, just say the word. I just thought …"

Way to go, Evvie. Could you show any less enthusiasm if you tried? But then she heard a telltale beep. She panicked. "Listen, it's Call Waiting. I'd better take it, in case it's my dad." She cut him off with the Flash button. "Hello?"

"Good heavens, that was fast." It was Moira. "Are you on the other line?"

"Oh, shit."

"Thank you very much."

"No, I'm sorry. That's not what I meant. I didn't mean 'shit' because it's you. I just hung up on somebody, thinking you were Dad on the phone."

"Oh, dear. Call me back."

"No, no, it's fine."

"How *is* your father, anyway?"

"If grouchy impatience to be released is any sign, he's doing great. No, honestly, he seems to be okay. They just have a couple more tests they want to do."

"That's good. And how are you doing, darling? I can't believe I have two Kerrs whose health I need to enquire after."

"I'm fine. Even my damned itchies seem to be calming down the last few days." Evvie rapped the wooden table with her knuckles.

"Your body must be getting used to less estrogen."

Evvie laughed thinly. "You mean, used to being a dried-up old hag."

"What nonsense. Who were you talking to, anyway?"

Evvie gave a sharp intake of breath. "I am such an idiot. It was Beady's co-producer on *Their Fathers' Sins*, Ezra Rosenberg. He actually called from London to … to invite me out for dinner."

"That's wonderful!"

"No, it's not. He probably called because Beady nagged him to. The weird thing is, Miriam said he and Beady were going together. But even if he called on his own steam, it's probably because he's just interested in being friends."

"Do you find him attractive?"

"He's not your typical pretty boy, but he's got a certain aliveness. He's really passionate about his work. Anyway, I think I've blown whatever …"

Moira's voice was imperious. "Call him back."

"I couldn't. Besides, I don't even know the number he was calling from."

"Call Beady on her cell, then."

"No. It'd just feel too weird."

"My God, you're like a teenager." There was an unusually long pause for a conversation with Moira. Finally, her stepmother spoke again, her tone suspiciously light. "You know, darling, I nearly forgot to tell you. I bumped into Simon Warwick a couple of months ago."

An electric shock whipped through Evvie. Her voice came out croaky. "You did?"

"He looks rather petrified. Like too many years of cigarettes have hammered the wrinkles into his skin. He's working as a clerk at Cody's Books, of all things. Right here in Berkeley. And, my dear, I have to say he's utterly pathetic."

But Evvie was hardly paying attention. She rang off with the excuse of something boiling over on the stove.

It wasn't hard to get the number of Cody's Books from Information, but it was torture waiting for someone to answer the phone. The person who finally came on the line was clearly harassed.

"Cody's," he spat.

"May I speak with Simon Warwick?"

"This is Simon. What do you need?" *Ah. You had to hand it to him—that was certainly the question.*

"Simon, it's Evvie."

"Who? Can you speak up? We're pretty busy here."

"It's Evvie."

"Evvie who?" *Okay, now she should get off the line.*

"It's Evvie Kerr."

A pause. "Was there some reason you called?" *Besides being a fucking idiot?*

"It was just that my stepmother said she saw you. I just … wondered how you were doing."

"Oh, you know, Evvie. What'd the man say? 'Life is very fair. It destroys everyone's dreams.'"

"Not everyone's, I hope." Her eyes narrowed. "You should see Ben."

"Who's Ben?"

"Your son. He's amazing. Smart, caring, full of energy. He's got a bright future ahead, that's for sure."

At least that got a decent pause out of him. "Listen, Evvie, I've gotta go. We're pretty snowed here. Unless you have something specific …"

She let the phone fall onto the table. Eventually, a clipped, recorded female voice intoned, "If you'd like to make a call, please hang up and dial again."

She stared sightlessly at the front page of the *Times,* vaguely aware that the room had become dense with humidity. Her sweat was dripping from her forehead onto the paper like an ominous wet web.

It finally dawned on her. She was having the mother of all hot flashes. The celebration of her body's adjustment to independence from estrogen had definitely been premature.

Twenty-three

BEN SLEPT POORLY in the week following Anna's miscarriage, haunted by the memory of Anna's blood splattered across Tash's white blouse. Sometimes, in the middle of the night, he became a dazed, nocturnal archeologist, obsessed with the certainty that everything would make sense if only he could descry the meaning of those vivid crimson hieroglyphs.

Now he felt like he was going to jump out of his skin as he sat in his car, waiting for Tash. She'd insisted on being picked up on the street behind her house. When she finally rounded the corner, hunched in on herself like a sick animal, he couldn't help but notice that the pink capris that had fit her so sexily a month ago hung loosely around her hips.

She slid into the Beamer and let him give her a quick peck on the cheek, but she didn't kiss him back. Somebody's car alarm went off, and Ben closed the sunroof, but he regretted it almost immediately. The interior of the car felt dark and claustrophobic.

Tash eyed him guiltily. "I called Anna's room at Cedars this morning. God, what kind of luck was that—getting a monster infection after losing the baby? I wanted to talk to her before she checked out, but her mom answered the phone. I'm such a chicken. I just hung up."

He stifled an expletive as he pulled away from the curb. "Look, it's okay. She's got the people she needs by her side. The best thing you can do is to take care of yourself. It wasn't your fault. If anything, you probably saved her life." He stole a glance at her. "Have you told your mom and dad yet?"

"No," she said bitterly. "And I've decided I'm not going to. My mom went through the whole sixties thing without even smoking pot. I'm gambling on the Sumters not calling my parents. They're the type that like to put on the total social front, so I'm guessing they won't." She stared out the windshield. "Anyway, where's this meeting?"

"It's up on Robertson. Tony says it's a pretty hip crowd. Actors, musicians, creative people. You should fit right in."

"Oh really? Is that what you think? A bunch of loser addicts? That's where I belong?"

"Tash. Don't"

"Don't what? Didn't you say I've been an idiot?"

"Yeah, but that was only to get your attention. Listen, I'm sorry. I didn't mean it."

"Yes, you did. And you were right." Her eyes began to pool.

He had to navigate across several lanes to pull over. "Move the fuck out of the way, asshole!" He turned off the motor.

Tash was crying hard now. But at least she let him hold her, her words muffled against his chest. "God, poor Anna. Who could tell that she was that far gone? She sure didn't look pregnant. She was so skinny. I can't stand thinking about it. If the baby had made it, it would've been born an addict." She shuddered. "Ben, it scares me to death. The choices we make without even knowing we're making them. God, we're so … fragile."

As he rocked her in his arms, Ben prayed she didn't notice that his own body was trembling. He didn't know what he'd do if she didn't make it through this. He'd seen enough kids at Uni who went through rehab, only to start using again. He kept reminding himself Tash wasn't as far gone as that. She'd only been getting high sporadically, and her resolve to draw a line between the past month and her future seemed pretty solid. She'd probably agreed to go to this Narcotics Anonymous meeting more for his sake than because she really needed it. But still.

He had two contradictory voices in his head these days, constantly shouting over each other. Everything was going to be okay; Anna's parents would keep mum about Tash … or else they wouldn't. Tash was going to stay clean and sober … or maybe not. When his grandfather had checked into the hospital, his doctors said he was suffering from gas, but if so, why hadn't he been released? Everyone said his aunt's cancer would be cured forever, but he knew deep inside there was no guarantee.

It was like a door had opened into a shadowy, unpredictable world, and he'd been thrust over the threshold. He had no idea who he was supposed to be anymore. Or how he was going to cope with so much dread.

Twenty-four

EVVIE WOKE WITH a peculiar sense of dread on her final day of radiation. She was acutely aware that, thanks to her father's medical crisis, the family seemed to have lost track of her treatment timetable. Not that she really cared. Her diagnosis had been enough of a big bang. She'd much rather this cancer treatment phase of her life go out with a whimper.

Still, it was depressing to have no one notice that she had to literally force herself out of bed this morning. Seven weeks of nuking had left her breast raw and rough-skinned, and she felt utterly drained.

Once she got moving, she noticed that Ben's bedroom door was ajar. She stood on the threshold, downing her orange juice. His room was in its typical post-hurricane mode, books and clothes strewn everywhere. She had to hand it to his drama teacher. Anyone who could get a bunch of teenagers out of bed at the crack of dawn for rehearsals had to be one hell of an inspiration.

She was looking forward to his school play, especially since it would coincide with the return to LA of her best friend, but she was relieved to have a week or so to gather her strength before opening night. The return of Ezra, whose call she'd never gotten around to returning, she preferred not to think about.

When she arrived at the Radiation Center, her graduation was far less ceremonious than Temple's. It wasn't that Helen and Russell weren't incredibly kind and effusive. Helen penned, "You are truly the best, the nicest and funniest patient I've ever treated," on her graduation certificate. And Russell—who knew how carefully she'd been eating by her consistent refusal to dig into the big bowl of Hershey's Kisses he kept by his desk—inscribed along the right margin of the certificate his list of ten favorite LA restaurants, claiming she'd lost so much weight that she could use a little beefing up.

But she didn't dare linger under the sweet parasol of their sentiment. The Millstone's relatives had asked for a special consultation, and if she wasn't on time for their meeting, they might actually start believing all the nasty things Millie had undoubtedly been saying about her. All she needed right now was some bogus lawsuit on her hands.

She rushed into the Home, flush-faced and panting, only to be informed by Maggie that the Stone family had evidently stopped to consider their source, phoning to say they didn't need to speak to Evvie, after all.

Maggie squinted at her suspiciously. "Why are you breathing like that? Gads, this radiation's really taking a toll, isn't it?"

"I'm done."

"What?"

"I'm finished. Got my graduation certificate today. I'm actually thinking of framing it."

Maggie wrapped her in a hug, screeching a little too loudly in her ear. "Thank the Lord! What you need now is a holiday."

Evvie pulled away. "Can't. My nephew's got a big part in the school play, and I'm not totally convinced my dad's out of the woods yet. Besides, who'd want to spoil a perfectly good vacation by being too damned tired to enjoy it? No, I'll wait till I get my energy back and then take off for Maui or something."

"You must be so relieved."

"You know, it's weird, Mag. That place was actually like a second home—a regular hangout for all us poor, sick bastards." She faked a laugh, but gave up the pretense when she noticed Maggie's pitying expression. "Actually, I think I feel a little more anxious now that it's done. I mean, as long as I was going there, I had this team fighting against my disease. But now—"

"But now you're cured."

"Jesus! I wish I could be as optimistic as everyone around me. Who the hell really knows? I *did* get the cancer in the first place. And then it was just my luck to get the weirdest menopausal symptom on the planet. Those itchies have been hell. When too much shit goes down, you can't help but feel like you're target practice for the dark side of God."

"Dark side of God? What are you talking about?"

"Well, doesn't it make sense, with all the shit in the world, that God is just as evil as He is good?"

"Oh, Evvie, you can't really mean that. I know you're Jewish, but I think even in the Old Testament it's pretty clear that we're the source of evil, not God."

"I wouldn't dream of insulting your religion, Mag, but I've been struggling for months now against blaming myself for this damned cancer. And it's dawned on me—would you really blame humans for things like earthquakes and tornadoes? I mean, I do believe what the scientists are telling us about climate change, but how could all the violence of Mother Nature throughout the ages be down to Adam and Eve?"

"But Evvie, that line of thinking's so creepy. If God isn't all good, how could we ever feel safe in the world?"

Evvie just shook her head. "Safe? I don't know about safe. Guess I left that country a couple of months ago." She gave a wan smile. "But keep trying, Mag. I sure wouldn't mind if you figured out how to link me back up with that blissful river of De Nile."

***

Across town, on the other side of the hill, a rousing refrain spilled from Uni High's auditorium.

The rehearsal for *Westside Story* couldn't be going better. Ida Rodrick, the portly but energetic head of the Drama and Speech Department, nodded emphatically in her upright chair, chosen to support a back that had been giving her the business since overseeing the school's production of *The Pirates of Penzance* in 1975. She didn't bother to restrain herself from clapping loudly and whistling through her teeth like a teenager as "Jet Song" came to a close. Responding to her praise, the herd of handsome young bulls of the senior class broke into self-congratulatory high-fives, perspiration streaming down their faces and soaking the red bandanas they wore to distinguish them from the blue-bandana'ed Sharks.

Mrs. Rodrick grabbed hold of Ben and directed her broad mouthful of lipstick-smeared teeth at him. "Ben! We're going to wow them, aren't we?"

Ben grinned, half in honest response to Mrs. Rodrick's earnestness, half at his girlfriend, who was beckoning to him from the wings.

He leaned down to kiss his teacher's springy gray head, then ran to Tash, who'd receded into the shadows. He spun her around in exultation. "Did we kill, or what?"

She squealed half-heartedly. "Stop, you're making me dizzy."

He put her down, anxiously scanning her face. Her expression betrayed nothing but simple enthusiasm. "You are so beautiful."

"I don't know about that. I'm getting fat. I can't believe I've put on five pounds already."

"Hey, don't knock those pounds. They're proof that you're being a good girl." She flicked him a wary look. "Sorry. That was uncalled for. Anyway, you know I like you better with those sexy curves."

Tash relented, snuggling into his arms. "Baby, you rock. The truth is, I don't know what I'd do without you. You know, Nicole called last night."

Ben pushed her to arm's length. "I hope you told her to fuck off."

"Not exactly. I said I was tied up with rehearsals. Come on, you don't know how hard it is to suddenly *diss* people who've considered you a friend. Yeah sure, Nicole and Tammy were total bitches to Anna, but they were just as high as she was that night, and it wasn't like Anna couldn't have driven to the ER when she started cramping, instead of going off to some club. I kinda feel sorry for Nicole. She's like a lost puppy without Anna to hide behind. But I kept telling myself how you'd bust my balls if I started getting into some codependent relationship with those girls again."

"Codependent, eh? A couple of twelve-step meetings, and you're already into the buzz words?" He looked around before passing a quick hand across her pubic mound. "Anyway, if you've got balls in there, I sure haven't found them."

She giggled. "That's because you cut them off along with the cocaine."

He snapped angrily, "Don't even say that fucking word."

"Ben, believe me, I wouldn't be joking about it if I were the least bit tempted. I can't believe what a loser I was."

"Actually, you weren't a loser. You were a little snot. But you know what? We've gotten a lot tighter through this. Maybe it all happened for a reason."

She looked up at him consideringly, but a line of bodies brushing past them put an end to their conversation. They became aware of Mrs. Rodrick's voice calling loudly, as if she'd been trying to get someone's attention for ages. "Maria! Natasha! Where is that girl?"

Tash broke free from his embrace and ran onto the stage.

Ben felt only the slightest twinge of jealously as she began her duet with her partner, Frank Tomasso. His lips moved silently with them as they sang. He hoped to Christ she meant it about not being tempted. If she got back into that shit, he knew it would be twice as hard to turn her back around.

Twenty-five

WHILE A VACATION in Maui might still be just a dream, the slow boat of nostalgia was about to deposit Evvie on a lush isle of memories at her father's Wonderland Avenue home. Michael was finally due to be discharged from the hospital, and Evvie had convinced Miriam that now was their chance to give his house the kind of spring cleaning he never would have sanctioned, had he known.

Michael's stubborn sense of privacy precluded him from allowing anything more than a bi-weekly cleaning by Carmella, who attacked his wood floors, leaded glass windows, and dirty linens with a determined domestic vengeance. It was a losing battle. The march of dust and grime both in and outside his shelves and cupboards was as inexorable as cosmic entropy. Michael took pride that he was still sufficiently ambulatory to keep his few dirty dishes in check and that he swabbed out his bathroom sink each night with his washcloth. But still, it was undeniable: his house was permeated with a signature old man's smell, vaguely reminiscent of dirty socks, cooked cabbage, and moldy cheese.

When Evvie and Miriam pulled onto Wonderland Avenue, Beady's car was already parked in front of Grann's house. Beady had promised to try to stay awake long enough after checking in on her *grand-mère* to say hi before going home and sleeping off her jetlag.

Evvie ran ahead of Miriam and rang Grann's bell. Beady flung open the door and grabbed her hands. She danced Evvie onto the lawn, whirling her in breath-taking circles and screaming loud enough to wake the whole neighborhood. "Free at last! Girlfriend, you are free at last!"

At least someone had remembered.

Once Evvie got past smoothing Miriam's ruffled feathers—she'd gone into a serious pout, as if it were Evvie's fault that she'd forgotten when her sister was scheduled to finish radiation—the three women walked across the lawn to Michael's house.

They ended up camped out in his little-used den, with its floor-to-ceiling shelving bearing awards and plaques propped up with idealizing zeal by a younger Moira. Before long, they'd managed to carpet the wood floor with helter-skelter piles of photographs documenting over half a century of the Kerr family tree.

Beady shook her head. "I don't know about you white folks. You've got more variation in skin and hair color than all my *tantes* and *oncles* back on the Bayou." She turned over several of the photos in front of her, reading aloud the names Riva Kerr had handwritten on their backs with a lively, feminine flourish. She gestured towards Miriam. "This Lemuel Kirschon. Red hair and freckles just like yours. Not exactly what you'd expect in a nice Jewish boy." She scrabbled for another photo. "Now look at Yehud. Could be Evvie's male twin, don't you think? But with kinky hair. Didn't you say they were brothers? Bet you a Häagen-Dazs they didn't share the same daddy. You think their mama had a little on the side and got busted when baby number two arrived?"

Miriam objected, "But what about me and Evvie? As you said, it's the same thing. There's lots of Jews with red hair."

Evvie broke in. "Yeah, just listen to you, acting like Soleil conceived your half-white ass via Immaculate Conception, like Baby Jesus himself."

"What is it about your Jewish ass that you can't get that the concept of Immaculate Conception refers to the Mother of God's birth, and not Christ's?"

"And what is it about your disgustingly high and tight little ass that doesn't get there's nothing immaculate about any of us? For all I know, one of my wandering Jewish great-great-grandmothers got detoured into Ireland somewhere along the centuries and got *shtupped* by some redhead from County Cork. The whole human race is a bunch of mutts by now, except for a few hundred thousand indigenous tribespeople and maybe five hundred perfectly proportioned white-blonde babes from Sweden." Evvie gave a tug at Beady's wild yellow frizz. "Who the hell are you to talk, anyway?"

"Okay, okay, you got me."

"Good, 'cause I was scared you were segueing into some rap about racial purity."

Beady shuddered. "Please. That's not even funny."

"What's not funny?" Miriam had wandered out to the kitchen and was returning with a six-pack of Bass Ales, a bottle opener, and a photograph pinched like a cigarette between two fingers.

Beady scooted to the side a little to make room for her. "Being reminded of that hellhole of a refugee camp. I don't want to even tell you what I saw there."

Miriam blinked. "Oh. Well, here's something that'll trigger some nicer memories. Would you believe this?" She waved the object in her hand. "I found it in the old coupon drawer, underneath about five tons of loose toothpicks, filthy takeout menus, and boxes of matches from restaurants that went out of business before we were even born." She held up a black and white photograph of a gang of kids goofing off on the sidewalk in front of Michael's house, painted the creamy tan it had been twenty years ago. "Ta-da!" she crowed, dangling it in the air just out of Evvie's reach. "Oh no, you don't."

"Shit." Evvie pulled back her hand.

Miriam seemed oblivious, but Beady touched Evvie's shoulder. "That right shoulder's still tight, isn't it, baby? Didn't you say you were going to get some physical therapy?"

"*Mm hmm*, next week. The therapist wanted me to wait till I finished radiation." Miriam looked chastened but said nothing. "C'mon, let's see what you've got."

Miriam laid it onto the floor, and Evvie and Beady stretched out on their stomachs next to her.

Evvie said, "Oh, my God, it's Sherry. I was just thinking about her a few weeks ago." She lowered her voice. "Do you remember …?"

Beady sat up, covering her round breasts with both hands. "How could I forget? That child was nasty!"

"Do you believe we actually let her feel us up?"

189

"Honey, it's not like we had a lot to feel."

Miriam looked puzzled.

Beady looked at her in surprise. "Don't tell me you don't remember. I know she hauled you into her garage for those 'prayer meetings,' too. She had a lot of nerve, messing around with the heads of a bunch of younger kids like that."

"What in the world are you talking about?"

"Do you mean to tell me it didn't stick inside that little red head of yours that we all got molested by some Okie child?"

Evvie snickered. "Don't even bother. Miriam doesn't remember anything she doesn't want to."

"What's that supposed to mean?"

"Never mind." Ashamed of herself, Evvie changed the subject. "How're things going with Paul?"

Miriam let out a groan. "Oh, Paul, Paul. I'm sick of worrying about Paul Welles. Why does every man become a bore after a couple of months?"

Beady laughed at her. "Honey, it'd take a whirling dervish to keep up with your fickle needs. Paul's a sweet boy, Miriam. A little young, but that's probably why you went for him in the first place. I knew I should have warned him."

"Why does everybody take his side? Am I supposed to be a nun or something? He goes ballistic every time he thinks I'm flirting with another guy. I swear he's paranoid. He still can't get over me going out to dinner with Nils Jergensen. For God's sake, it's going to be the high point of my professional life, working with someone of his caliber." She frowned. "Actually, he's a bit of a lush and a sloppy kisser, but what the hell." Seeing Evvie's eyes widen, she added, "Yeah, well, so what if I fooled around a little with him afterwards? Nothing serious. We were both pretty drunk and knew it didn't mean a thing. It was back to the business of pre-production the next day, and that was that. I never gave it another thought. And Paul never knew about that, anyway. His fantasy is that Nils Jergensen and I are having some kind of affair." Noticing Beady throwing Evvie a sardonic look, she said defensively, "You yourself would go crazy being with somebody as needy as Paul."

"Honey, I wouldn't go after a kid ten years younger than me in the first place. I don't want gravity doing anything to me it hasn't already done to my partner. What do you expect of a kid in his twenties, anyway? Some kind of father figure?"

"Ew, no. You know I can't stand older men." But then Miriam grinned cagily. "Though Ezra Rosenberg's pretty cool. He called this morning, and he was sweet enough to agree to come to Ben's opening tomorrow night. Since Paul's having such a hissy fit, I thought Ezra might as well use his ticket."

Evvie's heart stood still. Beady shot her a quick look.

Miriam put a hand on Beady's arm. "You're not interested in him, right?"

Beady responded with a clipped, "Right."

Evvie excused herself and fled to the bathroom.

The face in her father's vanity mirror scowled at her. One of the bulbs in the overhead fixture must have burned out, and Carmella must have installed a yellow-tinged one as a replacement. Under its ghastly penumbra, the pores on her cheeks were Martian craters, and the lines on her face looked as if they were outlined in kohl. She tried pasting on a phony smile. It *would* be a blessing for Ben if Miriam hooked up with a man of substance for a change.

She flopped onto the toilet seat. Who was she kidding? She supposed she should feel guilty for the evil thoughts she was having, but how could you always feel kindly toward someone as blindly self-involved as her sister?

Twenty-six

MIRIAM NIBBLED HER cuticles as she examined the two dresses she'd laid out on her bed. She picked up the hanger with the sexy little black number on it and held it up to her body, turning every which way before her antique pine-framed mirror. She knew she looked enticing in this kind of slinky crepe sheath, but was it a bit much? She didn't want Ezra thinking she was blatantly coming on to him.

She shoved the black dress back in her closet.

Clever of her, really, inviting Ezra to the play under the guise of treating Beady's new friend like family. She scrutinized the layered cream chiffon Harari outfit on the bed, rubbing a fold of its delicate fabric between her finger and thumb. Demure was good. It was so important to strike the right tone.

It was going to be tricky, though, trying to win him over with so many people around. Not only would Evvie and Beady be there, but Moira had flown into town this morning for the performance, and Miriam had been corralled by Ben into inviting his new girlfriend and her mother Brenda Lem to a celebratory dinner at the trendy new French restaurant, Tigre. Brenda was all right, she supposed. Miriam had sat next to her at the Uni High Senior Awards Banquet, and she seemed friendly enough, if a little uptight. Miriam hadn't exactly been surprised when Ben had announced that he had a girlfriend, but she realized it must be more serious than she'd assumed when Ben told his grandfather about it, adding the confidence that Brenda had been an activist during the sixties.

Was that weird, or what? Brenda seemed like any upper middle class Jewish attorney with frizzy hair and a tight gym ass. Thinking of her as a rabble-rouser stretched the imagination, and how she'd turned out a hot little number like Tash for a daughter was anybody's guess. Maybe Tash's Polish-born father Andrej was some outrageous hunk. Miriam still hadn't met him. He wouldn't be at the play. In fact, from what Miriam could gather, the man seemed to travel back and forth between Eastern Europe and the US half the time. Maybe he was a spy. She giggled, but a dark thought intruded, making her sit down abruptly at the edge of her bed. The Harari dress slid to the floor. Tash had better not be getting any ideas. Ben was still a baby. He didn't have a clue what he wanted to do with his life. He needed time to get to know himself at Yale—thank God he'd decided at last!—and to explore the world after college without being encumbered by a girlfriend who'd chosen to study art at some school in Minnesota, for God's sake. Besides, while she could understand Ben going gaga for Tash, what mother in her right mind wanted her son to get serious about a girl who was obviously such a slut?

***

In her own bedroom, Evvie sprawled across her duvet, consumed by a funk. When the phone rang, she reached for it reluctantly.

"Evelyn?"

Oh lord. They'd released him from the hospital just this morning, supposedly with flying colors. *Please tell me he's not in trouble again.* "Dad, are you okay?"

"I'm fine. Evelyn, listen. Tell Benjamin to do a good job, do the Kerr family proud."

She breathed again. "Of course. I'm so sorry you're not up for opening night. But you know it'll probably be better by Sunday, anyway, after they've ironed out the wrinkles."

"And another thing."

"Yes, Dad."

"The *tallis* and *yarmulke*. I forgot to give them to you. They're still on my desk, wrapped up in tissue paper."

She felt awful "Oh my God, I totally forgot. I'll make sure to get them next time I come over. You were really sweet to offer them."

"Yes, well … Listen, Evelyn."

"Yes, Dad?"

"I looked at my calendar when I got home. You must have finished your radiation by now. You're probably very tired. When people get tired, they get depressed. Try to have a good time tonight. It's a wonderful thing, you know, to have a whole life ahead of you." He rang off before she had a chance to respond.

Evvie stared at the receiver. My God, was age finally mellowing Michael Kerr?

She had to admit that hearing him say those words was surprisingly energizing. Before she could talk herself out of it, she sprung out of bed and marched into the bathroom. She was suddenly determined to style her hair the way Peter Hale had painstakingly demonstrated the last time she'd gone in for a trim.

At the very least, she'd show Ezra Rosenberg that Miriam's sister wasn't exactly chopped liver.

***

The Uni High auditorium was steaming, but nobody cared. What button-bursting parent (or, for that matter, grandparent, aunt, or uncle) gave a shit about a ruptured air conditioner when the young light of the family's life was delivering a socko performance in the play that was arguably the gold standard of American musical theatre?

Ben was scarily intense as the wild Riff, and gooseflesh fanned out across Evvie's arms as his character lay dying on the stage. Once Ben's part in the play was over, though, she was free to focus on her nephew's girlfriend. She had to admit that Tash made a beguiling Maria, and by the time she sang her final duet, Evvie was a little in love with the girl herself.

When the curtain fell, Evvie put a hand on the back of her seat and hefted herself up to stand on her chair. Her blond curls bobbed as she stamped and whistled. Ezra laughed up at her, but he automatically stationed himself closer lest she start to fall.

195

Embarrassed, and teetering a little, Evvie accepted his hand before lowering her high-heeled feet to the floor. But when Ben came out for his solo bow, she forgot herself again and let out a loud whoop, calling out, "Way to go, Ben!" She saw Ben's face flush as he heard his name above the cheering and applause.

"He's loving it," she cried.

"Who wouldn't?" Ezra offered her an upturned palm and gave her a wide grin as she responded with an uncertain high five.

Her hands stung pleasurably. Evvie looked away. She caught Moira raising an eyebrow at her and making a pointed little gesture at Ezra with her handsome chin.

In spite of herself, Evvie glanced back at him. He was staring at her. She could hardly bear the depth of expression in his dark, moist eyes.

"You know, your nephew looks more like you than his mother."

Evvie pretended she hadn't heard, and soon enough Miriam had managed to sidestep Moira's outstretched arms to give Evvie a teary hug.

"Wasn't he wonderful?"

Evvie could feel her sister's lean torso under her chiffon dress and felt a flicker of wonder at the lack of even a tiny roll of flesh between the bottom of Miriam's bra and the top of her bikini panties.

But now Miriam was turning in Ezra's direction, and she transferred her hugging arms to him as if it were the polite thing to do.

Evvie's cheeks were still burning when Beady pushed past some other kid's hysterical family clogging up the aisle. "Is that our boy, or what? Honey, he's a natural performer. I told Tony that Ben's aunt'll be fighting off the Hollywood agents in the audience to keep him going to Yale in the fall."

Beady called out to Moira to help shepherd their group backstage. Evvie felt like she was caught up in some alternately euphoric and dismaying whirlwind. She fought to keep her mind focused on her nephew, but it kept sneaking over to how Miriam was managing to stay no more than a finger's width away from Ezra.

It was chaos backstage. Girls with tears and perspiration tracing snail tracks down their stage make-up were hugging and declaring their undying love for one another. Jets and Sharks had transcended adolescent macho to embrace one another victoriously. In the confusion, isolated phrases floated over to her. "Oh, my God, Sharilyn, this was the best moment of our lives; it can't get any better than this." "Do you believe it? It was tons better than dress rehearsal." "You rocked, dude."

She tried to keep Moira's blue-black waves in her sights as she excused herself past bouquet-clutching men searching for their daughters. Somehow, she managed to catch up with Moira, Beady, Miriam, and Ezra just as they'd spotted Ben. He grinned over at them, then turned back toward a circle of castmates, all of whom seemed to be talking excitedly at the same time.

The family reached the periphery of the group just in time to see a radiant Tash grab Ben's hand and tug him toward a corner, where Tony and Opal stood waiting. Evvie and the rest of the group hesitated. Ben looked helplessly back at them over his shoulder, shouting, "Listen, I know we had plans, but everybody's going out to Miranda Todd's parents' beach house to celebrate. Do you guys mind?"

Before anyone could object, they were gone. And what was more, the rest of the cast had departed with them. The room went silent. It was as if the parents of the senior class had been thrown into sudden, collective mourning. They were getting their first real taste of the loss to come this fall.

Evvie saw a pant-suited woman with frizzy hair glare at the place where Ben and Tash had been standing, then glance doubtfully over at Miriam, whose face had turned starkly freckled with rage. Evvie edged close to Miriam. "Is that Natasha's mother?" she hissed. "Don't you think you should bring her over here? It's worse for her. She's all by herself."

With a resigned sigh, Miriam left her side to fetch Brenda Lem. Evvie sensed Ezra moving closer. He smiled tentatively. "Teenagers. Pretty unreliable, eh?"

"No, honestly, he's a great kid. You could see how torn he was." She made a humble dip of her head. "Why would he want to hang out with a bunch of old folks when he could party with his friends?"

"Old folks? Is that how you see yourself? I'd say you were still in the young category, just not seventeen."

"I don't know about that. These past few months I've been feeling about a hundred and ten."

"But that's just temporary. Beady said you're going to be just fine?" He'd made it a question rather than a comment, and there was an urgency to his tone.

"That's what they say, but—" Evvie clammed up. She'd said too much already.

"But it's hard to trust that more bad shit isn't going to descend on you from out of the blue." It felt like he could see right into her head.

"I don't know," she mumbled, and before she could censor herself, she added, "I think somewhere inside I've assumed all my life that things were going to go wrong."

Ezra looked pained, but before he could respond Miriam appeared with Brenda and made introductions all around. For the first time, Evvie registered that Moira and Beady had maintained a distance the whole time she and Ezra had been talking.

Trying to make the best of the situation, they began to make driving arrangements to the restaurant. Moira insisted to an annoyed-looking Miriam that she and Brenda come along in her rented BMW to navigate for her, since she'd never been to Tigre before.

Evvie went with Beady and Ezra. When they entered the glass-fronted restaurant, they were greeted by a chic Frenchwoman, who led them up a small staircase to the balcony, where a large, round table was set for a party of eight. Evvie glanced around nervously. There were only six in their party now. She couldn't help but appreciate this restaurant's charming Provençal style—spare white walls, unpainted wood molding, and hanging baskets with artfully arranged dried flowers. She watched a thirty-something man in a chef's hat zip up the stairs, taking them two at a time. He pumped her hand warmly.

"You must be the famous Aunt Evvie. I've heard so much about you." Evvie shot him a startled look. "I'm Tim Grenaldi. This is my place. Put my first and last names together to call it Tigre." He made a self-deprecating face. "I know Ben from surfing. It's my other passion. He's a great kid. You must be very proud of him." He introduced himself to the other two and then looked around. "Where's the guest of honor?"

Just then, Beady appeared on the landing. "That boy has gone off to Malibu with his homies, my own rat of a son included. So, I'm afraid we've made you set aside this big table for nothing."

Grenaldi, obviously a pro, didn't skip a beat. He gestured to a waitress, who together with one of the busboys unobtrusively whisked away the extra place settings.

Making a fuss over the beauty and youthfulness of Ben's mother (which seemed to go a long way in defusing Miriam's irritation that Ben wasn't even there), the chef pulled out a chair for her. Miriam caught Ezra's eye and confidently patted the seat beside her, but Beady whooshed Brenda into that chair and then sat down herself on Miriam's other side, smiling blandly and fluffing her yellow frizz. As if in concert, Moira quickly sat down next to Brenda and, ignoring Miriam's annoyed gaze, proceeded to compliment Natasha's mother on her daughter's talent and versatility.

Grenaldi took leave of them, murmuring something about surprises. Ezra held out one of the two remaining chairs for Evvie, a bemused smile on his face as he sat down beside her.

Beady passed a menu to a scowling Miriam. "I love their logo, don't you?" A clever sketch on the menu's cover depicted an arched-back tiger morphing into *l'Arc de Triomphe*. Before Miriam could respond, their waitress began passing out the first of a whole series of appetizing freebies. Beady nudged Miriam. "That Tim Grenaldi is something, isn't he? Tony tells me he's won tons of awards." She gestured to a delicate arrangement of pieces of moist lobster, little sliced moons of avocado, and a sweet ratatouille of exotic summer fruits. "I'm sure he's taking a personal hit in the profits department with all this. I just love a generous soul, don't you?"

Evvie had no idea what the rest of the table was talking about, but thanks to Tim Grenaldi's hospitality, she and Ezra managed to get nicely buzzed on champagne. Each time their waitress topped off their glasses, they took turns making wacky toasts. It was Ezra's turn this time. "To the geniuses in our government who pronounce nuclear *nu-cu-lar*. I always look at that one as a secret IQ test." They clicked glasses heartily, and champagne sprayed Evvie's face. Ezra leaned forward to gently dab at her with his napkin. "That's a really nice necklace you're wearing. Those stones look beautiful against your skin."

She blushed. "Ben gave it to me last Christmas."

"Christmas? I'm surprised a nice Jewish girl like you celebrates Christmas."

"It's my favorite holiday." She smiled mischievously. "You'd probably be even more surprised to know I used to pray to baby Jesus before going to sleep."

"Wait a minute. Let me get this straight. Your father was a Jew and a communist, but you celebrated Christmas and said prayers to Jesus Christ? Is that why you dyed your hair blond?" Startled, she threw him an embarrassed glance. "Just kidding. I like it. Sets off those big dark eyes of yours. But baby Jesus?"

If she hadn't been a little drunk by now, Evvie would undoubtedly have drowned in hair paranoia. As it was, she latched onto the complimentary lifeline he'd thrown her and kept paddling. "The prayer part was my little secret. Christmas was thanks to Moira. She had to drag my father kicking and screaming into that one. Oh God, you should have seen him, slamming his bedroom door like a three-year-old when a couple of deliverymen hauled a giant tree into our living room the first time. But for me and Miriam, it was like we'd died and gone to heaven. All those beautiful decorations. And the smell!" She cocked her head. "I take it, as a nice Jewish boy, you've never had a tree yourself."

"Not even a 'Chanukah bush.' My folks were pretty traditional. But I'd get one every day if I could watch your eyes lighting up like they are right now."

"Uh oh, I'd better watch out. All this flattery could go right to my head. Actually, it'll be the champagne that goes to my head tomorrow morning. But how many times do you get a chance to celebrate your nephew's musical debut?"

Ezra studied her intently, and she found herself blushing. "He really means a lot to you, doesn't he?"

"Am I that bad?"

"It's actually quite touching."

"Don't get me started. I've watched him grow from a tiny baby to a beautiful young man ..." She fumbled for her napkin, then realized it had fallen off her lap. "Forgive me. I always was a maudlin drunk."

Ezra took hold of her arm and pulled her back up. "Here." He patted her wet cheeks with the tips of his fingers. "There's nothing to forgive. But I have to admit, I was pretty curious when Beady told me you were the one who took care of him at the beginning."

Evvie slid a guilty look in her sister's direction, but fortunately Miriam was busy singing an off-key rendition of "La Marseillaise" with Moira. "My sister needed a little help to set up a life for herself."

He played with his champagne goblet, teasing the golden liquid toward the edge before righting the glass again. "You have a special affinity for kids?"

Evvie gave a little sound of recognition. "It wouldn't have occurred to me before, but you know, I guess I do. There was a little girl at the Radiation Center who captured my heart." She explained about Temple's situation. "Right now, we're all praying for a miracle. I'm afraid that's what it's going to take. It makes me feel so selfish, feeling sorry for what I've been through, when a kid like that …"

"And yet you work with old people. You'd think you would have focused on the other end of the age spectrum."

Her eyes sparked defensively. "It made perfect sense at the time. The grad school I went to had a special program in gerontology. And I was used to relating to people older than I was. My mom was only thirty-three, but my dad was forty-three when I was born, and most of his friends, who virtually lived at our house, were even older. Mostly writers, but some just fellow travelers. Noisy, vital, but definitely not young."

Ezra was slow to respond. It occurred to Evvie that he looked tired. He had his elbow on the table, his chin resting on his hand, and she took note of the dark circles under his eyes.

"You know, they're begging for volunteers at UNESCO, people with therapeutic skills willing to work with children."

"If I weren't drunk, I'd swear you were trying to recruit me."

He grinned and leaned so close that his arm pressed against hers. "Truth be told," he whispered, "I wouldn't mind winning you over for something."

Maybe it was the champagne, but Evvie found herself sitting very still, not wanting to relinquish the little island of warmth where their bodies touched.

***

"Come on in, baby, don't be shy."

Ben pushed aside the curtain of amber beads dangling in Tash's doorway. He had never been in her bedroom before, and if it hadn't been for her spur of the moment inspiration to come here instead of Miranda's, he probably never would. Despite having organized countless demonstrations in the sixties, Tash's mom was a terrible prude. She might not be able to control how her daughter dressed, but she wouldn't let Tash entertain any boys in her room.

Tash had clearly been in charge of decorating this space. It was a retro-hippy hive, swirling red and pink paisley fabrics covering everything from bed to ceiling. The room smelled thickly of jasmine incense. He approached the dartboard hanging on the opposite wall. She'd been telling him about it all semester. It was her senior project—built with her own hands in woodshop, then decorated with spot-on renderings of familiar faces with which she'd taken considerable liberty.

He looked closer at the ironic, pie-wedge montage. Tash had positioned a hangdog Bill Clinton uncomfortably squeezed between Day-Glo caricatures of Monica Lewinsky and Hillary. An oil pastel of George W's head was tacked onto an anatomically detailed version of a baboon's crimson ass. The bull's eye was a miniature version of one of those *Uncle Sam Wants You* posters, with a dollar bill emblazoned diagonally across it like a no-smoking sign.

"Jesus, welcome to our world. Tash, it really rocks. This is like something you'd see hanging at MOCA. Now I know why Leonards gave you an A plus." He pulled her to him so that they both faced the board, and he wrapped his arms around her slender waist. "And why every undergraduate art department in the country has been fighting over you. How did you even think of it in the first place?"

"I cannot tell a lie." She scratched her eyelid delicately. "It all came to me when I was high. Don't worry. I'm not even tempted anymore." She broke into a sly smile, seductively sucking her finger, then wiggling it at him. "But you have to admit, sometimes great things come out of something bad."

He lunged forward and pinned her onto the bed, burying his head in her breasts, which gave off the faint scent of gardenia. "What am I going to do with you? You're my devil woman. My bad, bad girl." He slid a hand up her thigh. "Now is this what you mean?"

She shivered.

He found his way around her panties and put his finger inside her. She moaned.

Feverishly, he began urging her dress over her head, his hands clumsy with desire. She unhooked her bra for him. He yanked off his shirt. Then she began lowering his pants down his legs. They got caught at his ankles, and he laughed nervously as he pulled them free and flung them onto the floor.

She gave him a long look. Though the room was warm, his skin was covered in gooseflesh. And then she did something she'd never done before. She slithered down toward the foot of the bed and began licking him, starting with his ankles and working up until he felt her lashes, like little wings, teasing his belly, her lips searing his balls. "I love you, baby," she stopped to whisper. "This is how much I love you."

Ben was on fire. He pulled her up so that she faced him, and he rolled on top, letting the full weight of his body claim her. He looked right into her eyes as he thrust himself inside her—wanting her, needing her, shattering everything that had gone before.

Twenty-seven

EVVIE FELT AS if she were waking from an exceedingly long hibernation. Every cell of her seemed to vibrate as she held her phone to her ear and registered what Ezra was saying. "So, do you mind being the one to drive? Beady's agreed to handle the dinner afterwards with the critic from the *L.A. Weekly*, but it'll leave me car-less."

She rubbed her bare toes over the ankle of her other foot and gave her nude body a thumbs up sign in the mirror, something she only felt free to do because Ezra was across town at Beady's place, while she herself leaned against the cool tiles of her bathroom wall. The fact that he wanted her to come to the screening of the rough cut of *Their Fathers' Sins* could be put down to courtesy. That he'd invited her to dinner afterwards had to mean something more.

She couldn't help but acknowledge that her trimmed down, olive skinned body and spiky blond hair looked striking against the wall's turquoise tiles. That is, if you ignored the puckered arch over the nipple of her radiation-coarsened right breast.

"Too bad your sister has to work this afternoon."

Evvie's balloon deflated with a whining fizzle. "Yeah, I'm sure she'll be sorry to miss it."

"No biggie. There'll be other showings before our theatrical release. Christ, I hope this baby finds its way to a decent-sized audience." As Ezra shared his nerves over how this preliminary version of *Their Fathers' Sins* would be received, Evvie's mind split onto two tracks. One listened with genuine interest, leading her to murmur sympathetically at all the right places. The other kept insisting that she'd made more of Ezra's invitation than he'd intended. What if she were just a momentary consolation prize while Miriam was unavailable?

Even as she started getting ready, she had to battle her instinct to call Ezra back and cancel. She really should stay home with Ben. The poor boy was sick with exhaustion. At least she hoped that was what it was. A phone call to his doctor had elicited the information that lots of kids suffer emotional fatigue around graduation time, but it seemed callous to just leave him. The fact that Moira had promised to come over in an hour or so with a host of herbal remedies didn't help. It would probably drive Ben nuts to have her around.

Evvie paused with her black silk slacks halfway up her thighs. What if Ben couldn't make it to his own graduation? It would be a damned shame to miss out on the applause for all the academic and athletic awards he'd earned. Given the way he'd dragged himself to his bedroom yesterday and crawled under the covers like a wounded animal, that wasn't completely out of the question. For once, her cynicism about homeopathy gave way to a fervent prayer that Moira would find some miracle cure in her holistic bag of tricks.

Evvie actually went so far as to dial Beady's number, but Tony informed her that both his mother and Ezra had already left for the AFI Fest. So that was that.

***

Evvie was right to worry about her nephew, but she didn't know the half of it.

Little more than six weeks ago, Ben had been high as a kite on a heady cocktail of gardenia perfume and the wizardry of Tash's tongue. But yesterday, on the day of his graduation rehearsal, he'd crashed.

He'd woken early and sped to school with the anticipation of a two-year-old heading for his first trip to Disneyland. The football field was a buzzing hive of hyped-up seniors. Ben pushed his way through the crowd, having to raise his voice each time he asked if anyone had seen Tash.

Promptly at 10 a.m., their principal's voice cackled out from her megaphone, "Ladies and gentlemen, you need to line up now. I'm trusting you can manage to get yourselves into alphabetical order without killing each other." Ben looked around wildly. Where was she? Tash was usually the one who gave *him* hell for not being on time.

It was spooky how she just materialized by his side. Ashen faced, she started pulling him away from the coalescing crowd.

"We've got to talk," she hissed.

"But …" He looked longingly back at the winding snake of his classmates, who'd gone momentarily quiet, as if mourning their upcoming eviction from the last outpost of childhood.

"Don't 'but' me, Ben. I'm late."

At first, he thought she was referring to being late for rehearsal. But then he froze. The guillotine of recognition sliced neatly down. He knew he was an asshole to feign ignorance, but he said it anyway. "Late for what?"

She flashed him a sharp look. "Don't even. You know exactly what I'm talking about." A mysterious screen shot up over her face, but her wringing hands told a tale of their own. There was so much he wanted to ask, so much he wanted to at least try to say, but he'd just stared at her until, finally, she'd walked off, looking disgusted. He tried following her, but his limbs were leaden. It was like trying to run underwater. He stopped, paralyzed on Uni High's end zone, faint echoes of old cheers in the air—"Wildcats rule!"—until a long wave sucked him under and washed him home.

***

When Moira arrived, she found Evvie nervously waiting at the front door. "Good heavens, you look like a ripe orange, just about to burst." Herself a dramatic confection of blue-black hair twisted into a thick long braid artfully trained over one shoulder of her white linen pantsuit, she'd murmured, "White is so conducive to healing, don't you think?" Moira stepped back to appraise how Evvie's orange silk tunic top shimmered against her olive skin. Her stepdaughter's breasts looked round and whole under the graceful drape of fabric.

"Don't stare at me like that. Do I look ridiculous?" Before Moira could respond, Evvie went on manically. "I'm like some Halloween decoration, aren't I? What was I thinking, black toreador pants and orange top? And it's summer, too. It's just that these pants—there's something miraculous about the way they're cut that makes my ass look a little less like a house. But I wanted some color, and the magazines all say orange is the thing right now. And they had this blouse on sale at BCBG, and even though most of their stuff only looks good on girls Ben's age, I thought it sort of fell nicely ..." Her eyes were pleading as she ran out of breath.

Moira, who'd been pinching her lips thoughtfully between thumb and forefinger, spoke with quiet authority. "He'll love it."

Evvie blinked. "You think?"

"I know." Moira put her hands on Evvie's shoulders and aimed her towards the door. "Now go. Get out of here and have a wonderful time. And tell Beady I'm definitely going to see her film when she brings it up to the Bay Area."

Evvie hesitated, and the pink splotches on her cheeks paled. "But wait. About Ben. I looked in on him a few minutes ago and he was still asleep. Do you think we should take his temperature before I go? What if he's really sick? I don't want to land you with a crisis on your hands ... I mean, this is your vacation ..."

"Hell with vacation, this is my family. Besides, what am I on vacation from? It's not as if I work for a living. It's Ben's theatrical debut and his graduation ceremony I flew down here to witness, and I'm going to make damned sure I get to see both. He *will* get well. Take a look at my bag of goodies."

Evvie looked down. The big black Barney's bag on the floor was bursting with little bottles.

Moira gave Evvie a gentle shove out the door and shut it behind her. She turned to the empty hallway and rubbed her hands together. "Now for Mr. Ben. We'll have that boy feeling like a million bucks in no time."

***

Ben woke to a godawful smell. His eyes sprang open to find his dim bedroom swirling with smoke. He leapt out of bed and dashed out of the room.

"Evvie! Get out of the house. The place is on fire!"

Plowing blindly down the hall, he ran right into his stepmother Moira, who stood with her hands on her hips, a Cheshire cat grin on her face.

"I see you've had a burst of renewed energy."

"We've got to get out of here!"

He'd never seen his stepmother more obliviously self-involved. She merely laughed in his face. "I've got to tell Evvie that I really am a miracle worker. I got you right up, didn't I?"

Concluding she was beyond self-centered—for all he knew she'd gone certifiably crazy—he turned on his heels and ran toward his aunt's bedroom, crying, "Evvie! Evvie! Where are you?"

"Wait, Ben." Moira had followed him and was grabbing at his wrist. "Forgive me. I really didn't mean to frighten you. It's aromatherapy steam. I thought it would do you some good." She started pulling him toward his bedroom. "Look."

She was right. There was no smoke in his room, merely a bizarre set-up on top of his stereo cabinet. A porcelain statue of an angel with a hollowed-out place in its stomach in which a little container of oil was suspended over a candle. Spicy steam billowed out of its pursed lips like a child blowing bubbles.

Ben's ears turned bright red. "Who said you could come into my room when I was asleep? And where's my aunt?"

Moira looked crestfallen. "Sweetie, you must forgive me. I just thought … we all agreed … Look, Evvie's gone to see Beady's movie." Her eyes crinkled in a conspiratorial grin. "Your aunt Evvie's on a date."

Ben narrowed his eyes. What the fuck was she talking about?

"It's true. Beady's film partner. Ezra Rosenberg. You should have seen him and Evvie at the dinner you missed. It was footsies under the table time." Ben took a step back at the image. He didn't even want to go there. But now Moira was poking him teasingly in the ribs. "By the way, why did you really pass on dinner that night? After you got Tash's mother involved? That wasn't like you at all. Now 'fess to Moira." She put her face up close to his, her smile just a little too knowing. "I'll bet you and that lovely girlfriend of yours wanted to celebrate without us old bats around. Frankly, I don't blame you. Would have done the same thing if I were you. But your mom was more hurt than she let on. I hope you've found a way to make it up to her."

Ben had always suspected Moira was a witch. Something about the herbs and the hair and the exaggerated mannerisms. Now, he was sure.

"My mom already let me know how pissed she was. I think that was penance enough."

"You think that's what it's all about? Anger and penance. Did you ever consider that she might have wanted to share a once-in-a-lifetime moment with her only child?"

"Come on! It was no big deal. Aunt Evvie didn't care. She didn't say anything about it, and besides, you're telling me now she had a great old time."

"Maybe that's just the point. I mention your mom, and you immediately talk about Evvie. Have you ever considered that your mother might need some confirmation from you that she has her own place in your heart, as your mother?"

"Mother? What kind of mother is it that deserts her kid as soon as he's born? And what's the point of giving birth to an unwanted child, anyway? Who always knows, no matter what they do or what they accomplish, they're going to end up like shit, because they are shit, and everything they touch turns to shit?"

Moira looked as if he'd slapped her in the face. "Ben, what is it?"

Before he could stop himself, the words were marching out of his lips of their own accord. "I fucked up big time. Tash is pregnant. That's where my bright idea for opening night landed us. In the total shits."

Moira slumped onto the side of the bed. Ben immediately regretted his words. It occurred to him that Moira usually looked half her age. She didn't now.

But then, as if by an effort of will, she straightened and motioned him to sit next to her. But she still looked haggard and raw. He felt awful. He let her hook an arm over his shoulder, actually taking some small comfort in the warmth of her touch.

"Listen to me. You're—we're—going to get through this. But you can't weather it alone. As soon as she gets home tomorrow, you've got to tell your mother."

He wrenched away from her. "No way! Tash is one hundred percent determined to have the baby. I can't let her down now. My mom'll want her to get an abortion."

"How in the world do you know that?"

"Oh, come on, don't play naïve. Isn't that what she wanted to do with me?"

"You poor deluded boy." She hesitated. "If you must know, it was your grandfather. He's the one who pushed for an abortion. She'd let her pregnancy get too far along to get one. The only reason she stuck with her plan to go to New York was to learn the skills to support you. Simon Warwick certainly wasn't going to do it, and Miriam wasn't so sure that Michael would come through financially. You know how self-righteous he can be."

"Bullshit. She was only too happy to leave me with Aunt Evvie."

"Oh, Ben. It's true that Evvie was a saint, and let's face it, she flat out adored you. And you're right about Miriam wanting to study at the Fashion Institute very badly. But she also would have loved to work with Gaultier after that."

"Gaultier? What are you talking about?"

"The designer. Jean-Paul Gaultier. He came to the final fashion show of her class at the Institute. Went absolutely gaga for her stuff. Offered her a chance to work directly under him in Paris once she graduated. There were even rumors he wanted to groom her as his eventual successor." Moira's eyes bored into his. "And she said 'no.' She felt it would be a terrible life for a child. And she wouldn't dream of any more separation from you."

"Why didn't I ever hear about this?"

"Because I'm the only one she told. She never wanted you to feel guilty, and believe me, she hasn't regretted her decision for one minute. As for Evvie not knowing, your mom made a judgment call, a wise one, I thought. She figured that if Evvie found out about it, she would have insisted on dropping her own career completely to be your nanny in Paris while Miriam's fortunes soared. She couldn't do that to Evvie. She made me promise never to tell a soul." Moira shrugged. "Your mother may be a little selfish at times, but she can respond like a champ when life gives her a wakeup call."

Ben buried his head in his hands, his voice muffled. "Yeah, but it's pretty shitty that I'm always the one to wake her up."

Twenty-eight

"JUST TRUST ME."

Evvie laughed, looking away from Ezra toward the broad white beach outside the Casa del Mar's opulent lounge. Off to the right, the Santa Monica pier amusement park offered an old-fashioned counterpoint to this art deco renovation of a once-exclusive beach club that had, indeed, once excluded Blacks and Jews.

"I'm telling you, the oysters will just slip down your throat. Anyway, how is it that a woman of the world like you has never even tried them?"

"Woman of the world? The farthest I usually get from West LA is the San Fernando Valley."

"We've got to do something about that. It's a great big world out there."

"For people like you and Beady."

Ezra began twirling the stem of his wine glass, spreading the kiss of condensed liquid between the glass and the polished wood table. He stared out the window for a moment, barely registering the sun's flamboyant decline.

"You know what really scares me? Ignorance. How in the hell are we going to survive if nobody pays attention to the fact that half the planet is trying to kill off the other half? For Christ's sake, more than seven million people were either killed or driven from their homes last year by war, domestic insurgencies, or political repression. It's a miracle there's anyone left." He stopped. "Forgive me. Here we are, finally getting our first time alone together, and I ..."

"And you've got some kind of courage in your genes that I didn't inherit."

"You've got it all wrong there. My parents are pretty simple people. Their idea of a good time is to rent a video and bring home Chinese takeout on a Saturday night. I always figured it was the Jewish thing. Never knowing when the next Holocaust would hit. But that didn't stop your father from going public with his art and politics. So, you can hardly use the excuse of genetics."

"No, you're right. Both my parents were courageous. My mom was one of the original Freedom Riders. But you know, there's more than one kind of fear that can shut you down. I've been sensing lately that my father had his own personal holocaust that I don't think he's ever recovered from." She hesitated, tempted to tell him about her dreams, but thought better of it. "Or even acknowledged. Oh, I don't know. It's so easy to sit back and judge someone else for how they've handled their suffering. When I think of how much more self-involved I've become since the cancer ..."

Ezra leaned back in his oversized rattan chair, which his big frame filled with a vibrant masculine authority. Evvie watched, fascinated, as he managed to balance the chair on its back legs without tipping over. "Sounds to me like a good thing. I have a feeling you've been much too self-sacrificing most of your life."

"And how much do I owe you for that armchair analysis?" She grinned slyly. "And speaking of chairs, I'm very impressed by the rocking maneuver, but there's a waiter struggling to get by behind you."

With a red face, Ezra straightened and apologized to the waiter, who was bearing a tray loaded with exotic-looking drinks and little squared-off bowls of nuts. He grinned at her. "Wise guy, eh? You owe me for that one. How about we split this joint and take a walk to the pier? You can win me a prize in the ring toss."

He stood up and held out his hand, leading her down a staircase that spilled onto the boardwalk.

She stole a sideways glance at him. He looked lost in thought, but she didn't feel alone at all. The sea breeze had fashioned a crazy mop of his black curls, and gooseflesh on his bare arms made the thick mat of hair on them stand up. On the whole, she had to admit that she preferred his frank and earthy roughness to the too-cool-for-school demeanor of Simon, who'd espoused such spiritual purity, but found a way to detach himself as soon as things got tough.

Ezra returned her gaze. "Penny for your thoughts."

"You don't want to know."

"Oh yes, I do. I want to know everything. And feel everything, too." Before she realized what was coming, his lips were on hers, his tongue prying in a way that made fire lick from her thighs to her belly button. The tiny part of her mind that was still functioning sent out a flare of alarm.

Before she knew it, tears were streaming down her cheeks. She stepped back, hiding her face with her hand. "Forgive me. It's not this. I mean, it's not you."

His eyes were dark wells. He pried her hand away from her face and enclosed it in his own, knocking it against his chest with each word. "Don't. Don't ever apologize for your tears. Especially tears of joy. Those, you should thank the Lord for."

She drew back. He knew exactly how much she liked him. She was well and truly fucked.

But there was something she had to ask. "You said, 'the Lord.' Do you believe in God?"

He glanced at her defensively but seemed to recognize that her question was in earnest. He looked pointedly in the direction of the ocean—now a glistening mirror to the rainbow-hued Ferris wheel— then up at the sky, fast transmuting into a velvet tent of the deepest aquamarine. "Do I believe in God?" He pulled her to him and uttered hoarsely, "At this very moment? Am I some kind of idiot? How could I not?" She didn't win the ring toss. Or any other game, for that matter. But they giggled their way through seven circuits of the carousel, threw four quarters into the guitar case of a filthy, but surprisingly sweet-voiced folksinger, and held sticky cotton candy hands at the very top of the neon Ferris wheel. Evvie was short on cash, so Ezra sprang for her trip beyond the beaded curtains of a chain-smoking gypsy for-tuneteller, who had a mole on her lip sprouting three long hypnotic hairs. When the woman announced matter-of-factly that she'd just met the man of her dreams, Evvie figured it was a sign. She brought Ezra back to the condo.

Making love with Ezra wasn't a bit like being with Simon. He seemed as excited by giving her pleasure as getting his own. She had a horrifying moment when he removed her bra, her neck seizing into a rock-hard spasm. Only when he ran a slow finger along the puckered length of her scar, inquiring about her blue sentinel node stain and then kissing it—tenderly, with a mother's booboo-kissing lips—could she breathe again. And then, a sudden urgency compressing the universe into one still point, Ezra was kissing her all over, touching her, tasting her, raising her from the dead.

***

They were alone in the condo. Miriam wasn't due back from her Santa Barbara shoot until tomorrow and Moira had left a note announcing that Ben was feeling much better and that she'd invited him and Natasha to spend a night in her lavish suite at the Four Seasons. How like Moira. Still, Evvie had fastened the chain lock. You never knew.

She felt deliciously decadent, walking around stark naked after their lovemaking. The condo was so quiet she could hear Ezra lift up the toilet seat in her bathroom. She grinned at the sound of his urine hitting the water. Funny how a little thing like that could make you glad you were born. She noticed that Ben hadn't picked up their packet of mail from the floor beneath their mail slot. She ambled over and knelt to retrieve the bundle of letters, casually running an eye over the envelope at the top.

She was so relaxed that, when the panic hit, it hit with a vengeance. Her face draining of all color, she ripped open the envelope. Two items fell out. The first was a terse letter from Sally MacBride. She pictured the hollowness of Sally's gray eyes as she wrote: "Temple has gone to God. I hope He gives her more peace there than she had in this world. I hope you are okay. Can't say that I am, but I guess I'll survive, if that's what you call it. P.S. Temple wrote this for you right before she went to the hospital. I'm sorry, but I was too insane to send it then."

Ah, Fate, you little fucker. You were just waiting in the wings, weren't you, for your perfect moment? Evvie picked up the postcard. It bore a familiar reproduction of Christopher Robin and Winnie the Pooh throwing 'pooh sticks.' Still crouching, she turned it over. On the back, Temple had drawn a plump valentine heart. Evvie had a vision of the bald child bent over the postcard, her pink tongue caught at the side of her mouth as she concentrated on making perfect parallel strokes inside the out-lined heart with her pink pen. And then printing atop the heart in a rainbow arch of violet, blue, green, yellow, orange, and red block let-tering: "U R 2-Good 2-B 4-Got-10."

That was a good one. The rainbow was an especially nice touch—hadn't that been the supposed sign of God's covenant with his chosen people? She looked up at the naked Ezra, who had appeared as if from a cloud and was towering over her, concern written all over his face. At least she thought it looked like concern; he seemed unaccountably blurry. The words tumbled out of her, along with a mounting uncon-trolled giggling. "I guess she just wasn't one of the chosen ones. Now isn't that a hoot?"

She felt herself being hauled awkwardly onto her feet. As if they had a life of their own, her fists made repeated contact with his chest. Someone was screaming. When his open hand made stinging contact with her cheek, everything stopped. The noise. The wild agitation. The blur.

She took her hand away from her burning cheek and bent down to pick up the letter. Wordlessly, she handed it to him and watched the lines of pain in his face deepen as he read it. Whatever she had felt for him a few minutes ago had been replaced by a curious sense of detach-ment. She found herself noticing flaws in his face and naked flesh. How had she missed the blackheads on his nose, the coarse pores across his cheeks, the spare tire beginning to burgeon around his mid-section, how disproportionately over-developed his calves were? He had a large pimple on his right hip, and the hair all over his body, wasn't it just a little too simian?

She looked down at her own nakedness. It was like she was cov-ered by some eerily hairless animal hide. Without speaking, she turned and walked purposefully toward her bedroom. She brought Ezra's clothes out to him. "I think you'd better go."

"Evvie, I can't leave you like this."

She shook her head. "Please. Just go."

"Evvie, love, I can't just … this is awful … Can I call your sister for you? Are you sure?"

But she was already at her bedroom door. She locked it behind her before roughly pulling her nightgown down from its hook and yanking it over her head.

Twenty-nine

MOIRA STARED AT Ben and Tash, sitting stiffly on opposite sides of her hotel room's king-sized bed, each of them looking positively funereal.

"Look, kids. I know it seems like the end of the world, but we'll sort this out. I'm sure Natasha's folks'll come around, and I know for a fact that Miriam will back you up, whatever you want to do. Couples who both work have families, so there's no reason why two full-time students can't. And with the kind of grades you have, there's no question you could both get into UCLA. Tash, I'm sure they have a perfectly fine art department there."

Tash, wearing hip-hugger jeans and one of those crop tops that left little to the imagination, folded her arms in front of her, as if the baby were already showing. Moira issued a silent prayer. Please let the girl remove that belly button ring before too long. She had a horrible fantasy of the baby being born by someone pulling Natasha's silver ring, like popping the cork of a piggy bank.

Moira excused herself to use the toilet. The bathroom was deliciously decadent, everything—including its huge Jacuzzi bathtub—paneled in cherrywood, with "his and hers" peacock-painted porcelain sinks scooped from a wide marble counter. But even the flattering lighting surrounding its beveled mirror couldn't soften the twin lines harshly etched between her eyes, the incipient jowls just beginning to detract from her cleft chin. She realized she didn't give a shit. Not really. The tyranny of being beautiful was getting boring. She splashed her face with cold water and, taking a deep breath, opened the door.

Ben and Tash still sat as if separated by some invisible Berlin Wall. Moira ran a hand through her hair. "Look. Let's walk through this again. Tash, you're absolutely sure you want to have this baby?"

Tash gave a curt nod.

"And Ben, you love Tash and want to marry her and bring up your child together? God, listen to me. I sound like a minister."

The smile died slowly on her lips. Nobody was laughing. Ben threw a pleading look at his girlfriend.

Tash, who'd been avoiding his gaze, suddenly faced him. "Yeah, but the baby'll be a burden for you, right? How can you be a good father to a kid who feels like a burden?"

Ben flushed with anger. "You think I'm just like my father, don't you? Some unfeeling asshole who wouldn't totally fall in love with his own kid? Christ, Tash, how could I not want a baby with the girl I love so much I'd die for her?"

Moira flinched. "Oh, come on, now. This isn't about death. Not about burdens, either. It's about love and relationship and creative problem solving." She began pacing the room, struggling for clarity. "Let's face it. You're scared shitless. And you know what? That's a good thing. Anybody who's thinking about having a kid should have a healthy amount of apprehension. Whoever we are, and whatever we're doing, we're doing it for the first time. Lord knows, you wouldn't be the first couple starting out a little young because of an accidental pregnancy." Her face softened. "You'll need a lot of support, and I swear to you, you'll get it. I know it's fashionable to make fun of her, but Hillary Clinton was right. It does take a village." She laughed. "And let's face it, if there's one thing old lefties do well, it's the village thing."

Moira studied their faces. Could it be she was getting through? She'd persuaded Ben to bring Tash to the hotel because she'd hoped to convince the girl to get an abortion. But it turned out that Tash had a mind of her own that reminded Moira of Miriam at the same age. Tash had put it pretty bluntly. "I know it sounds totally un-PC, but I'd be killing something inside me if I offed my own baby. It's not like I'm some martyr. I just couldn't do it to my feelings. To my body. To me."

Very lovely, but personally, Moira thought that Tash was being way too idealistic. These kids had no idea how much life itself, with its inevitable profusion of inner and outer conflicts, forced you to trash your precious feelings a million times before you died. But she wasn't about to try and play God. For all she knew, this was the first and last child the girl would ever conceive.

Watching Tash let Ben enfold her in a husky embrace, Moira began to breathe a bit more deeply. This old wise woman role was new for her. The whole thing had been an unbelievable strain. But then her cellphone rang. Frowning, she strode across the room and grabbed it. Who could possibly be calling at this hour?

At first, she thought it was a crank call. The words were so garbled. But then she realized it was Evvie—Evvie as she'd never heard her before.

"Evvie, what is it? Slow down. I'm so sorry to hear about Temple. But wait, I'm not following you. What is it about your father?" She tried to breathe. "You called the ambulance? All right, I'm closer to Wonderland Avenue than you are. If we're not at his house when you get there, meet us at Cedars."

***

Michael looked up anxiously as Moira rushed into his bedroom. "You. You shouldn't have to be here." His forehead was beaded with sweat. She put a hand on his bare shoulder. It was clammy to the touch. His pajamas were strewn on the floor, as if he'd feverishly shed them.

Where in the hell were the paramedics? She shouted down the hall to Ben to call them again. She didn't like how glassy Michael's eyes looked, nor the gray tinge to his face.

"Don't worry about me, Mike. How much pain are you in? Did you take an aspirin?"

She fished frantically in his medicine cabinet and flew back with the pill. He obediently opened his mouth, and she placed it at the back of his tongue. Luckily, he had a glass of water on his bedside table. "Just a little bit. Swallow? Good. Now, I don't want you to sit up, but do you think we can slip a pajama top around your shoulders?"

221

He looked down. He had a crinkled photograph in his lap. His words came out in breathy spurts. "Did you mind?"

"What?" Straining to pull him forward, she hastily slid one sleeve onto his arm. Where the fuck were the paramedics?

"That you couldn't…"

"Oops-a-daisy." She'd managed to get the other arm in its sleeve. Now for the bottoms. He was such a proud man. He'd be humiliated to have Ben and Tash see him naked.

"That you couldn't replace Riva."

She glanced down at the photo in his lap and felt a frisson of recognition. She knew that Dick Shea had taken the picture at Cedars in 1960, catching a moment of pure joy. An astonishingly handsome young Michael was leaning across a hospital bed to plant a kiss on the cheek of his first wife, who gazed in wonder at the newborn baby in her arms. Evvie was wrapped up like a little papoose. Her munchkin face was crowned by an astoundingly profuse aureole of curly black hair, and her already soulful eyes were locked onto her mother's as if they beheld the Holy Grail.

"Of course not." It hadn't been Riva she'd been threatened by, but the ghost of Golda Starekova and the trail of bitterness left in her wake. Once the bloom had fallen from Michael's infatuation with Moira, Michael had regularly used that ghastly pogrom as the centerpiece to his rant that the bastards always won out in the end.

As she threw back the top sheet and struggled to coax the pajama bottoms up her ex-husband's frail old-man legs, it struck Moira how unfair the whole deal was—being shaped by things that happened before you could form a cogent thought. If there were a God, he had to be pretty primitive to come up with such a ridiculous arrangement as that.

Thirty

SWOLLEN-EYED AND yawning, Evvie squinted at her wristwatch. Jesus. Three a.m., and this capacious barn of a restaurant was nearly filled. At least the young Adonises and Persephones who giggled and flirted at the other tables had the excuse of sheer youth for being out so late. It certainly wasn't hers.

After being kicked out of Cedars' Cardiac Intensive Care Unit several terrified hours after an ambulance had delivered her father to the ministrations of the ICU staff, she and the rest of her exhausted family had ended up meeting Miriam at funky Canter's Deli by default, having found the more upscale Jerry's even more jammed to the rafters with youthful émigrés from the city's club scene.

The Intensive Care Unit had been jammed itself. Evvie had only agreed to leave after a sequence of nurses reaffirmed that Michael was stable and needed to be left to sleep. But the clincher had been the head nurse's woman-on-the-edge warning that something dire would happen if there were too much emotional action in the ICU. Even then, Evvie had tried arguing with the staff, but the fact that another man, an ancient rabbi, was actually dying in the unit didn't exactly help her cause. His family of what looked to be about a dozen adult children and four times as many grandchildren, along with scores of quietly *davening* members of his synagogue, were congesting the halls and ICU waiting area like an attack of summer ants.

Evvie glanced across the table at her sister. Miriam looked about as bad as she felt. Thank God she'd had the wits to ask one of the unit drivers to bring her here from her gig in Santa Barbara. In the shape she was in, she probably would have driven her car right over the cliff into the Pacific.

Miriam's driver had one of those classic corn-fed faces. He looked about as relaxed in this deli as a Mormon missionary at a Grateful Dead concert. He'd had the good grace to insist on sitting at another table. Evvie watched his protuberant pink-hued ears work up and down like little lobster claws as he gnawed away at a thick corned beef sandwich.

They were halfway into their own voluminous portions of food before her sister actually registered Tash's presence. Evvie watched her rake her eyes over the girl, who sat silently at Ben's side with one of Moira's shawls wrapped around her.

Miriam turned to Ben. "What's *she* doing here?" Then, as if she hadn't realized how rude she sounded, she compounded her felony by asking Tash, "Aren't you hot in that thing?"

Ben's face went beet red. "How can you talk like that?" He slid a protective arm over his girlfriend's shoulder and whispered something in her ear.

Miriam looked around the table. "Am I missing something?"

Evvie stared blankly back at her. What was the big deal? So, what if the two teenagers had been together when they'd all learned of Michael's heart attack? Was that a crime?

But Ben looked like he was going to be sick. He drew a deep breath before declaring, "You might as well know now. Everything's going to shit anyway."

Evvie looked at him apprehensively, noticing out of the corner of her eye that Tash was rolling her eyes at him and Moira was slicing her hand in the air like some uptight orchestral conductor.

The bones of Miriam's neck were sticking out like an old woman's. "What else could be going to shit as much as your grandfather having a heart attack?"

Evvie had an idea or two on that score, but she wasn't about to bring up Temple's death right now.

"I'm going to be a father. Tash is pregnant with our baby."

Ben's words came out so baldly that it took a moment for any of them to react. They'd also been fairly loud. The tables around them fell silent.

Evvie knew now what people meant by an out-of-body experience. It was as if she'd been launched like a helium balloon to the restaurant's cheaply tiled ceiling. She observed the scene below with an uncanny neutrality. There was so much energy concentrated at their table that it might have been the nuclear core of the universe.

Ben wrapped his arms around a now weeping Tash.

Miriam took her silent, eyebrows-arched case to where Evvie's body sat, despite her spirit still floating above. "Tell me this is some weird, inappropriate adolescent humor."

Moira shot her a warning look.

Miriam stood abruptly, her chair rasping the linoleum like shark's teeth, and staggered over to her driver, who was staring intently down at his plate.

"Frank, I want you to take me home."

Evvie landed back in her seat and realized she was trembling uncontrollably. She sensed a presence hovering just behind her. She turned, and their waitress hesitantly proffered her bill. Evvie gave her the ghost of a smile. "God. I guess you wouldn't mind us getting our soap opera out of here." She fished feverishly in her purse, then looked up with a blank expression. "Anybody got some money? My wallet's gone, and, I don't see my cell phone or organizer, either. Jesus, could I have lost everything at Cedars?"

***

Not nearly enough hours later, it was as if some sneaky God had installed in each of their brains a set of synchronized alarm clocks.

The jangling duet of Miriam's high-pitched titters and Moira's early morning ex-smoker's laugh grated against Evvie's reluctant wakefulness. With considerable effort, she raised her head. She tugged her pillow to her chest and molded its plump contours against her body. What the fuck were they laughing at? They sounded like a couple of kids on a sleepover. She herself had slept intermittently. Having peeked into Miriam's room a little past midnight to see Moira cradling her sister in the bed like a baby, she figured Moira had decided to spend the night. But laughter? Now?

She heard Ben's toilet flush and then his heavy footsteps striding down the hall. She held her breath, picturing him marching out of their lives forever, until she caught the reassuring suction-breaking *whup* of the refrigerator door opening and the sounds of Ben caught in a sneezing fit. She waited for Miriam to call out, "Get a tissue, for heaven's sake," but heard instead Moira's hearty, "Up already?" followed by Miriam's faltering, "Sweetie, I know we need to talk, but I think we'd better call the hospital first, don't you?"

Jesus, Evvie thought, *I'm really losing it. My father!*

She picked up her bedside phone just as the Cedars' operator was putting Miriam through to the ICU nurse's station.

"He's holding stable, Ms. Kerr. We're all very heartened. Why don't you take your time this morning? I'm sure none of you got much sleep last night. With any luck, Doctor Shapiro will downgrade his condition to serious sometime today."

Evvie lifted her eyes to the ceiling. *Thank you, God. And please, please don't let him be in too much pain.* Her hand went to her breast. Her scar had begun to throb. In spite of Dr. Manning's assurance that this was pretty much par for the course with keloids—sensitivity to the touch and aching on their own from time to time —she herself was of the opinion that her scar was an invisible umbilicus to the people she cared about.

It hit her then, like a Cossack's boot in the belly, how terrified her father must be. The staff at Cedars would be viewing him as just another patient, lucky to be alive at his age. What did they know of the universe of experience inside that withered skin? What *could* they know of his struggles, his history?

Pushing herself out of bed, she prayed fervently that her father's failing heart would hold out a little longer. *Lord, I can't take another loss. Not now.*

She'd been fighting for months not to blame God for what had happened to her, but what if her father were right? What if there was no God, after all? Or maybe God was just the sum total of what the Fates threw our way. If there *was* a God, she prayed He wouldn't give her any more shit to contend with for a while.

But God must have been occupied elsewhere. The doorbell rang, and within seconds she picked out other voices joining her family's in a noisy clamor: Beady, Tony, and—oh no, it couldn't be, but it was—Ezra Rosenberg. Fuck. She threw herself onto her duvet and stuck a pillow over her head.

By the time she finally forced herself out of her room, wearing a pair of unwashed jeans, a wrinkled turquoise blouse, and a heavy set of bags under her red-rimmed eyes, Ben had already escaped with Tony into his room, and Beady and Moira were excusing themselves to whip up some breakfast. Which left Miriam and Ezra standing together in the hall. Miriam's back was turned to her, so she couldn't see the bitter expression with which Evvie watched her fling herself into Ezra's arms. Evvie turned away in disgust and headed for the kitchen.

Moira and Beady were murmuring together in low tones. They looked up guiltily when she entered the room. She figured they'd been talking about her, but she didn't care. Her mouth tasted like garbage. She stalked over to the Sub-Zero, found some orange juice, and took a slug straight from the carton. She swiped a hand across her mouth. "Right. I'm off to see Dad."

Moira arched a caustic eyebrow. "Good morning to you, too." Then she murmured in a placating tone, "Listen, we just talked to the hospital. Praise God, he's okay." She made the sign of a cross on her chest. "I promise. We can all go after breakfast."

"I know about the call—I listened in. But, really, how can you guys think of him lying there, helpless, while you're pigging out on lox and cream cheese?"

"Dear heart, I know you're upset, but let's be logical. We'll probably spend the whole day with your father. Don't you think it might be wise to get a little sustenance inside you first? So, you can really be there for him? Besides, you're still in a healing process yourself."

Evvie responded bitingly, "Really? I hadn't noticed." She did, however, register that Moira had evidently dressed as hurriedly as she had. Her olive silk pants clashed with the Kelly-green threads in her turtleneck sweater, and her dark tresses were barely held together by their tortoise shell clip as she whirled toward the cutting board and began fiercely dismembering a tomato.

Evvie was less aware of Beady, silently sizing her up. Now her friend glided over and wrapped her slender arms around her. "Honey." Beady's breath was a tickle in her ear. "I'm so sorry about your dad, but it does sound like he's okay for now. Let's just take half an hour to have a bite together. Ezra's here. He really wanted to see you."

Before Evvie could respond, Miriam swept into the room, followed by a guilty-looking Ezra.

Evvie couldn't help but notice the barely suppressed excitement on her sister's face.

"Good morning, Evvie." Ezra's voice was strained.

She couldn't—daren't—look at him. Instead, she directed her words in an obtuse angle over the side of his head and out the kitchen window, marveling—as she returned a muted "Good morning" back to him—that the sun had risen as if nothing had happened.

Before she knew it, he was at her side. "God, Evvie, this is too much for one human being. I hardly know what to say."

He seemed oblivious of Miriam, crossing the kitchen toward them. To Evvie, the single-mindedness of her expression seemed menacing.

But Moira was taking hold of her sister's elbow. "Miriam, dear, will you help me set the table?" Beady looked only too relieved to follow them out of the kitchen.

Ezra hadn't taken his eyes off her.

She flushed. "Shit. I'm not going to be able to avoid you any more than I can avoid … I can't …"

He leaned in so close she could smell the coffee on his breath. Tenderly, he brushed away her tears with his fingertips. "Evvie, maybe you just think you can't. What if you actually had someone rooting with you for your father's recovery? Sharing your grief over Temple? Over what's happened to *you*?"

She wanted to take his hand and hold it, hard, against her cheek. But, instead, she flung it away. "You don't get it. I'm not like other people. I can't open up like you want me to. I'm a bottomless pit. Whatever you think you have to offer would never be enough."

"Is that what you think?"

"It's what I know."

"What happened between us last night? Wasn't I enough then?"

She just stared at him. She couldn't let herself melt. She didn't know exactly why—only that it felt like her life depended on it.

"No," she said flatly. "You weren't enough. But I'll wager you'll be more than enough for my sister Miriam."

He stared at her in disbelief, then turned on his heel and left the room. Moments later, she heard the front door slam.

She told herself she was a fool to be shocked that he'd left without saying goodbye.

***

Evvie realized that Moira had been right. They did end up spending the whole day, and then some, at the hospital. Michael was still wearing an oxygen mask when they arrived, not quite able to breathe on his own. He was dozing most of the time, but every once in a while, his eyes would flick open, and she'd wipe his clammy brow with what she hoped was a reassuring smile. During his bouts of sleep, she dredged up every memory of him she could, as if she were cramming for some cosmic final exam.

It was as if each memory of him had been registered, not just in her mind, but in her body. She felt again the fullness in her flat, little-girl chest when earnest-faced grown-ups crowded her family's living room to hear her daddy talk about social justice. She recalled her earliest scent of him as a male animal. Experienced anew the envious excitation of watching him put his arm around her mother's shoulder, lighting a mysterious flame in her mother's dark eyes. How many times had she heard her father singing along mournfully to Paul Robeson's "Shenandoah," while her mother brushed her hair before bedtime?

Had he been singing to her mother or to her?

The hours of waiting accumulated like a swarm of flies. In her musings, she was a gawky six-year-old, walking hand in hand with her father up one of San Francisco's famous hills, the moment captured by a street photographer, who'd caught her—gap-toothed and goofy—grinning up at the father who must have been more than fifty, but looked a heart-stopping thirty-five. Just a few years later—older, more subdued—she sat between her parents on the couch watching the first moon landing. Despite her dad's predictable rant about the starving people who could have been fed instead, his moist eyes betrayed him, and when Neil Armstrong's feet made bouncing contact with Luna Firma, she'd felt in her gut that she and her father were kindred spirits, filled with the same flat-out awe.

Cedars started to feel like an unwanted second home. Contrary to his doctors' optimistic expectations, her father stalled for several days on the runway of recovery. His vital signs weren't catastrophic, but they didn't begin to improve until day five. By then, the family's vigil had taken a stark toll. Miriam's slenderness had subtracted its way into that kind of icky does-she-have-an-eating-disorder hollowness, and Moira and Evvie had carbohydrate-comforted themselves into the human counterparts of a couple of overstuffed sofas. The weather didn't help any. It was more like London than LA that week.

When Michael's beleaguered body finally won the beachhead of a regular hospital room on the cardiac floor, his relieved clan gathered for dinner at the condo. Even Ben, who'd stunned them all by refusing to go the hospital after the first day.

Moira had whipped up a quick *salade Nicoise* for the four of them, luring Ben into the dining room with the promise of his favorite apple cinnamon crepes for dessert. As they wiped the powdered sugar from their mouths, she propped her elbows on the table and rested her chin on the steeple she'd made with her interlaced fingers.

"It looks as though we're through the worst of this, but, you know, there's a lot of work ahead. Even if he ends up returning to virtually normal, it's going to take a while for Mike to recuperate."

Evvie knew she was right, but Moira was way ahead of her. Evvie's own thinking had slowed to a crawl half a week ago.

"And, of course, we have another family challenge facing us."

Oh, no, do we have to? Now?

"This is what I'm thinking. I'm sure each of you will have your own ideas, but it might help for one of us to start the ball rolling. Mike will probably require actual nursing in the very beginning, but after a week or two, he'll still need a lot of live-in care, to cook for him, get him walking, help him bathe himself. Maybe even use the john." She gave a bright smile. "My thought was that I could do it." She scanned their faces, each of which bore some measure of disbelief. "I know it sounds like an unusual arrangement, but, really, hardly anyone knows your father's little quirks and habits better than I do. You know he'd be a bear with a stranger. "And"—Evvie sensed now that the real clincher was coming—"once he's a little better, Ben and Tash could take the other two bedrooms in his house. Lord knows, it's just wasted space right now."

Miriam's face had gone a shade of purple Evvie had never seen before. Her voice was pure vitriol. "You've thought of every angle, haven't you? It's good, Moira, just terrific. Especially since I'm certainly not going to have a couple of babies trying to raise a baby in my house."

Evvie felt her face grow hot, and, sure enough, she found herself snapping, "Wait a minute. Your house? Is it just your name on the mortgage? You think I might rate a vote, too, on what happens here?"

"I'm sorry, but there's no way I'm going to have a couple of kids playing house together— *la di da*, isn't this fun?—then freaking out the first time the baby screams or has an attack of diarrhea."

"Why's that? Because they might need you? You have to admit it would be something of a novelty—actually helping to care for an infant."

Miriam took a full minute to respond. "You know, I've been biting my tongue, trying to give you some slack ever since you got cancer. Kept telling myself it was natural for you to become completely self-involved. I didn't realize you'd turned into a total bitch, too."

Ben hurtled up from his chair, blocking his ears with his hands. "Stop it! Stop hurting each other. This is all my fault. I've ruined everybody's life with this fucking baby."

Miriam was quick to take him up on it. "Then why don't you try to persuade your precious little girlfriend to have an abortion?"

Ben directed a meaningful look at Moira, as if to say, "See? I told you."

Evvie sat very still. "There's no such thing as a 'fucking baby.' Not in this family. Not anywhere."

Miriam burst into tears. "Oh, God. Of course, there isn't. Don't you think I know that?" She turned a pleading face to her son. "This isn't about me, really it isn't. It's just that I had such dreams for you, Ben. That you'd be free to taste life fully before settling down. Have chances I didn't. Is that so much to ask? Isn't that what every parent wants for her child?" Her gaze drifted to Moira. "He doesn't even know who he is yet."

Ben stared at her, his fists clenched.

Evvie intervened before he could speak. "I don't know if any of us do. I certainly don't know who the hell I'm supposed to be anymore. You're right, Miriam, I have been pretty self-obsessed lately. But what about you—fooling around with one pretty boy after another as if *you* were the seventeen-year-old? And Moira? I don't know what you think you've been doing, futzing around up north when everybody you love is down here. So here we are. Fate did a little matchmaking between Tash and Ben. Wasn't it John Lennon who sang about life intruding when you're busy making other plans?" Her voice shook. "There's something I haven't told you. Remember Temple? I got a letter last week. She died. No more future. Nothing to stress over. *Nada*. Five years old, a spirit as kind and true as an angel, and just like that, she's gone. Maybe there's something fated about Ben bringing a child into the world right now, with Temple going out, and Dad ..."

Miriam stuck out her chin. "Dad's not going to die. They said he's going to come out of this just fine."

"Come on. You know we're on notice. Contrary to what we've all believed, he really isn't God. He won't live forever. Maybe it's a kind of karmic justice that the next generation of Kerrs is preparing to come into the world at this time."

Miriam shuddered. "Christ, how did life get so heavy all of a sudden?"

"All of a sudden?" Evvie's laugh was harsh. "Welcome to reality, dear heart. You've just joined the rest of us on planet Earth. Maybe the change of scene'll do you good."

***

That night, Evvie was squeezing the dregs of a tube of Crest onto her toothbrush when Miriam opened the door to their shared bathroom. They saw each other's startled faces in the vanity mirror. Miriam mumbled, "Sorry," and turned to leave.

Evvie managed to lurch forward and grab her sister's elbow. "No. I can do this later. We should talk." She gestured toward the toilet. "Do you need to pee first?"

Miriam's eyes flashed, but she kept her voice down, clearly concerned that Ben or Moira might hear. "Oh, please. I'm not five years old, and you're not my fucking mother. You don't have to ask me if I need to pee, for God's sake. You take care of your needs. I'll take care of mine."

Evvie's voice was drier than dust. "You know, you're right. If only I'd applied that advice years ago."

"What do you mean?"

"I should have let you have it when you took my lover to your bed."

Miriam took a step back, eyes wide. "How dare you."

"How dare I what, Miriam? Speak about that dirty little secret—your unbelievable selfishness? You had to have everything, didn't you? Moira's adoration. Dad's favoritism. Being the pretty one, the talented one, the one who everybody gravitated to. You just couldn't stand it, could you? That I actually had something special of my own for once. You just had to take that, too."

Miriam nervously twirled a lock of hair. "Evvie, that's not how it was. You and Simon were winding down by the time that he and I …"

"When did you come up with that one? Before or after you fucked him?"

"Come on, Evvie, this is totally unfair. If you were still going strong with him, why in the world didn't you say something?"

"Why should I have to? You knew he was my boyfriend."

Miriam gave her a helpless look. She fled the bathroom and collapsed onto her bed. Evvie was right behind her, an avenging Fury. She halted, arms akimbo, in front of Miriam's dresser, which was covered with photographs of the two sisters from every stage of their lives.

Evvie coldly eyed Miriam, who had curled into a tiny ball in the middle of the bed. She could almost smell her shame.

But suddenly, Miriam sat up. "Wait a minute. Something about this isn't right. If it was as simple as me stealing your wonderful boyfriend, why the hell *didn't* you just say so? Who were you protecting? Me? Him?" She nearly spat out the words, "Or you?"

Evvie thought she had a lot of nerve, but her heartbeat quickened. "What do you mean?"

"I don't even know what I mean, but there was something else going on when I got together with Simon besides me being a selfish sixteen-year-old. Something about you. Something kept you from fighting for Simon Warwick. What was it, Evvie? Think about it. I dare you."

In spite of herself, Evvie did. She felt around inside her head the way you probed a loose tooth. She licked, and she pushed, and she levered. And what finally broke free made her slump against the dresser. She glanced guiltily at Miriam. Her sister's face was scored with tears.

The truth wasn't simple. It was unbelievably twisted and complicated. Miriam's challenge had thrown her back to the moment right before Miriam and Simon had first met. Simon was kissing Evvie in the car, and she, and she ... was dying inside ... hating being kissed, loving being kissed, not quite able to ignore the little signal in the pit of her stomach that the kiss was her payment for allowing him to use her father's house—her father's house!—as a warehouse for storing the weed he was planning to sell. And then Miriam had waltzed up to the car, perfectly prepared to accept Simon's worship as she did their father's love. And something dark in Evvie, not just her resignation, but something far more pernicious, let Miriam have that snake of a man because she'd sensed he would find a way to let her sister down, too.

Evvie ruefully shook her head. "God forgive me for thinking of myself as smarter than you. You're right, you know. I knew he'd break your heart. What I didn't know was that you'd get Ben out of the deal."

Miriam's eyes became vengeful slits. "Well, you made damn sure you didn't get shortchanged that time, didn't you?"

"Miriam, that's not fair. I've loved Ben like he was my ... You can't think everything I've done has been out of selfishness."

"How could I think that? *I'm* the selfish one. That's the drill, isn't it? Miriam's shallow, Miriam's vain. Don't turn to Miriam when it comes to the big stuff, because she's too frivolous, she doesn't have what it takes." Evvie opened her mouth, but Miriam forestalled her with an upraised hand. "You think I haven't felt it? And you—you dumb ass—have made the assumption that everybody thinks I'm the pretty one." She shook her head. "Do you have any idea how many

234

times your precious Simon Warwick told me how intimidated he was by how beautiful you were? Fortunately, Moira did me the favor early on of letting me know I was good looking, so that didn't kill me too much. But, honestly, Evvie, how do you think it's felt to always be looked at as the self-centered one of this family?"

"Fuck the excuses. You should've known better. It was a cruel thing to do."

"I know it was. I can't tell you how sorry I am. All I can say is, I probably thought it would elevate me to some of your exalted status if I could attract a man who'd been interested in you. Come on, exercise some of that psychologist's compassion of yours. Do you have any idea how humiliating it is to be the younger sister of someone so unrelentingly deep and soulful?"

"You must be joking." But Miriam wasn't smiling. Evvie felt her own rage start to dissolve. She flopped onto the bed next to her sister and gently took her spindly arm, stroking it. "Christ, Mir, I'm sorry. For the both of us." Then a shadow crossed her face, and she propped herself up with her elbow. "There's just one thing, though. You'd better keep your hands off Ezra Rosenberg, or I will personally wring your precious little neck."

Thirty-one

HIS BLEAK MOOD aggravated by a wedding party in full swing down-stairs, Ezra sat in a dimly lit hotel room whose stale cigarette odor mocked the prominent no-smoking sign in the hall. He stared blindly at a blank television screen, nursing his third Samuel Adams and a pained grievance against the woman he'd been fool enough to fall in love with. Still, when his cell phone rang, he nearly knocked it to the floor in his hasty reach for the receiver. Could it be?

"Ez, it's Tom."

Damn. "Hey, man, isn't it kind of early for you?"

"Don't worry, I'm not dying or anything. I'm on my mobile, so I'll make it fast in case it cuts out on us."

"What's up?"

"You've got to get your ass over here. Neil Sheldrake called from the Beeb. They want you on it right away. By the way, boyo, he let something else slip. You never told me you were negotiating a contract. Sounds like he's ready to deliver on the deal. I'm creaming with envy. Anyway, I'm on my way to Number Ten right now. What a mess."

"I'm not following you."

"What are you doing over there, living in some kind of bubble? Hey, I didn't catch you in bed with some babe, did I?"

Ezra went silent.

"Ah, hole in one, eh? Well, I hate to spoil your party, but you might consider turning on the TV. Israel's latest clampdown on Hamas has provoked a vicious backlash here. A bunch of synagogues have been torched, and over the last twenty-four hours, a mob's been gathering outside the PM's. It's ugly, man."

"Christ, I had no idea. It's not like it's been all over the news, or anything."

"Why am I not surprised? People in the US don't give a shit about what goes on in the rest of the world unless it directly impacts the US. Anyway, how fast can you get here? Or is the little woman going to put up a fight?"

Ezra reached for a Tums. "Nah."

"Sorry, mate. She must be something special if she's felled the mighty Ezra."

Mighty? More like mewling, cowardly, pathetic. "Listen, tell Neil I'll get over there as soon as I can, but, just between you and me, I might need you to hold him at bay for me. There's one thing I've got to do before I leave."

***

Arriving at Cedars the next morning, Evvie was disappointed to find her father fast asleep. The head nurse had cautioned that he'd been restless most of the night. Evvie stared at him, mesmerized by the faint lifting and falling of the small mound of his chest.

The flesh on his face was taut, and his skin had a deathly translucence to it. It was as if his illness had rendered him back into the rickets-dwarfed child who roamed her nightmare landscapes, an uncomforted ghost. He looked weightless, as if she could just slide one hand under the slight rise at his lower back and lift him into the air.

There was a hush to this room that felt ominously funereal. Hearing a vague rustling behind her, she whirled around.

Ezra stood in the doorway. He looked tentative, uncertain of his welcome. Her heart began to beat far too quickly. She turned back to her father, unnecessarily pulling up the top sheet as she struggled to compose herself. When she turned back around, Ezra was gone.

Panic overtook her. She ran into the hall, but he was nowhere in sight. She rushed to the nurses' station. "Did you see a dark-haired man …?"

He was just getting into the elevator when she found him. "Please. Ezra. Wait. I'm sorry. You came all the way here, and I …"

He stepped back out. His expression was clouded. "How's he doing?"

She tried to still her heart. "They say he's okay, but I'd feel a lot better if I could hear that directly from him."

"I'm sure you would. But it makes sense that he needs lots of sleep right now."

"I guess so, but still …"

"Evvie, I … if there's anything I can do." A tired-looking nurse pushed a medication trolley in their direction, one of her thick-soled shoes unaccountably squeaking with every other step. "Look, can we go somewhere a little more private for just a minute? It's just … I've been called out of the country, and I want to … I have something for you."

She led him out of the building onto the windy third-floor pedestrian bridge between the hospital and Cedars' twin outpatient towers. Strong gusts uncurled Ezra's hair and pushed it up and out to one side. Evvie had to lean close to his lips to hear what he said.

"I've been called back to London for a gig. Who knows how long I'll be out there. The BBC has made me an offer that's pretty tempting." She stared at him, uncomprehending. "Anyway, I'll be bunking at my pal Tom's place until I know what's what. Beady's been there. She knows where it is. When your dad gets better, I kind of hoped …"

That was it. He was leaving. She rubbed her bare, goosefleshed arms. She sensed him wanting to reach out to her, but she kept him away with a sharp look. "Oh, Ezra, Ezra." She gave a hollow laugh. "Ezra Rosenberg. You know what I thought of when I first heard your name? The Rosenberg children. When I was little, I was terrified I'd lose my parents just as they had. Being a Red Diaper Baby in the sixties wasn't easy. I felt so alone. You sure you're not Ethel and Julius' son?"

Ezra took her hand and held it lightly. "Evvie, you don't have to be alone. Give me the word, and I'll tell them to find somebody else …"

It was as though he were speaking another language, a freewheeling patois she'd been forbidden to utter. Her heart ached with the temptation of it, but the habit of constraint was too strong. "Don't be

239

ridiculous. We barely know each other. Of course, you must go." She pulled her hand away.

His face went slack with resignation, and he stared at the ground. She saw that he had a weather-beaten briefcase with him. Now he knelt down and carefully unbuckled it, holding something out to her as he straightened.

"I've got a little going away present for you."

"I'm not going anywhere."

"I noticed." Then he urged his gift onto her, softening his tone. "But I am. Here. Beady told me you lost yours."

It was a finely crafted oversized wallet, made of elegant brown leather. She played it over and over in her hands, caressing its sleek surface. When she looked up again, he was already walking away. From the back, he could be a doctor, briskly heading off to his day's worth of patients.

"Ezra!" He looked back. She gave him a silly wave with her fingers. "Thank you. And … take care of yourself."

He nodded once, then turned and stepped through the automatic doors.

The wind was stinging her eyes. What else could it be but the wind? She started to shove the wallet into her purse when something sliced across her palm, giving her a nasty paper cut. *What the hell?* The sharp edge of something was protruding from the wallet. Cursing, she pulled it out.

It was a business class ticket issued by British Airways to Evelyn Kerr for return passage from LAX to Heathrow.

A piece of paper had been folded over it. "Evvie," Ezra had written, "when things calm down some, you might like a little change of scenery. I would've made it a one-way ticket, but I didn't want to pressure you too much. Just come. And by the way, signing off with the phrase 'Love, Ezra,' is not a mere figure of speech. You can take it both ways, with and without the comma. Love, Ezra."

The wind pushed her, making a blond froth of her hair, but she held her ground, sucking her cut until the bleeding stopped. Then she inserted the ticket back into the wallet and carefully folded Ezra's note in two. Darting a quick glance around her, she made sure that no one else had entered the bridge. She slipped the paper inside the left cup of her bra, settling it like a snug bandage over her heart. She allowed herself a little smile of satisfaction. She felt like a pre-teen stuffing her bra with cotton, but she didn't care.

But then her worry breezed back from its brief hiatus. What if her father had woken to an empty room? Mentally kicking herself for her selfishness, she sped anxiously back to his bedside, heedless of the small slip of paper, pulsing like the wing of a tiny bird to the drumbeat of her heart.

Thirty-two

OVER THE NEXT several weeks, Michael's medical status shot all over the map. The family began to regard with distaste the generally kind Cedars' nursing staff, whose almost daily revisions of his condition were studded with words like "upgraded" and "downgraded," as if he were an airline passenger about to embark on some doubtful journey. It seemed to Evvie as though her father's body were making up for a lifetime of physical hardiness by developing every possible infection and organ malfunction to which a heart attack victim might fall prey. Mercifully, Michael himself was out of it most of the time, only the mist inside his ventilator and the sounds of the respirator pump and monitors attesting that he still lived. Evvie couldn't rid herself of the fear that he was cycling through Dantesque layers of some inner hell while his body was pumped with an unending series of drugs. She kept whispering into his ear how much she loved him, how much she needed him, how much she always had.

But her father was a very old man. While his sturdy spirit fought successive waves of insults like the Red Army at the Russian front, he was contending with a more implacable winter than Rokossovsky's forces. Inch by miserable inch, his beleaguered body lost ground.

It went on long enough that they took to staying with him in shifts. The bills, after all, still had to get paid. There came a time, though, when, no matter what Evvie was doing, she had one ear just waiting for the dreaded call that Michael had finally lost his war.

When it came, she discovered she was completely unprepared.

She had just concluded her latest round of peace talks between Millie Stone and Sarah Weitzmann and had collapsed as much as possible into her desk chair. The cell phone was right beside her. It was in her hand before it finished its first ring. It was Aurelia Balaban, the family's favorite ICU nurse. "Evvie, you and your family had better get here. I have to say I think it's time."

Alerted by some sixth sense, Maggie Rimes materialized at the doorway. Evvie's hand was trembling so much that Maggie had to step forward to take the phone from her and set it down. Evvie slumped against her desk. "Oh, God, Mag, my dad's dying. I can't believe it. Will you be all right here? I don't know how long I'll be gone." She knew she needn't have asked.

Maggie gave her arm a quick squeeze. "Just drive carefully. Promise."

Drive? Now that it came to it, Evvie felt like she barely remembered how to put one foot in front of the other to walk out of the room.

"Oh, Mother of Jesus. Catch your breath a second. Do you want me to call the rest of your family?"

Some ancient balance restored with the thought of her loved ones, Evvie grabbed her phone and hastily dialed Miriam's number. By the time she unlocked her car door, she'd managed to reach Moira, as well.

They were already at the hospital when she got there. Miriam looked up blankly as Evvie approached the ICU bed, but Moira said, "Thank God, you made it. I was beginning to worry that you wouldn't get here in time." She gestured to Miriam and Ben. "Let's give Evvie a moment with Mike by herself."

The bunched keloid under Evvie's scar throbbed as she stood over her father's bed. He looked like a child playing dead, his arms tucked by his sides like a little soldier. She bent down to kiss his soft, worn hand, and held on to it tightly as she spoke to him through her tears. "Daddy, I love you, I don't think you ever knew how much. I know you don't believe in God, and please don't be angry with me, but I hope your soul knows boundless joy where you're going. I wish you could tell me what to do. I met a man a while ago. I think you'd really like him. Oh, Daddy, how am I going to survive with you gone? I wish I could have been a more pleasing daughter to you."

To Evvie's horror, her father fluttered his fingers within her tight grip and managed to loosen his hand entirely from hers.

But then his fingers felt around until he found her hand again, this time enclosing it within his own, giving her three squeezes in emphatic succession.

And then, he let go, his face turning white as a sheet. He was gone.

There was a faint rustling at her side. Evvie turned to see her step-mother. Evvie looked at her and shook her head. Moira began to cry.

Evvie noticed that her father's arm was hanging down the side of his bed. She carefully replaced it alongside his inert body. On a sudden impulse, she put her first and second fingers together, touched her father's hand with them, then solemnly pressed them to her lips. Moira raised her eyebrows, curious. Evvie said simply, "It's what they do with the Torah."

Then she knelt by the side of her father's bed and prayed.

***

That night, Evvie dreamed of her father again. Except he wasn't a little boy this time, but a grown man, looking wise and strong, as he had last year. Her father was standing on a strangely still plain, so vast that it extended beyond the horizon in every direction. It was just the two of them there, and they were facing each other. Her father was holding a parcel, wrapped in a woven fabric glistening with golden threads. He reached inside and thrust its contents into her hands.

She stepped back with the weight of it, cringing in disgust and dismay. What he'd given her was big and gloppy and viscous, a quivering, pulsing thing, and somehow she knew that it was her own heart. Her father smiled sadly at her and refused to take it back. "Evvie," he said, and she cried out in her sleep, because even in her dream she knew he shouldn't be talking. He was already dead. "Evvie," he insisted, "you have a beautiful heart."

She woke with a start and sat up, breathing heavily. She had the faintest sense of someone in the room with her and squinted, trembling, into the darkness, seeking her father's ghost.

But there was nothing. Nothing but the memory of her father enclosing her hand with his own.

Thirty-three

THE DAY AFTER they buried her father, Evvie curled under layers of rumpled bedclothes while Beady stretched out her long legs on top of the covers. The rest of the crew were in the kitchen, cleaning up piles of dirty dishes left over from the small gathering following Michael's interment by the side of his first wife at Mt. Sinai.

The more public memorial service befitting a man of Michael's stature, with Dick Shea the main speaker, would be held in a month or so. That would hopefully be enough time for Moira to pack up all her possessions and put her house in Berkeley on the market, and for Evvie and Miriam to sort through the accumulated remains of a lifetime on Wonderland Avenue before Moira and the two teenagers moved in. The redecorating would have to take place quickly. Miriam and Moira were already collecting magazines and catalogues, from *Architectural Digest* to *Baby Gap Home*, and would no doubt be lingering in *futzing*-with-design-heaven until the moment the baby was born.

Evvie's eyes were red-ringed from non-stop crying. She'd gotten so good at grieving she could talk, do a whole host of chores, even laugh while an endless river of tears riddled her face.

The weather was turning chilly. Evvie tugged her new blanket from Moira up from the foot of the bed, so that its forest green fringe just covered her breasts. "I don't know. Don't you think it's a little psychotic?"

"What's psychotic about it?"

"I can't just leave my whole life, my work …"

"Just think about trying it for a year. You'll even be back for a few days for the Memorial. It's not the Ten Commandments. You don't have to etch it in stone. Surely Maggie can hold down the fort for at least that long. You've told me how much you've come to rely on her …"

"But Ben …"

"Ben's going to go through what he's going to go through, whether you're here or not. You can't put your body between him and all of his train wrecks."

"Jesus, what an image. I feel like I'm leaving the whole family facing the monster of all wrecks."

"C'mon, Evvie. Let them sort out a few things without you. Exercise their own coping skills for a change. They've been taking you for granted forever. Time to leave the plantation, honey. Let Miss Scarlett clean up her own shit."

"Beady! That's not why I'm thinking of going."

"It's still altruism all the way for you? Not even an eensy-weensy smidgeon of self-interest here?"

"For heaven's sake, is everybody in my life bent on educating me on my less-than-saintliness? I guess you're right, at least a little. The idea of so much freedom sounds utterly intoxicating. This could be a new start on a lot of levels."

"But your daddy, God rest his righteous soul, wouldn't have been so big on the level that starts with s and ends with x, right?"

Evvie thought about that one for a moment, then burst into a fresh bout of tears. "Oh, Beady, you've got it all wrong. I think my father wanted more for me than I ever knew."

"Well, then, if even Michael Kerr would have approved, what the hell are you waiting for?"

It wasn't just Beady who was encouraging her to go. When Evvie broached the subject to Moira, her stepmother was thrilled. They were standing at the curb of the United Airlines terminal at LAX. Moira was on her way back home to pack up her things.

Moira gave a wild shriek, dropped her Prada overnight bag onto the sidewalk and wrapped her arms around her, nearly lifting her off her feet. Waves of Chanel No. 5 assailed Evvie's nostrils. "Darling, that's the best idea I've heard in years. When are you going?" But then, as if something had just occurred to her, she pushed her away to arm's length and subjected her to a scrutinizing gaze.

"What?"

Moira ruffled her curly locks. "The hair. Charming, but it'll have to go."

Evvie, who could think only of Temple, stepped back in horror. "What do you mean?"

"I mean, my dear girl, that there probably won't be too many decent hairdressers in Kosovo, or Macedonia, or wherever the hell you're going. You'd end up with those disgusting roots ..." She patted her own wavy black head. "I ought to know. And, with a man in the picture now, that will never do. You'll have to go back to dark brown."

When Evvie returned home from the airport, Miriam was sitting cross-legged on the living room floor. She had scores of magazine cuttings spread haphazardly around her feet and was frowning at them as if she were contemplating the fate of the world.

"She get off okay?"

Evvie nodded and dropped down next to her.

Miriam pointed to a photo of a child's bedroom. "I get carried away imagining what a beautiful room we're going to create, then I remember that this is for Ben's baby. Ben's baby! Evvie, do you really think he's going to be okay? What happens if he and Tash are a terrible match? What if they can't handle the stress of it? How are they going to focus on their studies?"

Evvie stared at her.

"I know. I did it. Thanks to you. And they *will* have Moira. But Moira's ... Well, you know Moira. She's not exactly big on mess and chaos. And while I'd like to be a hands-on grandma, I don't know how much Tash wants me in the picture right now, not after what I said that night." She leaned over and gave Evvie a quick peck on the cheek. "I'm just glad we've all got the expert here to guide us through the scary bits."

Evvie looked down guiltily.

"What's wrong?"

When Evvie told her, Miriam leapt to her feet, hands curled into fists. "You can't. Not now."

"Miriam, you'll do fine. Moira's really into this, and, well, there's the Lems. They've already said they'll help. And you've got Beady. You heard her say she expects to be a very involved godmother."

"Fuck all that. What about Ben? He's going to go nuts having Moira around all the time. You're the only one he'd feel comfortable really turning to with … oh, I don't know … all the stuff he confides in you."

"Wasn't it you who reminded me recently that he's *your* son?"

Miriam's voice was ice. "Fine. But don't think I'm going to be the one to tell him."

It took Evvie a week to summon the courage. She decided to ask Ben to collect her from Fragonard. Her car was getting its six-month servicing, which she figured was a necessity if Moira was going to try to sell it for her, and Beady had dropped her off at the salon on her way to doing some pick-up shots for a Coke commercial. Rather than ask Miriam, who was pretty much giving her the silent treatment these days, she tempted Ben with the trade of a ride from Fragonard for a lunch at Mangiare, one of his favorite West Hollywood restaurants.

As they followed the *maître d'* past the sweeping marble bar onto the terracotta tiled patio, Evvie caught Ben's eye and gave a slight gesture to the right, where Candice Bergen was conversing with a gray-haired man. Ben nodded slightly, looking like a male model in his Levi's and open collared white shirt. It was a running joke in the family that every time they went to Mangiare, there was at least one celebrity dining there.

When they sat down, Ben flashed her a crooked grin. Evvie's heart sank. How was she going to bear being away from him?

A lean waiter handed them their menus, and a young waitress followed on his heels. Clearly flustered by Ben's good looks, she nearly dumped her basket of sourdough bread into his lap before setting it down on the colorful tablecloth next to a small Deruta bowl of extra virgin olive oil.

Evvie tugged a thick piece of bread off the loaf, dipped it into the oil, and took a bite. "Shit." She stared ruefully down at her chest, where a splotch of oil spread like a Rorschach across her pink silk blouse. She laughed. "Oh, well. My eating disorder strikes again."

Ben glanced at the spot and then quickly looked up, as if embarrassed to be staring at her breast. "Aunt Evvie, you look great with your hair back to its old color."

Evvie touched her head. "You think?"

"I really like it. What made you decide to do it after all this time?"

This was her chance. If she didn't take it, she was going to regret it later. But still, she stalled.

"I don't know." She flourished her menu. "What looks good to you? I think I'm going to go with your old standby this time. Do you think they'll put some *prosciutto* on the *pizza arrabiata*? I hate to be one of those high maintenance LA diners."

"C'mon, Aunt Evvie, you're easy. You're never high maintenance. That's why everybody loves you." She blanched.

It was only after she'd dulled herself with a whole pizza and a decadent *tiramasu* that she got up the nerve to broach her topic.

"I'm so glad to hear that you and Tash are going to get some counseling. It makes everything so much easier when you keep talking and working things through."

Ben nodded, brushing the crumbs off his shirt with his napkin. "I hope so. But we'll still be counting on you a lot. I've told Tash a million times that it was you who made my childhood a lot less weird than it could've been."

She slid her hand across the table. "Sweetheart, there's no way to say this but flat out. You know I'd love to be here to watch you discover the joys of fatherhood—and, believe me, I know you're going to surprise yourself at how you're going to take to it. You're such a good and sensitive soul." She squeezed his hand to emphasize that she meant it. "And who, knows, maybe I can fly back for the birth ..."

He stared at her.

She scooted her chair around so that she was sitting right next to him. "Ben, I have the opportunity of a lifetime. I don't know if you even knew—so much has been going on—but, you remember Ezra, don't you? Beady's filmmaking partner? He came to your show."

Ben's eyes betrayed that he sensed where she was going.

She pushed on. "You saw the tape of *Their Fathers' Sins* yourself. What those kids go through. Ezra put a little flea in my ear. He does most of his work in Europe. I'm thinking about doing some stuff for

UNESCO. Dust off my old play therapy textbooks and try to make a difference. I'm pretty burnt out from working with seniors. I didn't even realize it until the cancer. I could also see whether Ezra and I could make a go of something meaningful together."

Ben swallowed. "God, Auntie. You don't have to apologize for wanting to have somebody of your own. I just never thought ..."

"I know." She laughed shakily. "I guess the joke's on both of us. I've been dreading *you* going away. I can't believe that *I'm* the one—"

She became aware of the waitress hovering nearby. Evvie motioned with her hand.

"You sure you're finished?"

"At home I might actually lick the last crumbs off, but seeing as we're here ..." The waitress laughed on cue and deftly cleared the table.

Once she'd gone, Evvie put an arm over Ben's shoulder. He hadn't cracked even the faintest grin during her repartee with their server. "I know it's wretched timing."

He replied unhappily, "I was so stoked in January when we entered a new century, but everything seems to be running on bad timing these days."

But when the day came, Ben insisted on driving her to the airport, with Evvie and Miriam holding hands in the backseat. The traffic was terrible, and Evvie didn't know whether to be worried or delighted that she might not make her plane. All three of them went silent when the odd-shaped tower at the center of LAX loomed into view.

As soon as Ben pulled up in front of British Airways, she and Miriam slid out of the car and were immediately assaulted by honking and diesel fumes. They hauled suitcases from the car like a couple of automatons.

Evvie slammed the trunk shut before Miriam could notice the bulky tissue-wrapped package she'd left inside, with an envelope on top addressed to Ben. Despite what her father had said, she knew he wouldn't begrudge her passing along the ancient *tallis* and *yarmulke* to his grandson. She couldn't explain it, but it made her feel a little easier about leaving.

Glaring at the buses and taxis surrounding his BMW, Ben shouted, "Evvie, don't set foot on that plane until I get up to the boarding gate. It'll take a few minutes to park, but I'll get there in time, I swear."

She yelled back, "Don't worry. Don't get in an accident. We've got plenty of time." A skycap materialized and asked for her ticket and ID. After he loaded her bags onto his trolley, she glanced around for Miriam, who was holding both their purses.

All too quickly, she and Miriam approached the escalator to the departure terminal, shaking their heads in unison at one of the ubiquitous professional beggars stationed at the bottom like Charon at the Styx. Miriam stumbled, and Evvie shot out a hand to steady her, knocking over her rollered overnight bag. Miriam righted it, but she seemed unable to move until Evvie stepped onto the escalator first.

"Evvie," she heard her sister say from behind her, "I'm afraid I'm never going to see you again."

Evvie threw Miriam an encouraging smile over her shoulder. "Don't be ridiculous. Of course, you will."

"I'm afraid you'll die in some shithole."

"Honey, a shithole's where you make it. I was as safe as houses in LA, but then I got cancer. That's pretty shitty. Lately I've been thinking that God is finding sweetness in the midst of the shit. I figure going to the thick of man's murderous hatred for his brother is as good a place as any to start the sweetening."

Someone coughed, and the sisters exchanged glances, recognizing that their neighbors on the escalator had been craning to catch their conversation.

"Dammit, Evvie, even when you're crude you're wise. I don't know what I'm going to do without you."

Once they stepped off the escalator, the crowd pushed them along. It was only when they hit the security check logjam that Evvie spied Ben running toward them. She was afraid she was going to lose it. From inside the metal detector, she said gruffly, "Miriam, you guys are going to do just fine."

Miriam got through right after her, but Ben was still stuck in the line.

"Here." Miriam thrust a piece of paper into Evvie's hand.

"What's this?"

"It's the number of Adam Phones. I've arranged for them to deliver a mobile phone to you at Heathrow. I want to be able to reach you, wherever you are on that crazy continent. And if you get into some kind of jam, call me. Promise."

Ben broke free at last. He rushed forward and grabbed Evvie to him. She reached around for Miriam and pulled her into their circle. Her throat was tight with a strangled sob. "I love you guys so much."

Ben murmured, "Auntie, I've been so selfish. You could have died."

"But I didn't. I got a second chance, didn't I?" *Thank you, God.*

"Tash made me promise to tell you. If it's a boy, we're naming him Michael." This was too much. They huddled together, bawling like babies. Strangers jostled them from every side, but they didn't care. They were shoots of an ancient root system—intricate, interwoven.

A voice came over the loudspeaker announcing that her flight was boarding. With a slow reluctance, Ben and Miriam let her go. Evvie kept looking back at them as she pulled her overnight bag toward the gate. It was okay. They were holding onto each other tightly, their waving hands like angels' wings.

She surrendered her boarding pass and entered the tunnel. She was being moved along some vast, invisible stream. And everything in her was dissolving.

THANK YOU FOR READING

We hope you enjoyed this book. If you did, then we would be very grateful if you would please take a moment to leave a review wherever you purchased it. Thank you.

JOIN OUR MAILING LIST
https://www.thomasjacobbooks.com/let-s-talk

FOLLOW SHARON ON SOCIAL MEDIA
https://www.instagram.com/4fleurandfriends

MORE BOOKS BY SHARON HEATH

The History of My Body
The Fleur Trilogy Book 1

Tizita
The Fleur Trilogy Book 2

Return of the Butterfly
The Fleur Trilogy Book 3

The Mysterious Composition of Tears
The Further Adventures of Fleur

Chasing Eve

Acknowledgements

Enduring threads of soulfulness, resilience, humor, compassion, and the wisdom born of suffering are woven from my Jewish ancestors into the essence of their Karson, Heath, and Noble descendants. They comprise the root system of all my novels, but most visibly in this one.

I call the younger generation of my family the Adorables. Chris, Claire, Tray, Tahlia, Braden, Jennifer, Sarah—nothing would be possible for me in this life without them. My cousin Wayne Karson has been a marvelous ally of my work. My passion for writing has also been generously supported by my chosen (and more distantly related) kin—Linda and Martin Tidd, Mary Hallman, Judy Altman, Constance Crosby, Robin Wynslow, Deborah Howell, Pamela Kirst, Suzanne Ecker, Frances Hatfield, Jane Reynolds, Diane Eagle Kataoka, Carolyn Raffensperger, Naomi Ruth Lowinsky and Dan Safran, Leah Shelleda, Joey Madia, Patricia Damery, Smoky Zeidel, Malcolm Campbell, Claire Allphin, Jim Bessey, Alison Crowley, Pat and David Eisenberg, Wendy Anderson, Gary Anderson, and Sue Rodgers Hammond.

I have Chris Heath to thank for his keen editorial eye; Harriet Friedman for her early enthusiasm for this project; Janet Muff for her consistent advocacy of my creative daimon; my publisher Melinda Clayton for her devoted stewardship of all my books; publicist Dessy Pavlova for my beautiful author website; the members of the C.G. Jung Institutes of Los Angeles and San Francisco for invaluable experiences of communal caring and depth; Tom Singer, Shoshana Fershtman, Lynn Franco, and my fellow presenters at the 2024 Presidency Conference—Politics in a Traumatized World: Dystopia and the Creative Imagination—for offering profound reflections and glimmers of hope during these disturbingly dark times.

This novel began to take shape after I survived breast cancer twenty-six years ago and got its second wind after a more recent brush with the disease. I am deeply grateful to Dr. Michael Van Scoy-Mosher, Dr. Joseph Lebovic, untold numbers of dedicated scientists across the globe, and the heroes of the Cedars-Sinai Medical Center for keeping me alive.

To this home planet and the stars that seeded it, as well as the strong and fragile body that carries the load of my spirit's intensity, I bow forever in gratitude.

About the Author

Sharon Heath is a Jungian analyst in private practice and writes both fiction and non-fiction exploring the interplay of science and spirit, politics and pop culture. The author of five previous novels, she's an environmentalist, a voracious reader of British crime fiction, a Yaya to two adorable grandchildren, and a certified (if not certifiable) cat lady. She has blogged for *HuffPost* and also maintains her own blog at www.sharonheath.com.

www.ingramcontent.com/pod-product-compliance
Lightning Source LLC
Chambersburg PA
CBHW060538260626
47161CB00003B/961